THE BLACK MASK LIBRARY

THE EARLY YEARS (1920–26)

The Man in the Shadows: The Complete Black Mask Cases of Terry Mack *by Carroll John Daly*

THE SHAW YEARS (1926–36)

Blood on the Curb *by Joseph T. Shaw*

Black Harvest: The Complete Black Mask Cases of Jules Tremaine *by Norvell W. Page*

Boomerang Dice: The Complete Black Mask Cases of Johnny Hi Gear *by Stewart Sterling*

Dead Evidence: The Complete Black Mask Cases of Harrigan *by Ed Lybeck*

Laughing Death *by Raoul Whitfield*

Luck: The Complete Black Mask Cases of Oscar Sail *by Lester Dent*

The Price of a Dime: The Complete Black Mask Cases of Ben Shaley *by Norbert Davis*

South Wind: The Complete Black Mask Cases of Jerry Tracy *by Theodore Tinsley*

THE LATER YEARS (1936–51)

Dead and Done For: The Complete Black Mask Cases of Cellini Smith *by Robert Reeves*

Let the Dead Alone: The Complete Black Mask Cases of Luther McGavock *by Merle Constiner*

Murder Costs Money: The Complete Black Mask Cases of Rex Sackler *by D.L. Champion*

BLACK HARVEST

The Complete

Cases of Jules Tremaine

NORVELL W. PAGE

---

introduction by Will Murray

primary illustrator: Arthur Rodman Bowker

cover by Jes Schlaikjer

BLACK MASK
2021

Visit STEEGERBOOKS.COM for more books like this.

Thanks to Rob Preston

Table of Contents

Introduction

NORVELL WORDSWORTH PAGE was the perfect writer for *Black Mask,* as it was issued in the days when Joseph T. Shaw was skippering the magazine, during the tumultuous period when Prohibition gave way to the Great Depression. Page had nearly a decade of experience as a big-city newspaper reporter when he sold his first fiction manuscript, which grounded him in current events, especially as it pertained to gangster era.

Born in Richmond, Virginia, early on Page set his sights on a literary career. His father, Charles Wordsworth Page, had visions of Norvell becoming the next Edgar Allan Poe, but the newspaper game is where he got his start. Early in the Roaring Twenties, he joined the Richmond *Evening Dispatch* as a young cub reporter, later moving over to the Norfolk *Virginia-Pilot* and then the Cincinnati *Post* before landing in New York City. This was the gangster era, and he covered it thoroughly. Page knew cops and crooks, and was intimate with the sordid world that inhabited.

"I don't know why it is, but men who aspire to write the Great American novel always become newspapermen," Page wrote in 1935. "I did, too, and for the last twelve years have been sliding about the country doing one dirty job after another. I didn't know, when I was patting corpses familiarly on the shoulder in the morgues, that it was all going to come in mighty handy some day. In fact, when I began to write fiction finally, I chose the one part of these United States I knew absolutely nothing about: the West. I wrote Western stories and, what's worse, sold 'em!

"One day the editor who purchased them looked at me sourly and said, 'Why don't you write about something you know... like gangsters.' Well, he paid for that remark—for I've been writing detective stories ever since. Amazing how many midnight murders can chill your blood after a lapse of many years when at the time they happened it was 'just another stiff.' And we newspaper men grumbled about leaving our cans of coffee in the press room and pushing out into the night. We thought that was *work.* I could get wistful about newspaper work and I would swear that when I sidle into a police-headquarters press room and whisper 'I'm an old newspaper man myself,' my voice is positively *mournful.*"

While working on the New York *Herald-Tribune,* Page sold his first pulp story, "Corralled," to *Western Trails.* Perhaps as a nod to Poe, he signed it N. Wooten Poge. His motivation was desperation. His father, an executive at the Wurlitzer Company, lost everything in the 1929 stock market crash. Turning to the fictioneering to support his parents, Page grew prolific fast. Family lore has it that Norvell's pseudonymous middle name, Wooten, was a pun on "owe ton," but no one alive truly knows. "Woe ton" as in a ton of woe seems equally plausible.

Shortly thereafter, he broke into *Detective-Dragnet* magazine, a title that straddled the gangster sub-genre by giving due credit to the forces of law and order. Soon, Page was turning out stories for that title and a competitor, *The Underworld Magazine.* There, Norvell found his metier: Crime stories.

Late in 1932, Page sold "Those Catrini" to the prestigious

Black Mask and decided that the world of pulp magazine readers should know his true name. His close friend, Theodore A. Tinsley, had just broken into the magazine via a series character, Jerry Tracy, who was closely patterned after gossip columnist Walter Winchell.

"Cap" Shaw was an exacting editor. He demanded a writer write leanly, and ruthlessly cut his manuscript to the bone. Whether this was Page's personal own approach or he had learned it during his brief period writing for Shaw, Norvell was an inveterate rewriter.

"I turn out 100,000 to 120,000 words a month for the 'pulps,' he explained. "These words—the pulp writer always talks of words—because he's paid on a wordage basis—are written as well as I am able to write them. I try constantly to improve the quality, the forcefulness and the keenness of character interpretation in my stories. I spend twice as much time on rewriting as on writing."

Page got off to a strong start in 1933 with his *Black Mask* sales, along with a pair of short stories featuring detective Mark Curtis for the back of *The Shadow Magazine.* N. Wooten Poge was temporally retired. Norvell W. Page was an emerging star. His writing was marked by a brisk forcefulness and emotionally driven characterizations

Jules Tremaine was one of the most peculiar characters to stalk through the pages of *Black Mask.* During this period, Dashiell Hammett was still occasionally contributing to the magazine. Raymond Chandler would debut later that year. Shaw understood that he could only have so many private and police detective protagonists. No doubt he encouraged new writers to think outside the traditional pulp parameters.

Page's character is the brother of a disreputable politician, who takes an interest in the affairs of Little Italy, standing on the street corners, strumming his guitar and singing traditional songs. This brings Tremaine into close contact with the poor Italian people of Manhattan's Italian quarter and, over the course of his three recorded adventures, the Catrini crime family who preys upon them. Witnessing their cruelty first-hand, Tremaine sets out to whittle the Catrini down to size—violently.

These battles put him at odds with his older brother, Andrew, and a bitter hatred percolates between them. An even more bitter hatred is directed toward what Tremaine called "those Catrini." Trouble brews among this triangle of bitter rivals, and tragedy appears to be in the offing.

Over the course of three consecutively published stories, Page built a compelling narrative of gut-wrenching crimes and brutal street justice. Where he was going with all this is impossible to deduce now, for in the middle of an unfolding storyline, Page abruptly ceased contributing to *Black Mask.*

It's regrettable that the author did not take Jules Tremaine's war with the Catrini to its bitter climax, nor did he resolve the blood-feud between Tremaine and his unsavory brother. If he had penned sufficient chapters he could have combined them into a classic hard-boiled hardcover novel, as Dashiell Hammett was doing with his serials.

A few months later, Jules Tremaine made his final bow in one of the brief puzzle stories then running in *Black Mask.* It's an inconsequential effort and adds nothing to the understanding of the character and where the series was going.

The month after Page's third Tremaine episode ran in *Black*

Mask, he broke into *Ten Detective Aces* with a very different type of novelette, which is included in this volume. "The Green Death" features a one-shot character, King Landers, but it sets the stage for the ongoing adventures of Ken Carter, who appeared every month in subsequent issues of *Ten Detective Aces,* which was a retitled reformulation of *Detective-Dragnet.* That editor had lured Page back into the fold.

In those stories, the definitive Norvell Page style emerges. Ken Carter is a proud, sometimes arrogant wealthy private investigator who wages war on the criminal element. Carter's cases edge into a new sub-genre, the Menace story, soon to be called Weird Menace.

Why did Page abandon *Black Mask* for *Ten Detective Aces?* He may not have meant to. Inasmuch as he was writing part time to support his extended family back in Virginia while simultaneously working full-time as a newspaperman, he may simply have gone where the best pay was, intending to return to *Black Mask* later.

His pulp career was veering resolutely in different directions, however. By the summer of 1933, Page was writing the *Spider,* a new vigilante hero in the vein of The Shadow. Wealthy criminologist Richard Wentworth, alias the *Spider,* was not created by Page, however, despite the similarity between Wentworth and Wordsworth. He was instead a rough reimagining of a famous thriller character of the 1920s, Aurelius "Secret Service" Smith.

Popular Publications publisher Harry Steeger was eager to start an imitation of *The Shadow,* but feared a lawsuit from Street & Smith. Reportedly, he went to his lawyer for advice on how to proceed.

Steeger's attorney suggested he hire a seasoned writer who owned a series character and have the writer convert his character into a new personality, this creating a legal shield. The writer turned out to be R.T.M. Scott, who had great success with Secret Service Smith in the previous decade. Scott's son worked at Popular.

That September, the first issue with *The Spider* appeared, followed the month later by the second, both stories carried the byline R.T.M. Scott. Apparently, from the beginning, Steeger planned to replace Scott once the series was established and made bulletproof from lawsuits.

Fortuitously for Norvell Page, a fellow writer had hit a snag with the lead novel he was writing for Popular's *Dime Mystery Book Magazine.* The format was being changed and the showcase novels were being replaced by novelettes. Over drinks at a speakeasy, the unhappy pulpster complained to Page that he didn't want to cut his in-progress story.

"Mind if I have a shot at it?" Page asked. "I've never written for that editor, but I can give him 35,000 words in a week, if that's what he wants."

Page's substitute story, "Dance of the Skeletons," appeared in the October issue of the retitled *Dime Mystery Magazine,* which went on sale the same month that *The Spider* debuted. It kicked off the Weird Menace sub-genre. It probably also spelled doom for Jules Tremaine and Norvell's *Black Mask* career.

This fortuitous sale put Page in touch with Rogers Terrill, the editor of both magazines. Page sold him a short story for the first issue of *The Spider,* and before long Terrill tapped Page to write the *Spider* lead novels.

Page took over with the third issue, writing as Grant Stockbridge. Almost immediately, hero Richard Wentworth began taking on the forceful personality of Ken Carter. Just as Jules Tremaine had disappeared from the pages of *Black Mask*, Ken Carter, too, vanished from *Ten Detective Aces*.

The early *Spider* was more of a name than a personality. Prodded by his editors, Page began moving him in the direction of being a simulacrum of The Shadow. Since Popular Publication remained leery of lawsuits, they carefully and gradually Shadowized the *Spider*.

This led to an interesting development. In one early story, *Citadel of Hell*, Richard Wentworth takes on the disguise of the street violinist named Tito Caliepi, who haunts Little Italy. He wears a black cape and a slouch hat and serenades passersby while he spies on the criminal element.

This hunchbacked figure slowly evolved into the public image of the *Spider*. So in a sense Jules Tremaine was revived in the person of Tito Caliepi, and Richard Wentworth became a combination of Tremaine and Ken Carter. "Hard as a Pharaoh," as Page first described Jules Tremaine. Yet also as chivalrous as a Southern gentleman.

Page's exacting writing practices did not flag after he turned his efforts to writing a *Spider* novel every month.

"On my *Spider* stories," he revealed, "fifty-five thousand lead novels for the magazine of that title which I write monthly under a house name, I have written as many as six different opening chapters, and spent a full day getting the first two thousand words on paper. I may have written eight, ten, twelve thousand in getting those two, and even then, I don't always like them."

The demand for his work became so intense and the money so good that, at the beginning of 1934, Norvell Page resigned the New York *World-Telegram* to become a full-time pulpster, as fiction writers of the latter Prohibition liked to style themselves. In the time-honored fashion of the prolific pulpster, he began dictating his stories instead of typing them directly on the typewriter. Before long, he purchased an electric typewriter to help facilitate his output. He purchased an expensive Daimler automobile in emulation of the one his alter ego, Richard Wentworth, drove, and traded in his .22 target pistol for a matched pair of .45 Colt automatics like those the *Spider* whittled down Underworld mobsters.

As with so many young writers entering the field in the early Depression, Norvell Page's rise was meteoric. If writing more that 50,000 words of white-hot pulp prose every 30 days wasn't enough, he co-founded the American Fiction Guild, an organization for freelance writers which was headquartered in New York. To qualify for admission, one had to have sold more than 100,000 words. There were times when Page did that in a single month.

Page served as secretary and later became president of the Guild's New York chapter, and eventually National President. All while supplementing his *Spider* output with numerous detective and Weird Menace stories. He also found time to write for radio. It's suspected that Page scripted the short-lived *Spider* radio program, but the family recalled that he contributed to *The Shadow* broadcasts.

The AFG's first president, Arthur J. Burks, was one of the most prolific producers of his time. He liked to say, "The life of a pulp writer is seven years. At the end of seven years, you've got to go on to better writing, or go downhill."

For Norvell Page, six years of steady production passed before he ran into trouble. In the middle of 1936, he stopped writing the *Spider* and virtually everything else. Rumors persist of a nervous breakdown caused by writing a monthly novel and supplementing it with short stories and novelettes.

It was nearly a year before Page got back into his old routine, becoming Grant Stockbridge once more.

One AFG colleague noted his return in 1937, writing, "Norv is back at the old tempo now and his name is once again popping up on covers of lots of mags. Best of luck, old-timer."

Page was only 30. But in the pulp game, you became a veteran damned fast.

Norvell Page continued to write over the next decade, having at least one more brush with a nervous collapse in 1939. That year, he was yarning for multiple magazines under his own name and the revived byline, N. Wooten Poge.

It proved too much. When his doctor told him to take a much-needed break from writing, Page went on a cruise of the Caribbean. Unfortunately, the passenger ship was German owned. When World War II broke out, the captain made a break for South America in order to escape British warships patrolling the Atlantic.

The Page family and the other passengers were let off in Cuba, from which they found their way home while the liner S.S. *Columbus* was eventually scuttled by her crew to avoid falling into British hands.

By this time, Tito Caliepi had not serenaded New York citizenry in years. He had become the familiar figure the Underworld hated and cursed as the *Spider.*

Before his trip, Page had Richard Wentworth pick up his violin and once again and disguise himself as a street musician. But this time, Wentworth called himself Casimir Belotti. He might have been the ghost of Jules Tremaine, now all but forgotten.

Page soon returned to his writing grind, but at a more sedate pace. In 1943, with the pulp market shrinking and his wife having passed away unexpectedly, Page moved to Washington, D.C. to work for the Office of War Information, bringing along with him fellow pulpster, Ted Tinsley.

One suspects that after switching to writing dry reports for the government, it was a relief. When his O.W.I. service was over, Norvell returned to freelancing in 1947–48, writing reports for various presidential and congressional commissions. It is not known if he sold any fiction at this time. The pulps were dying. Page joined the Atomic Energy Commission in 1949, where he worked on and off until his death by heart attack at 57 in 1961. It was a strange spot for the author of the *Spider* to land. Or perhaps not. For *Unknown* magazine, he had penned *But Without Horns*, universally hailed as one of the finest science fiction novels built around the superman theme.

After his death, Page's second wife, Gean Purcell, later revealed, "My husband did not keep a single example of his pulp work, and when he met with those who worked with him in the pulps, such as Rogers Terrill, the conversation never turned to the pulps."

This was typical of newspapermen and many pulp writers. They considered their writings ephemeral, throwaway stuff. Yet at one time, a colleague said of Page that he "Talks of his 'Spider' characters as though they were members of his family, or boon golfing-drinking companions."

Curiously, when he walked away from the pulp jungle, Norvell Page did so absolutely and without a backward glance. None of it appeared to matter to him anymore. This from a man who, after he lost his file of *The Spider* magazine in a fire, asked his loyal readers to send him their personal copies, writing, "I cannot bear to think of losing one word that has been written about your hero and mine—the *Spider*."

During his dozen or so years toiling in the pulp jungle, Norvell Page made a vivid impression on everyone with whom he came into contact.

Popular Publication President Harry Steeger described him as someone who would "show up at the office with a black cape and dark slouch hat, wearing a Spider ring and stalking about as though he were going to perform some miracle of fiction."

Fellow writer William R. Cox recalled, "Norvell Page, who wrote 'The Spider,' wore velvet pants and a wide-brimmed hat, was a firm believer in reincarnation, and confessed to anyone who would listen that he communicated daily with his wife, who had died some years before...."

Ted Tinsley, who perhaps knew him best, painted a more balanced picture, while admitting, "Norvell's personality was not 'subdued' in the manner of a young blondish bank clerk. He *did* like to wear a Spider ring. He *did* like to wear a cape. He *did* like a slouch hat. And he did wear a beard, a black scrubby one. At times his flamboyant cape suggested he might be a Bolshevik, with a small bomb concealed for socially corrective action. Actually he was a nice guy, with a yen toward theatrics, who simmered down considerably after he took his talents (they were many) to Uncle Sam during and after WW2."

Norvell once wrote, "Writing for a living is hard work, but I wouldn't trade with any man living.... It's a great life if you don't run out of words." He never did, but it is a semi-tragedy that he turned his mind to less exiting words in his last decades.

Page was an exceptional writer for his time, drawing realistic characters with vivid emotional lives and not the cardboard clichés that many of his contemporaries trafficked in. His early work puts him firmly in the hard-boiled school of detective writing. Even though Page never returned to *Black Mask,* his contributions deserve to be preserved. If he had taken the high literary road instead of the lower pulp one, Norvell Page might today be remembered in the same way that Dashiell Hammett and Raymond Chandler are. Instead, he is celebrated as the author of nearly 100 frenetic, over-the-top *Spider* novels.

In order to round out this regrettably slim volume, we have included several detective stories Page wrote during his early career, including his contribution to the first issue of *The Spider* and his only sale to *Detective Fiction Weekly,* "Copper's Cross." His 1935 memoir, "How I Write," rounds out this book.

Those Catrini

Jules Tremaine promises to be a notable addition to the Black Mask *character group. Himself, his mission, are both a little mysterious. He walks boldly where one without courage would scarcely venture. He appears at odds with an established order of ruthless political power and of wealth drawn from such sordid source. At times he is as soft-spoken and sympathetic as a woman; at others, he is dynamite unleashed.*

JULES TREMAINE STOOD erectly on the curb of Mulberry Street, facing a row of dirty red tenements, and plucked three preliminary chords from his black guitar. He began to sing *M'appari.*

Before and behind him carnival crowds pushed and gabbled. To each side stood a pushcart odorous with high stacks of clams. It was the Festa di San Gennaro and the September night was soft. Women leaned from windows shouting at children who scrambled in the street under the arches of blue and red and yellow lights.

Jules threw back his head and his full voice soared. Before him a girl stopped. She was fifteen. Her breasts pressed roundly against the flamboyant pink of her dress. Her eyes were dark and liquid and they regarded the street singer somberly.

Jules sent the last note of the aria vaulting above the babble of the street, plucked an ultimate vibrant chord and bowed to her, a vital figure of a man just over five feet five and dapper in a modeled suit of dark gray. He swept off a black felt hat.

"Ah, *bella mia,*" he said, laughter behind his eyes. "You have tonight the face of a very, very tired madonna."

The girl's lips parted slightly, showing white teeth.

"Every time I try to sit down the floorwalker gets nasty," she explained.

Jules clapped his hat back on his head and made a wringing motion with his two hands. His voice threatened. "If I ever get my hands on that floorwalker, I'll...."

His wide teeth flashed beneath the black of his small mustache. Angela's lips curved. She threw back her head so that her throat was a sweet white line and laughed three contralto bell notes.

"That is better," said Jules. "Now what is it that makes these dark shadows under your pretty eyes?"

The girl's smile diminished but still quivered at her mouth corners. She nodded her head gravely.

"I'm worried, Mr. Tremaine," she said.

Jules pursed his lips. When he did that the militant points of his mustache moved forward slightly. His blue eyes stared beyond the girl into the dingy bricks of a tenement front.

"I suppose it's that lazy Antonio again," he said, his syllables short.

Angela clasped her hands and watched her long, tapered fingers as she moved them slowly.

"What's your brother up to now?" Jules demanded.

The girl drew a deep breath so that her breasts strained against the sleazy silk. Her eyes remained stubbornly on her hands.

"He has not done anything, Mr. Tremaine," she protested. "It is those Catrini. They say they will do something because Tony drives his beer truck into their part of town...."

Her words accelerated. She unclasped her hands and gestured with them. Her wide eyes, dark and frightened, met Tremaine's directly.

"—if Antonio works he must drive where his boss tells him. If he does not work we cannot eat. Ah, those Catrini...."

She raised her right hand with the thumb uppermost, the fingers spread, and clicked the nail of the thumb on her upper

teeth with an outward gesture. For the moment her eyes were bright and narrow.

"I know those Catrini," said Jules softly.

The girl's body lost its tension and became supplicant. Her hands, palms upward, the slim, tapering fingers bent outward, pleaded with Tremaine. There was a pucker between the black, straight brows, between the dark, questioning eyes.

"What can I do?" she asked. "What can I do!"

Tremaine looked down at his guitar and plucked the G string, turned a white ivory peg, cocked his head to the side and touched the string again. He looked up at the girl.

"Go home, Angela," he said. "I will sing three more songs, then come to talk with you and Antonio."

Angela spun on her heel, whirling out the thin silk of her skirt. A boy with a laughing mouth showered confetti over her and she threw back her head and laughed and snatched at the colored snow with quick hands. Three white pieces of paper and a star-shaped pink one settled on her black hair. She turned and looked gravely into Tremaine's round blue eyes.

"I know you will make everything all right," she said. "I am so happy I could dance."

She spun completely around on her heel and walked with little skipping steps three doors down the street. She waved to Jules before she went into the darkness of the tenement.

THOSE CATRINI! JULES TREMAINE looked down at his guitar and his lips smiled with little mirth. His fingers touched the strings soundlessly, then twanged a chord and two more and he threw back his head and began to sing *La donna e mobile.* His fingers were lean and white. They had squared ends.

Behind him in a vacant lot across the street, a fireworks cannon made a muffled concussion. Children screamed and squirmed between the pushcarts, hurrying to get nearer. A whirling spark soared, hesitated and burst into a jagged splotch of yellow fire. Spider legs of light spanned out from it and at their ends bombs burst in dazzling streaks of white. The explosions tortured the ear drums.

Jules shrugged and stopped singing. He drew the black guitar down under his arm and up on his back so that it hung suspended from his shoulder by a crimson braided cord. He looked over the crowd and laden pushcarts and moved slowly down the street, a short man but with power in the square set of his shoulders, the erect poised arrogance of the head.

The pyrotechnic display faded momentarily; there was another muffled concussion, then clear and high a girl's scream tore the night. Jules whirled, staring up at the third-floor windows where Angela and her brother had rooms. A succession of deadened explosions that were not fireworks beat on the air, then every sound was drowned in the ripping burst of more bombs.

On the walk where Jules stood people no longer stared at the colored fire in the sky. They faced the door of the tenement where that scream had sounded. A handful of children gathered silently. A fat man with wide red silk bands holding up too long sleeves waded through them. He entered the door. He staggered back, fell down the one step and sprawled supine. His feet jerked up and his heels thumped on the pavement.

Three men boiled out of the doorway. They had guns in their hands. Two raced down the street and separated. The third ran past Jules. He was a short and broad man. As he lifted and flung down his feet heavily Jules saw that the right shoulder was twisted so that it was at least three inches higher than the left. The man whirled about the corner.

Jules strode towards the door from which the three had come. The fat man who had been hurled to the street sat up and held his head in his hands. For five seconds he sat there, then reeled to his feet. His fat quivered with the speed of his flight. A boy bounded out of his way, staggering blindly towards Tremaine. Jules caught the boy with one arm and set him gently aside. He did not stop. His lips were pressed in a thin hard line, and a path opened before him among the thickening crowd. He entered the dark doorway.

Halfway to the second floor he was taking the steps two

at a time. On the third floor he thrust through an open door and stopped and stood, his right hand gripping the end of the keyboard and holding in place the guitar on his back. The air was acrid with burned gunpowder. A single yellow light bulb dangled from the center of the ceiling by a twisted wire. It threw a glare on walls that had been scrubbed until they were streaked gray. Jules kept his eyes on them for a moment; then he looked down.

There were two bodies on the floor. One had crumpled near him, a knee drawn up towards its belly. That was Antonio. From under him a dark liquid pool spread. Angela lay over by a door beyond which the kitchen gleamed. She lay on her back, hurled close against the wall by the six-hundred-foot-pound impact of .45-calibre bullets. Her head was thrown back and her throat was a white sweet line and there was a blue hole between her wide, frightened eyes. Jules saw there were two pieces of confetti in her hair, one white and square, the other a pink star shape.

Jules' right hand was on the keyboard of his guitar. There was a snap as a white ivory peg broke and he stooped slowly and picked it up and looked at it. The peg was smooth and cold in his fingers and it had broken off just under the head. In the street a brassy whistle skirled. Jules dropped the peg in his pocket and the right corner of his mouth twisted so that a single sharp incisor showed. Heavy feet pounded on the stairs and mounted swiftly. Jules shook his head sharply, glanced once around the room, then plunged through the door. He saw the policeman at the head of the stairs, and ran for the dark back hall.

"Halt!" the policeman shouted. "I'll shoot!"

A pistol glinted in the dim light.

Jules moved slowly towards the policeman, his hands raised well above his head and the guitar bumping against his right side. His eyes were narrowed, watchful.

"I'm just a street singer," he said. "I heard the shooting and came to see if Angela and Antonio were all right. They were friends of mine, and—"

"Shut up!" the cop ordered.

His heavy fingers clamped on Jules' shoulder and whirled him about and he patted his hips and sides and under his arms.

"Threw your gun away, did you?" he said. "That won't do you no good."

Jules allowed himself to be shoved back into the room where Angela and Antonio lay.

"You louse!" the cop rasped. "You shot the girl, too!"

Lights blazed before Jules' eyes and blackness followed.

TREMAINE HAD ONLY partly recovered his senses when he was roughed into the patrol wagon. The rush of air as it sped with a softly whining siren back to the station-house largely restored him, but he staggered as he was booted into the white square office of the captain. The breath of his captor was harsh and fingers vised on his shoulder.

Jules measured the captain under heavy lids. The man was fat and his white hair was pomaded into a smooth pompadour. He ran a hand over it.

"Well, well, what have we here?" he asked, and his voice was fat and oily.

"O'Reilly caught him running away after them two was bumped," said the patrolman, his hand still on Jules' shoulder. "He'd throwed his gun away."

"Running away, eh?"

The captain was seated in a swivel-chair tilted back before his desk. He leaned forward and rubbed white, puffy hands up and down his thighs. Then his mouth opened in a little pink "O" of surprise; his small black eyes went flat.

"——!" he said. "It's Jules Tremaine!"

The captain straightened, stumbled to his feet and slid a chair out from the wall.

"Sit down, Mr. Tremaine," he said. "I'm sorry about this. O'Reilly didn't know you."

Jules heard the patrolman behind him gulp and the hand flinched away from his shoulder.

"Jeeze, Cap'n, did we pull a boner?" the man asked.

"Get out!" the captain yelled, and the door opened and closed quickly. The fat man in the dark blue suit looked at Tremaine and smoothed his pomaded hair and blinked.

"I'm sorry about this," he said.

Jules continued to stand. He balanced his guitar carefully on the chair, eased off his black felt hat and fingered the back of his head. He winced and his lips pressed hard together.

"I think you said O'Reilly was the cop's name?" he asked softly.

"He's just a dumb flatfoot," the captain spoke hurriedly. "He don't know no better. I'll take it out of him."

"Don't bother, Captain," said Jules gently. "Don't you bother at all."

He placed his hat on the chair beside his guitar and looked about the office slowly.

"I want to wash up a bit," he said.

The captain skipped his fat sides across the room, swung open a door with a flourish and revealed gleaming white tile.

Jules doffed his coat and doused his face and head with cold water. The welt left by the cop's gun on his scalp stung. Jules cursed softly as he stroked his black hair to smoothness with a thin comb from his pocket. He pointed his mustache, shrugged into his coat and strolled back into the office. He adjusted his hat jauntily and slung the guitar over his shoulder.

The captain regarded him with troubled eyes. He opened his mouth and closed it again like a goldfish drinking air. He said: "You didn't see anything up there, did you, Mr. Tremaine?"

Jules revolved on his heel and looked up into the small black eyes. The captain shoved a puffy hand over his hair.

"I saw a boy and a girl had been murdered," he said, biting off the words. "Then O'Reilly slammed me over the head with his gun."

The captain frowned at his fingernails, though they were perfectly polished.

"You know how these young cops are," he murmured.

"Yes, I know," said Jules, and left.

A taxi weaved uptown with him and stopped at an address in the East Fifties where a dead-pan butler opened the door. Tremaine surrendered a gingerly removed hat but held on to the guitar, padding deliberately up the deep carpeted steps.

"That you, Jules?" a resonant voice boomed.

Jules retraced his way without answering, walked back through the dim, dusty-smelling hall and at its end entered a door to the right. The room was ten feet square and its walls were shelves of brown-backed law books. In its center was a desk, a reading lamp and a face that had the curious effect of floating disembodied in the air. Presently Jules could make out the spread shoulders of the man seated at the desk.

"Ah, it is you, Jules," came the resonant, slightly mocking voice.

Jules' face was expressionless as he studied the cadaverous countenance. A few strands of black hair had been oiled and laid carefully side by side across a bald dome-like forehead that lengthened the thin face extraordinarily.

"Who's the captain at the Houston Street station?" Jules asked.

The mouth corners of the man's face made creases like parentheses and strong white teeth showed momentarily.

"Going to use my influence at last?"

"No. The louse recognized me as a Tremaine. I was afraid I was beginning to look like you. My fears, I see, were groundless."

The creases about the mouth deepened; the head tilted back so that black smudges of shadow from the low desk lamp erased all the upper part of the face and made teeth gleam. The laughter was a faint roughened breathing, nearly soundless. When it stopped the face looked down again.

"My charming brother!" the man articulated. The creases smoothed themselves and the lips pursed. "The captain's name is Jimson."

The man stood and the shadows smudged his face again; the light revealed his length and the powerful sweep of his shoulders. Jules had to look up to meet his eyes. He smiled slightly and his mustache pointed forward a fraction of an inch. He bowed ceremoniously.

"My *dear* brother," he said, then swung about. The hall echoed the regular beat of his feet.

The room he entered was all gray and nearly barren. He laid

his guitar face down on a couch bed and took a screwdriver from the top drawer of a Sheraton chest. He looked across at his guitar and smiled.

IT WAS AFTER ten the next morning when Jules slid out of white silk pajamas and stepped into his shower. His stomach sucked in and the muscles of his chest and upper arms flexed and jumped under its cold pelting; then he dodged out from under and punished his tight lean body with a rough towel. As he bent forward his abdomen tensed into six ridges of muscle. He dusted himself with bath powder and hummed *M'appari.* He cut it short in the middle with a small tightening of mouth corners. A pulse throbbed in his throat.

A polite tap at the door caught Jules with his trousers just belted. He grunted: "Come in."

His brother, in striped morning trousers and cutaway, bowed himself in, clicked the door shut. Jules glanced at the domed forehead.

"I keep hoping those six hairs won't be exactly parallel." He sighed.

The mouth corner creases deepened in his brother's cadaverous face but the thin lips did not part. Blue eyes were sardonic. Jules drew on a linen shirt, thrust the tails into his dark gray trousers and plucked a heavy silk tie, gray, too, from a rack on the closet door. The taller man continued silent and Jules eventually toed about and faced him, his eyes half shut.

"Yes, my dear brother?" he queried.

"You aren't going back to Little Italy today, Jules?"

Jules brushed his left mustache with his right thumbnail. His still veiled eyes were amused. His voice was gentle.

"Surely, Andrew, you aren't at some thirty-and-six years of age beginning to worry about your younger brother?"

Andrew cursed in mild tones. He said with relish: "Some day you are going to get your well-muscled abdomen shot full of messy holes. Those Catrini—"

Jules lifted his right shoulder fractionally, moved deliberately to the closet. He tipped a vest off a hanger and drew it on. Buttoning it with lean, square-tipped fingers, he opened his eyes wide and focused their round blue gaze on his brother.

"Catrini?" he mouthed slowly. "Catrini? No, I don't believe I know anyone by that name."

Andrew smiled like a politician about to kiss a baby.

"I think I'll tell Captain Jimson I don't mind if you are picked up for those murders," he said, and added as an afterthought: "You louse."

Jules' lids drooped over his eyes again.

"Tell my dear friend Jimson," he said, "to have O'Reilly do the picking up, will you, Andrew?"

The eyes of the two brothers locked like slithering rapiers. The elder's tone was like May.

"Dear Jules! Don't tell me you're up to something?"

Jules laid the spread fingers of both hands on his chest, his eyebrows crawling up.

"I? My charming brother!" he exclaimed, shocked surprise vibrant in his words. "You can't mean your younger brother?"

Andrew's right hand, tense and straight as a knife, sliced across the air before him. He rasped a single monosyllabic obscenity and followed it with the word "you" and jerked open the door and slammed it shut behind him. Jules threw back his head and laughed with little sound. He shrugged into his coat, adjusting his black hat jauntily on his head, and turned towards his guitar. The door again swept open. Jules continued towards his guitar.

"Jules"—Andrew's voice was incisive—"you're probably as hard up for money as usual. I'll pay you to quit this stuff."

Jules lifted the guitar with both hands, then with one passed the red cord over his head, shoved his right arm through the loop. He turned slowly, eyes on his brother's lean, hollow-cheeked face, and said nothing.

Andrew thrust a bony hand into an inner pocket of his coat and drew out a black leather wallet with gold corner pieces. He fingered out five yellow-backed bills with 1000 in each corner and spread them out like a poker hand and held them towards Jules. "Lay off this comic opera stuff, will you? You're hunting trouble and I can't afford to have the name mixed up in anything so near election."

Jules eased the guitar under his right arm and up against his back, where he held it with a hand pressed against the end of the keyboard. The red cord was across his chest like an ambassador's riband. He bowed, his mouth corners depressed.

"My dear brother, you ask too much. Always I have long' to seeng een the streets. I make of eet my buseeness."

"Horsefeathers!" said Andrew. He put the money carefully back into the black wallet and restored that to his pocket. "You began this street singing to queer me with the party. You've always hated me. When you first started I figured you'd get tired of it. But you are a persistent louse. It may be that I shall have to take steps."

His face was wooden, but there were malevolent sparks in the depths of his eyes. Jules' face did not lose its mocking smile, but his eyes went flat and hard. He strode forward three paces until he stood within two feet of the taller brother, looking up into the cadaverous mask. A pulse throbbed in his throat.

"The truth is, Andrew," he said softly, "that I first sang in the streets for a lark. I was half tight and somebody made a bet. The wops were decent to me. They cheered when I sang. If it was sad, they wept. I like people like that, people who aren't afraid to have emotions. You and your politicians, friends and hirelings, can't figure that any man does a thing for the obvious reason. You always see intrigue.

"That's the truth of the matter, but if my street singing annoys you, I'm glad. I won't stop. Now get the hell out of my way."

A PALL OF white roses ornamented the weathered doorway of the tenement where Angela had lived. A baby of three stood and stared at it with grave eyes. As Jules walked slowly by he caught the faint sweetish odor of the flowers. Children scampered and cried. Tremaine stopped a half square away and stood on the curb with his back to Mulberry Street. His black hat sat at an angle. He touched his mustache with his thumbnail, considered a moment and struck a chord from his guitar that had curiously little resonance.

A fat man, his sleeves held up by red bands, sat on a chair on the walk. He heaved up and padded across to Jules.

"A man was here looking for you," he said.

Tremaine struck another slow chord.

"He say you come to Joe's place on Tenth Street he get you a job regular."

Jules showed his white teeth under the black militant points of his mustache. He said nothing, began to sing softly, plucking out a twanging bass accompaniment. He stopped and put his hand flat on the strings.

"What did this man look like?" he asked. "He was short and broad, eh? His right shoulder"—Jules hunched his own forward and upward three inches—"it rides like this, eh?"

The fat man blinked and regarded Jules' hunched shoulder and looked back to his round blue eyes.

"I give you the message," he said.

He eased back into his chair. Jules' head went back and he laughed almost soundlessly. The fat man sat and blinked at him. He looked up and down the street, then blinked again, put his hands on his knees, leaned far forward and levered himself to his feet. He picked up the chair and carried it into the tenement. Jules laughed again.

Militant chords leaped from the strident strings and he swung into the *Soldiers' Chorus.* A man in a rust-brown suit and with broad-toed black shoes and a derby jammed forward over his eyes halted before Tremaine. The street singer finished his song.

"What would you like me to sing?" he asked, his fingers walking over the strings.

The man growled in his throat. He was young and blond and weighed about two hundred and twenty pounds. His blue eyes glowered from a florid face.

"My name's O'Reilly," he said.

Jules bowed gracefully.

"I have heard the name before," he said, "but there seems to be some Freudian obstruction in my cerebration."

The young man frowned.

"Don't crack wise," he warned, "or I'll bang you over the head again."

"Ah, now I recall!" Happiness shone on Jules' face. "You are the gallant young policeman who last night apprehended me as I was calling on some recently demised friends. I am so glad to renew the acquaintance, Mr. O'Reilly."

The cop's scowl deepened. He grunted: "What was you telling the fat wop in the chair?"

Jules moved his right hand from left to right, palm upward, fingers spread, and shrugged his right shoulder.

"I tell him the day is lovely. I tell him it is too bad Angela and Antonio cannot see it. I tell him—" Jules shrugged delicately again, his hand completing the gesture. "I talk with him."

"Then why'd he go inside?"

"He, perhaps, do not like the song I sing."

"Huhn!"

O'Reilly stood with straddled legs, his head thrust forward. His hands swung at his sides, a slight rigidity in his arms.

"You bumped that girl because you couldn't get gay with her, then put the heat on the brother when he walked in on you."

Jules stopped smiling and his fingers stopped their soundless wandering over the strings.

"You fool!" he snapped. "I liked Angela. She was a nice kid, a clean hard-working little wop. The men who killed her were lice, and I'm going—"

"You're going to do what?"

Jules looked at O'Reilly from under half-lowered lids. He said softly: "It took you two minutes to get from the lot across the street to the door of the tenement where Angela was shot. I wonder why that was, Mr. O'Reilly?"

The policeman advanced his right foot a half pace, his left hand clenched into a fist. His eyes were bright and small.

"I've a good mind to run you in," he said, his words rasping.

"I wish you would," said Jules gently.

The florid color of the policeman's face deepened.

"I know your name is Tremaine," he said, "and I know you got off last night, but it won't work today. The captain said—"

Jules raised polite eyebrows as the man broke off. So there was another score against Andrew to be settled. Jules pursed his lips, the amusement in his eyes shaded by anger.

"Nevertheless," he said, "I wish you would run me in. There are a few other things I'd like to tell Captain Jimson, such as why it took you two minutes—"

"That's enough of that!" O'Reilly was tense, his voice hoarse. "If you know what's good for you, keep your mouth shut!"

Jules sighed deeply, with a theatrical lift and fall of his chest.

"I'm afraid, my dear O'Reilly, that it's too late to do that. I told the dear captain—"

"You told him what?"

"My dear fellow, you are so precipitate! This continual interruption grows irksome."

"You told him what?" O'Reilly's eyes were flat and menacing.

Jules returned the man's glare from under sleepy lids, his hands motionless on the guitar. The policeman's gaze flickered finally.

"That is much, much better, Mr. O'Reilly," said Jules softly. "As I was about to say, I told Jimson that I could identify the man who shot Angela and Antonio and that I would testify when they were arrested."

"You're lying," O'Reilly said hoarsely. "Jimson didn't tell me that!"

Jules shrugged, swung half about so that his left shoulder

was towards the policeman, strolled up the street, plucking soft chords. O'Reilly's heavy stride kept pace with him.

"You're rough on a guy that's trying to do you a favor," he said, placatingly. "I came to tell you that Joe—he's got a place up on Tenth Street—says he's got a job for you."

"My dear fellow!" Jules exclaimed. "That is charming of you!"

He swept a lean forefinger across the five strings but the catgut gave forth a tinny sound as if the resonance of the wood were damped.

"But just why am I so honored, and why has not my good brother's suggestion that I be arrested not been carried out?"

O'Reilly walked stolidly along beside him.

"Jimson said you had an alibi. Said somebody saw you in the street at the same time they heard the shots. And the chief told me to tell you about the job."

Jules pursed his lips so that the black mustache thrust forward. A frown drew his brows together.

"You'll be glad to get the job, eh?" O'Reilly suggested.

"Perhaps," Jules said. "I do not know. If you see this Joe tell him he can find me here."

"He can find you here, eh?" O'Reilly was carefully casual.

Jules threw back his head; his mouth opened but only small laughing sounds emerged. He said: "Yes."

O'Reilly said, "Okey," and marched off.

HALF AN HOUR later, at the corner of Mulberry and Spring streets, Jules Tremaine was singing. For the moment the street was clear of festa crowds. Two children, the younger barely two with a meditative thumb thrust into his mouth, regarded him seriously. Something hard nudged into Jules' back. His eyes half closed and he moved a half pace forward and continued to sing. The nudge was repeated. He ended his song, swept his whole hand across the five strings, then turned slowly.

The man behind him was about his own height, but much broader. His eyes were black buttons under the edge of a gray fedora. His right shoulder was at least three inches higher than the left.

"Joe sent me around to see you about taking that job," he said.

His right hand was in his pocket. Apparently he had nudged Jules with whatever was in that pocket. Jules looked at it. He said: "But I do not think I want a job. I want to sing out of doors."

The left corner of the man's mouth lifted slightly, but he was not smiling.

"This job would be out of doors," he said.

Jules shrugged. "I do not know this Joe."

"Well, he knows you. Come on."

Jules began a protest he did not finish. The man stared into his eyes. His right hand was in his pocket and he thrust it forward a half inch. He said: "Come on."

Jules looked into the button eyes and at the man's pocket. Very carefully he maneuvered the guitar under his arm and up on his back, held it in place with his right hand pressed against the end of the keyboard. He cleared his throat. He said: "All right, I'll come."

The man jerked his head to the right and Jules walked that way, across Mulberry Street, the man moving stiffly at his left side, his hand still in his pocket. They walked one square east, then two north and turned to the left. Near the corner a large closed car was parked. The sedan looked very heavy. There were two men in it. When Jules was opposite the car, the back door swung open.

"Get in," said the man beside him.

Tremaine cast a furtive over-the-shoulder glance back down the street; then he looked the other way. A man in a rust-brown suit and a derby stood on the far corner. When Jules looked at him he walked slowly away, the heavy, studied tread of a policeman. Jules swallowed audibly.

"Get in," the man said again.

Jules removed his hand from the keyboard of his guitar and it swung around under his right arm. He held it with both hands and thrust it ahead of him and put his foot on the running-board. He looked about again with a panic-stricken face. The man in the rust-brown suit had disappeared. There was no one else in sight. Tremaine saw that the glass of the car door was thick and had a slightly yellowish tint. Bullet-proof glass. The man with the twisted shoulder jostled him and thrust something hard into his back.

Slowly Jules climbed in. The two men already in the car said nothing. The driver had a dead-white face in which were dry, feverish eyes. The man in the back was bony. Bunches of muscle knotted on his thin jaws. Jules sank down into the deep upholstery of the rear seat beside him and carefully placed his guitar between his knees. The man with the twisted shoulder got in and clicked the door shut. The car lunged forward. Still no one spoke. Jules watched the dingy buildings slide past as they jounced the length of the block, crossed Mulberry and swung right on Lafayette and picked up speed. Jules caught a flash of a street sign at a corner. It read *E. 10 St.*

When they sped past Twelfth Street, Jules spoke timidly: "I thought Joe's was on Tenth Street."

The man with the twisted shoulder snorted a laugh. He said: "It is."

The car swung around Union Square, beating a red light, and jockeyed through Broadway traffic.

"What's Joe's last name?" Jules asked.

The man's button eyes looked at him with no expression. "It won't do no harm to tell you. It's Catrini."

Jules screwed down in his seat. The car slewed to a stop on a red light, the brakes snubbing its nose down. The motor purred and a faint odor of exhaust gas crept into the tonneau.

"Couldn't we have a little more air?" Jules asked.

The man on his right leaned forward and cranked the door window tight shut. The left corner of his mouth lifted slightly. He put his right hand in his coat pocket. When the car sprang forward again he took it out with a snub-nosed revolver in it.

"I'm afraid you can't have any more air," he said.

He rested the gun across his left forearm so that the muzzle gaped at Jules' stomach, and he cringed away from it, raising his right hand so that the palm interposed between the revolver and his abdomen.

"Don't," he whispered. "It might go off!"

The man snorted another monosyllabic laugh. He said: "It might."

TRAFFIC STREAKED PAST the windows and more buildings, flossier and expensive now. They swung east, then north, then swept up the ramp of Queensborough Bridge. The air sweetened, freshened by the water of the East River. It was filtering in from a ventilator in the car's roof.

Jules' eyes kept swinging back to the gun that was held carelessly cocked, the man's finger on the trigger. He pressed his body back in the deep softness of the cushion, shoving his feet against the floor. The snout still was leveled at his belly. He leaned forward, his hands clasped about the neck of his guitar. In this way he interposed his elbow between the gun and his body.

His left hand slid down the strings; his fingers inveigled themselves into the round sounding hole just below them. His lips trembled still. His sidelong glances at the gun were furtive and frightened but there was hardness at the back of his eyes. The car slid off the bridge, turned south, then east again. Jules saw that the continuous backward glide of buildings was interspersed now with trees. Traffic thinned. The car's speed picked up. Tremaine hunched forward over the guitar, fondling it. He swayed forward a little as the car slackened speed, but he was tensely braced when it swung around a corner and began to jounce over a rough road with long, heaving dives.

"Please uncock that gun," Jules quavered, glancing again at the black mouth of the snub-nosed revolver. "This bouncing might make it go off!"

The man with the twisted shoulder lounged back in the seat and said nothing. He allowed his eyes to slide about and looked at Jules out of their corners. Tremaine caught a flash of the chauffeur's white face in the small rear vision mirror above the windshield. He was grinning. The man beside Jules laughed outright, the knots of muscles on his jaws rippling.

The car swerved again and shoved its long snout up a narrow

lane among trees. In fifty feet it was completely out of sight of the main road. The machine stopped and slowly turned around. The car was long. It took a lot of maneuvering. Jules' hands gripped the guitar until they ached. He could feel the bite of the strings across his fingers. When the car pointed back the way it had come, the driver, a sly grin on his white face, leaned back and opened the right rear door.

"What—what are you going to do?" Jules babbled. His legs were tense under him. He lifted the guitar slightly from the floor, his left hand sliding down to the sound opening. His lips trembled and his shoulders cringed.

The man with the twisted shoulder swung his head slowly about. The corner of his mouth lifted. He spoke gently, unpleasant laughter lurking in his voice. "We think we've got a flat tire. We want you to get out and look at it."

The chauffeur laughed aloud. Jules looked at him. The feverish eyes were mocking. He looked into the bony, grinning face of the man at his left. Neither of these two had a gun but both were looking at the gun in the hands of the man with the twisted shoulder. Jules looked at it, too.

"I don't think the tire's flat," he said, in a pleading tone. "I didn't hear anything like a flat tire."

The man leaned towards him slightly, his button eyes flat, and the gun pointed unwaveringly at his stomach.

"This is a good car," he said. "You wouldn't be able to hear anything like a flat tire."

Jules looked wide-eyed at the gun and opened his mouth and closed it again. He gulped and said: "All right."

He got to his feet, crouching with his head against the low roof. He did not turn his back to the man but kept his eyes on the gun and lifted the guitar so that he held it crossways in his hands, the big end to his left. His left hand slipped the cord loose from its button at the base, then slid to the sound opening again and the first finger inserted itself in a ring there which could not be seen.

"All right," he said again.

He struck down with the guitar. Its base bonged on the wrist of the hand that held the gun. It discharged and the bullet tugged at Jules' left trouser leg. In the same instant he leaped from the car and his right hand seized the inner handle of the door and slammed it shut as he whirled behind it.

Shouts and hoarse curses burst out in the car, slightly muffled by its heavy doors and the thick glass. Jules was sprinting on his toes at a diagonal from the back of the car, sprinting with his head back and his chest out. As he ran he counted slowly to himself: "Three—four—fi—"

Wind struck him from behind and hurled him face down on the earth. A twig jabbed his cheek and a muffled ripping concussion burst in his ears. For nearly five minutes Jules lay as he had fallen, the earth cold against his face; then slowly he thrust himself up from the ground, gravel biting his palms, his shoulders humped, his head sagging. He heaved to his knees, then reeled to his feet, steadied himself with one hand on a tree. He breathed deeply a half dozen times, shaking his head sharply; and then he stood erect and moved heavily around towards the car.

The sedan was not quite where he had left it. It seemed to have been lifted off the ground and dropped about four feet to the right. It listed to that side. The top was blown out and jagged ends of metal thrust spear points up into the air.

One door sagged crazily and another was missing. The bullet-proof glass had vanished. Something red dripped on the right running-board, dripped and formed a sluggishly widening puddle. Jules' lips were pressed together in a thin hard line. Three men had been in that car. That left only O'Reilly to pay for Angela's death. And there was that score against dear brother Andrew....

Jules looked down at his left hand. A steel ring an inch across was on the forefinger and from that ring dangled a steel pin.

"Well, well," he said, and threw back his head and laughed with little sound. "That grenade must have ruined my guitar. I'll have to buy a new one."

The Confessional

"Hard as Pharaoh—soft as a woman," and he walked with a guitar among killers. That was Jules Tremaine

JULES TREMAINE STROLLED eastward through the cluttered smelliness of Bleecker Street. His new guitar lay comfortably against his belly and his fingers twitched smothered minor chords. Fat Italians waddled out of his path and smiled back at him.

Tremaine was not singing. His round blue gaze was fixed on two men who stood where the out-thrust jetty of a fruit stand made an eddy in the flow of humanity past pushcarts and stalls. One of the two men was lean in austere black, and hair like white floss glistened beneath the straight brim of his hat. The other was small in a flashy, wide-striped suit, and his jerky side glances were furtive.

The street singer leaned his erect shoulders against an iron railing fifteen feet from where the pair stood in a shaft of warm October sunlight and began softly to sing Schubert's *Ave Maria.* His eyelids were lowered. The man in black put a veined thin hand on the resplendent sleeve of the other. He bent forward, his lips murmuring, the pressure of his fragile fingers emphasizing words Tremaine could not hear. The furtive one stared up with concentrated fright. The muscles of his upper lip and the left side of his nose twitched and quivered like a rabbit's. His head began to jerk from side to side in negation as if some mechanical violence beyond his control was rotating it, and his lips framed a soundless "No! No!"

Behind the tall and the short man the crowd flowed on, a moving tapestry of subdued colors. To Jules it seemed the monotonously mute chorus of a grotesque show throwing into mocking emphasis these two spotlighted in sunlight. But this was not comedy. The stage was not set for comedy.

Tremaine's voice swelled into a dramatic crescendo. "A-a-ve Mar-*ri-i-i*-a-a," and he tilted back his head. When he looked again, the furtive man's stare was panic-stricken and fixed at some spot up Bleecker Street towards Seventh Avenue. As Jules watched, he pulled his eyes away, whirled and, doubled forward, tore a swift way through the sluggish river of people, leaving a wake of staccato curses.

Tremaine glanced quickly where the man had stared. The crowd was thinner towards Seventh Avenue. On a doorstep a man with a mustache like rusty bicycle handles was laughing with a child of three. A matron and a pushcart vender argued with outflying hands over the price of chicory. And down Bleecker towards him lounged a low, black limousine. Jules' eyelids dropped as he regarded it. He pursed his lips on the dying strain of his song and the black sword points of his militant mustache shifted forward a fraction of an inch.

He plucked two ultimate chords, straightened away from the iron railing and strolled, an alert, short figure in dapper gray, towards the fruit stand where the man in black shook his head slowly.

"Good evening, Father Boniface," said Jules.

The priest raised a care-carven face. Its scanty flesh was a translucent white as if a calm death had touched it and had been kind.

"Ah, Jules," he said, and there was a quaver behind his voice.

Tremaine smiled up into the worried pale gaze, his fingers walking soundlessly over the strings of his guitar.

"You and the sunlight, Father," he said, "seem the only things beautiful in this dreary patch of world."

The old man shook his head again so that the silvery floss of his hair showed first on one side, then the other. A fragile hand slid across the black coat, a Gothic Christ in ivory on an ebony cross, and Tremaine knew the fingers pressed the outline of a crucifix.

"Jules," he said, "the world is beautiful. The hard things are in the hearts of men. And there is where we should seek to help even if our help is scorned."

The street singer spoke slowly with tight words: "Vermin like that Bunny Riggs don't need your help or mine. Bullets end all their troubles... and should."

The priest's head went up sharply and anger darkened his pale eyes, puckered his brows. He opened a mouth that had gone taut, then did not speak. His gaze searched Tremaine's and slowly the tightness of his lips faded into a slight, weary smile. He smoothed a dry, veined hand across his forehead.

"Ah, Jules," he said. "You are two men. You are hard as Pharaoh and you are soft as a woman. Because Angela was a little thing that had touched your heart you went into the very jaws of death to kill the men who had murdered her. And that was a fine thing and a foolish thing, for vengeance is not for man."

Jules' mouth wrinkled in a grim, small smile, advancing the tips of his black mustache just a little.

"Occasionally," he said, "the Lord's vengeance needs a little mortal help."

A DOOR OPENING metallically spun Jules around. That lounging, low sedan was stationary just behind him. A man in a tall silk hat unfolded out through the opened door, a spare strong body delineated by a cutaway and gray striped trousers.

"Ah," said the man, "my charming brother!"

He bowed a second time.

"And Father Boniface! Good day."

Jules' smile was stiff. He thrust the guitar back under his right arm and up on his back, pressed his hand against the end of its keyboard as against a sword hilt and bowed rigidly.

"My *dear* brother," he returned formally.

"Could I persuade you to take a walk?" the elder Tremaine asked.

Jules, straightening, stared up into the expressionless, long face, stretched into the abnormality of a freakish mirror by the high sheen of the hat.

He said: "You should never wear tall hats, Andrew. They really aren't becoming."

Parenthetical creases deepened about Andrew's mouth corners, his lips surrendering to a meager smile.

"Could I persuade you to take a walk?" he repeated.

"Not with you."

"Oh, no, no." Andrew's tone was shocked, his face distraught with exaggerated concern. "I wouldn't think of asking that."

Jules bowed again with a ceremonious flourish of his black slouch hit.

"I want you," his brother continued, "to walk alone so I can confer with Father Boniface."

Jules' eyes ascended the formality of striped trousers and cutaway to the mockery of Andrew's face. Behind him the priest broke his silence. He said: "No!"

The elder Tremaine's eyes flicked past the street singer to Father Boniface. He removed his hat, holding it with careless accustom in his left hand, exposing the bald high sweep of his forehead.

"This is not a personal matter, Father. It concerns your parish."

Jules' head swung about. A frown worried the old man's face. His eyes were a pale torment. Tremaine deliberately thrust between Father Boniface and his brother.

"On your way, Andrew," he said.

"Jules, you are rude."

"On—your—way!"

Andrew's glance lifted to the priest. "Would you come to my

home tonight, Father?" he asked. "Or shall I come to you? It is most important."

Jules slipped a crimson cord over his head and laid the guitar gently beside the fruit stall. He straightened, his arms swinging at his sides. He said gently: "I had the honor to address three words to you, Andrew, and you compelled me to repeat them. I hope you will not make it necessary for me to say them again?"

The glitter in Andrew's eyes was like chipped topaz, but harder. The mouth creases were tight V's from the thin hate of his lips. He said: "Some day, Jules—"

"Yes?"

The elder Tremaine turned away. "I shall phone you later. Father." Urchins scattered jeering from his path. He inclined his head with dignity and entered his car. The chauffeur shut the door smartly, the motor's drone deepened and the limousine slid away. Andrew did not look back.

Jules bent slowly over his guitar and the crimson cord again pressed familiarly into his left shoulder. He turned to the priest, a smile on his lips, his eyes masked by heavy lids. He touched the left half of his mustache with his right thumbnail.

"I cannot understand," said Father Boniface slowly, "how a man like you...."

"... can be the brother of a slimy politician like the one who just left?" Jules supplied.

The smile on his lips tightened. He thrust the guitar behind him sharply, the clench of his fingers white on its end.

"It is precisely because he is such a man," said Jules, "that I am the man I am. Why else do you think a man of wealth sings in the streets like a beggar?

"I did it first on a bet one night when I was a little tight, and

I found out how good these people—" he swept his right hand in a broad gesture—"how kind these people could be."

"And it has seemed to me, Jules," the priest said softly, "that always you are searching—searching for something you have not yet found."

For a fleeting instant Jules' eyes showed hard as flint, then they grew mocking again, slowly, as if he was forcing that expression into them. He continued, very quickly, as though the priest had not spoken:

"And I learned the havoc wrought by gangs that my brother's politics fosters. This is not heroic, but... wouldn't I be less than a man if I did not do my best to counteract the evil my brother permits?"

The priest shook his white head as if it were heavy.

"It is not well for brother to turn on brother," he said slowly. "It begets hate, and hate can cause... can cause many things."

Jules threw back his head, and teeth showed white beneath his mustache. His laugh made little sound and neither then nor afterward was there amusement on his face. The right corner of his mouth lifted slightly.

"I am my brother's keeper," he declaimed.

Father Boniface's thin hand groped again to his crucifix.

"You are a queer man, Jules, a queer, hard man, and a soft man. Come; I wish to talk with you."

Tremaine bowed with stiff dignity and dragged slow feet behind the old priest as the marketing crowds opened a path for him—ranks of fat Italian women with the precocious obscenity of dirty children at their skirts, a line of mustached pushcart venders, chains of striding, brassy young girls. All stood aside for the Father. Jules was heavy-footed behind him, moving through the slanting dusty rays of sunlight, the guitar silent on his back, his eyes on the pavement and a tight hate on his lips.

IT WAS EASY to see that here the priest found sanctuary. In this austere room with its scrubbed pine table and the musty mellow smell of its shelves of books, pounds and pounds were lifted off those thin, high shoulders. Jules Tremaine balanced his guitar against the white plaster wall and through the room's single window inspected the dingy limestone walls of St. Mary's, across Sullivan Street.

"Jules," came the priest's gentle voice, "you must curb this hatred against your brother."

Tremaine toed about. His eyebrows lifted, but he did not speak.

Father Boniface let himself down into a chair behind the table, pushed his hands out before him and interlaced their brittle fingers. His white abundant hair was parted on the left and made a silvery scroll across the parchment of his forehead.

"Hate between brothers is bad business," he said. "Bad business, Jules, as I have reason to know."

Jules thrust both hands in the side pockets of his coat, his head arrogant above set shoulders. His blue gaze was wide and direct on the pale eyes of the priest.

"Father Boniface, you don't love my brother, yourself."

The white head nodded reluctantly, the brow puckered.

"That is true. It is one of my many sins."

"Baloney!" snapped Jules. "Father, you are a beautiful man, but there are times when you talk sheer nonsense!"

The old man's frown faded into a gentle smile.

"In my father's house—" he began. "I know," Tremaine broke in, "but the hell of it is that my brother and I probably will be in the same mansion... and it won't be big enough!"

He took his right hand out of his pocket and flung it in a sweeping gesture.

"Father Boniface, don't talk to my brother when he phones you."

"But he said it was about my parish!"

"Don't talk to him."

Father Boniface spread his two hands with palms upward, fingers slightly bent and apart and there was the same gentle smile.

"My boy, if it's about my parish—"

Jules stared at him hard, then lifted both shoulders. He turned and moved slowly towards the window, brushing his mustache with a thumbnail.

"What was it you wanted to talk with me about?"

He stared again at the gray walls of the church, still fingering his mustache. The priest answered nothing and presently Jules glanced towards him. Father Boniface was telling the beads of his rosary with white, accustomed fingers, his lips moving soundlessly, his eyes closed in a lifted face. Jules turned back to the dingy wall. A child had scrawled adolescent eroticism in white chalk letters a foot high, a single four-letter word reiterated for the entire length of the building. A blind beggar at the street corner held a cup in which were five yellow pencils.

"Of that of which I have spoken—the unnatural hatred between those of the same flesh and blood, which often is of evil consequences."

Father Boniface's voice was low, but it brought Jules pivoting around on his heel, and a frown to his face.

"It is not unnatural," he said, a little sharply, "when every instinct in one is opposed to every principle in the other. The mere accident of relationship does not alter that."

"If that were true, perhaps not," said the patient voice of the old priest; "but it cannot be so. There are inevitably kindred instincts, perhaps unsuspected where wills have clashed and the very closeness of such blood ties and of association have developed misunderstandings that might not have had birth between strangers."

Jules made an impatient movement; but the expression in the kindly old face choked his interruption.

"Leave that aside for the moment, Jules, but ponder upon it often. This I wish more to point out to you—where there should be greater affection, greater love, and this emotion is turned to hatred, that hatred will be deeper, more deadly, more destructive, unless it is rooted out and cast aside."

"Sophistries, Father." And Jules' tone did not wholly conceal his impatience; neither was it too convincing.

"Not sophistry, Jules," the priest said softly. "Truth."

Tremaine shrugged, and the silence of a full minute lay between them.

Jules raised his eyes and found Father Boniface's glance upon him.

"If it were not," said the priest softly, "for the inviolability of the confession—of which even you, a layman, are aware, I might convince you."

Jules' brows corrugated in swift thought. The confession. Hatred of brother against brother. Jules' mind flashed back to the two men on the street; Father Boniface and the furtive-eyed rat, Bunny Riggs. But Bunny's real name was not Riggs.

It was something else—and a man with that other name had died, died very slowly and very horribly as do men who offend those Catrini.

Jules' lips formed soundless words— "His own brother...." Abruptly he smiled, with a hard light deep in his eyes.

"And still I tell you," he said with curious lightness, "do not talk with my brother if he phones you—do not go to see him. There is no good in it."

"I have a duty, my boy," said the old priest patiently, "my parish, my people. I shall follow it in the way that is shown me. Follow yours as carefully, Jules—" he smiled—"and my worry of you will be less...."

GUITAR ON HIS back, Jules Tremaine, some hours later, paused on the curb of Sullivan Street and searched the chilling October night for a taxi. He saw none, crossed and walked slowly along Prince towards Sixth Avenue. The way was dark and a blundering wind was damp in his face.

Tremaine eased the pressure of his right hand and allowed his guitar to slip forward under his arm. He drew it up and, strolling even more slowly, touched the gut to soft resonance. His music was largo and sombre. His feet scuffed heavily.

Behind him along West Broadway, the Elevated slammed, sending echoes crashing like blind birds through the canyon of Prince Street, against the huddled brick warehouses and tenements. Jules bent his head so that he still could hear the vibrance of his guitar and in that position, in midstride, he halted. His fingers paused motionless above the strings while the rattle of the Elevated died. His heels settled solidly.

His eyes probed the darkness. A feeble light from Sixth

Avenue faltered into the jumbled shadows against the wall and lost itself in a blackened doorway and there picked out a gleam of silvery white. Gradually Tremaine made out a recumbent man.

Nothing unusual in that. Every block of darkened side street found four or five of the unemployed hunched in awkward postures of exhausted sleep. But there was that silvery gleam. It looked like the brittle hair of an old man and old, homeless men do not sleep with their heads uncovered.

White hair! Tremaine tiptoed nearer. He thrust the guitar behind his back again, bending closer. Suddenly he dropped to his knees, his guitar jarring into deep resonance.

"Mother of Heaven!" he muttered.

He lifted the white head of the old man in his arms and bent his head over the chest then jerked away sharply. Something cold and metallic had bruised his ear. Slowly Tremaine laid the stiffening body back on the walk and his hand groped for the metal that his ear had struck. It closed on a handle that fitted his palm neatly. His fingers clutched it, then flinched away and he sprang to his feet.

"Stabbed!" he muttered. "Good Lord! Stabbed!"

Jules glanced about him. A cruising taxi droned by on Sixth Avenue, half a block away. The approaching clatter of an Elevated train grew into bedlam and died. That was all in the dark street, the stooping street singer and a man dead in a doorway with a knife in his breast, a man with a scroll of silvery hair, with a fragile hand across his breast like a Gothic Christ in ivory upon an ebony cross.

Tremaine's mouth was a cold line. Driving legs took him to Sixth Avenue. A red and black taxi crashed a traffic light at his signal and shot northward with him, switching in and out among the striped stilts of the Elevated, swerving east when the lights opposed, whirling into Fifth Avenue and weaving on through the streams of traffic. Jules dropped out at an address in the East Fifties, took the brownstone steps two at a time and used a key.

The door bumped shaking against the wall and his beating feet sped him down the dim reaches of the hall to a small square room lined with books. There was no light.

"Mr. Jules, sir?" a grave voice, slightly alarmed inquired from the front hallway.

Tremaine strode back. The butler's face, tilted above his dark green livery, was carefully expressionless but his back was stiff.

"Where is my brother?" Jules rasped.

"Begging your pardon, sir. He won't be in for dinner."

"Where is he?"

The stiffness extended to the butler's neck. He looked down a thin nose.

"I don't rightly know, sir. Perhaps at his club."

Jules ducked his head out of the looped crimson cord and thrust his guitar into the butler's hand with a vehemence that sent the man back a half pace.

"Put this in my room, Burke," he said, "and phone the police there's a murdered man on Prince Street, between Sullivan and Sixth Avenue!"

The butler's jaw sagged. His mouth formed a lopsided cipher.

"Begging your—your pard...."

The door clapped shut behind Tremaine and the butler completed the sentence vaguely, stood staring down at the guitar cradled in his arms like a prize Pekinese.

JIMSON, THE DOORMAN at the *Clinton Club,* was portly and ruddy with years and good living. He stood squarely on his two feet in his dark blue uniform cap and coat and used a cold gray eye to better advantage than lesser minions their brawn and violence. But when Jules Tremaine slammed out of a taxi and leaped up the steps at him, he had no opportunity to use that frigid glance.

"Hey!" he attempted.

Tremaine was beside him before the syllable was out, past him, as he turned, and through the doors before those solidly planted feet could move.

Jules strode across the red and gold lobby. A page sprang forward from beside a high-arched doorway to the right. He had his instructions, that boy. Jimson, the doorman, had trained him. He stood squarely in front of Jules and asked, very loftily: "Someone you wished to see, sir?"

Jules' eyes shot beyond the trig uniform, spotted a tall, spare man in a tuxedo standing before the formal fireplace with an elbow on the mantel, a tall man with a high, bald forehead. Jules took off his hat slowly and for a moment stared under his lowered lids.

"Someone you wished to see, sir?" the page insisted.

Tremaine withdrew his gaze from the softly lighted room where a half dozen men in evening dress lounged in big plush and brown leather chairs and fixed it on the page. He clapped his black slouch hat on the boy's head.

"Put that in the check room," he said, and stalked across the wide, carpeted floor.

His sharp movements were an affront in that room. Irritated eyes were raised, shocked brows were lifted at the gray sack suit among the formal clubbiness. Tremaine saw none of this. His eyes were fixed on the tall man who glanced up now and locked gaze with him across the expanse of the room. The man took his elbow off the mantle.

Jules stepped close to him and said: "You lousy murderer!"

Andrew straightened from his bow sharply, elbows flexing and hands half clenched. He relaxed them but his voice was hard.

"What new madness is this, Jules?" he snapped.

The younger Tremaine stood on braced feet, fists rammed into his coat pockets. His eyes were nearly hidden beneath the weight of his lids and he spoke with tight hoarseness.

"I walked home tonight past the corner of Sullivan and Prince," he bit out.

Andrew sent polite eyebrows crawling up towards the high reach of his forehead. "I passed Forty-second and Fifth Avenue," he said.

"Did you see any murdered men there?" Jules asked softly.

Behind him he heard the subdued mobilization of the club's guardians, the irascible voice of a member. He did not swerve his gaze from its fixed, bitter regard. Andrew glanced beyond him.

"Perhaps," he murmured, "we would better conclude this pleasant little conversation in a more secluded place."

Jules said: "We'll finish it here."

Andrew sighed, a ponderous buffoonery of tried patience.

"No, Jimson," he spoke in a slightly louder voice. "It's quite all right. My brother was in a hurry."

The muffled marshaling of men retreated behind Jules' arrogant back and Andrew bent his long face slightly forward.

"Don't you think," he asked carefully, "that it would be less tiresome if you would detail your newest accusation instead of speaking in innuendo?"

"If you insist."

"I'm afraid I must."

"Stop me if you've heard this one," Jules jeered. "You tried to talk to Father Boniface this afternoon and he refused. You asked him to call on you tonight and said you would phone him later. . . ."

The elder brother slowly drew a Perfecto from a Florentine leather case, snipped the end with a gold pocket-knife and snapped a lighter into flame. Holding the cigar in one hand, the lighter in the other, he said gently: "I also ate lunch today."

"Damn you!" said Jules, his level voice edged. "Damn you! You asked for this, now you're going to listen if I have to club you to the floor."

Again the polite upward crawl of brows. Andrew put the cigar in his mouth, applied the yellow flame and puffed, rolling the Perfecto in his fingers until it was well ignited. He snapped cut the lighter.

"I trust," he pronounced, removing the cigar temporarily, "that no such extreme measures will be—er—necessary."

Jules took his hands out of his pockets and advanced two stiff steps. Andrew turned his head, expelled slow blue smoke, then allowed his eyes once more to meet Jules'.

"Andrew," said the younger man with slow emphasis, "you had an engagement with Father Boniface tonight, *and I found him murdered!*"

Andrew stopped the cigar halfway to his lips and pursed them so that little converging wrinkles made miniature darts around them.

"Now that," he said, "is curious."

Jules closed and opened the fingers of his right hand at his side. He raised it above his head, clenched into a shaking fist, the elbow crooked and tense. His voice was hard.

"So help me God, this is one crime that not all your politics can cover up!"

Andrew puffed deliberately and exhaled an indolent blue cloud.

"My charming brother," he deplored, "you seem to be all worked up."

Jules leaned even closer, his eyes darkly furious.

"Murderer!" he spat out and pounded from the room.

Andrew inspected the burning end of his cigar with its thin gray spiral of smoke and flicked ashes carefully into the fireplace.

JIMSON, THE DOORMAN, rigidly ignored Jules Tremaine as he made a slow exit down the stone steps of the *Clinton Club.* Midway down, he paused, adjusted his black hat, and surveyed the cars at the curb. A taxi swung in, the driver leaning forward with a raised forefinger. Jules shook his head and the cab eased back into the traffic. Near the corner a long, low limousine was parked and towards this Tremaine presently walked.

As he drew abreast of the front seat, the chauffeur glanced at him casually, then quickly again, a narrow sharp face under a uniform cap's visor.

"Yes, sir, Mr. Jules?" he asked.

"I am using the car tonight," Jules said slowly. "I won't require you."

The man sat silent a moment. "But, Mr. Jules—"

"Thompson!" said Jules.

"Yes, sir?"

"I won't require your services."

"I'm sorry, Mr. Jules—"

Jules leaned across the side and his voice was very gentle. "Get out, Thomson."

"Mr. Andrew said—"

Jules opened the door deliberately and stood in the meager light from the dash, his right hand in the side pocket of his coat, his head bent forward so he could see under the low roof. He looked into the chauffeur's eyes and his mouth was tight.

The man fumbled hurriedly with the catch of the door at his side. He stammered: "This may cost me my job."

"You're going to lose that shortly anyhow," said Jules, and ducked in as the chauffeur slid out the opposite door.

Sinking into the velvet of the seat, he kicked the starter and the Mercedes purred. He swung its pointed nose from the curb, turned left at Forty-ninth, north on Lexington and wove through the traffic with smooth speed. At Eighty-fifth he turned east and parked. He walked three doors farther eastward, went down a short flight of stairs and pressed a black button. Within a buzzer whirred. The door's opening outlined in dim light a man with high, square shoulders. The man said: "Hello, Jules," and moved back and to one side.

Jules stepped past him, eyes meditatively on a strip of green carpet, walked twenty-five feet down a narrow hall and turned left into a low, long room with a beamed ceiling. It was lighted comfortably with three lamps. He laid his hat on a Chippendale desk and sank into a brown davenport before a hooded fireplace. He leaned forward and put his elbows on his knees.

"Frank," he said, "I need your help."

The tall man stood on the hearth with braced feet. He wore glasses and a brush of a red mustache. His hair was a red brush, too. He grunted: "Fine."

Jules looked up at him from under tight brows.

"A priest with whom my brother made an engagement tonight was murdered while probably on his way to keep that engagement," he said.

Frank was not looking at him. He peered off into the juncture of the ceiling and the far wall and rubbed the palms of his hands slowly together. On the wall above the mantelpiece a sword and an old pistol opposed each other.

"This priest was talking to me this afternoon," Jules went on.

Frank continued to massage his palms. He asked: "Why did you mention your brother?"

Jules clasped his hands, elbows still resting on his knees. He looked at his hands.

"I think a gangster confessed to this priest and that gangster is Bunny Riggs."

"Oh!" Frank's chin raised an inch, his mouth opened, the tongue touching one corner. His eyes narrowed a trifle.

"Yes," said Jules, "Bunny Riggs has been used by those Catrini... before this. When Riggs was talking to the priest this afternoon and Andrew's car rolled up, Riggs ran like the devil." Frank smiled with a gleam of slightly irregular teeth. He walked to a corner and from a book shelf took a flat black box about nine by six inches. He opened it and slid out a Colt .45 automatic.

"Have you seen this one?" he asked. "Test barrel."

Jules inspected the gun as the other held it out on the palm of a large hand.

"Nice," he said, "but I'll want you to keep it in the holster tonight. Our work calls for blanks. Those two .45 revolvers now—"

Frank frowned and sighted the automatic at a speck on the opposite wall. He sighed. "I've been wanting to try Ruby out."

He held the gun flat in his hand again, looking at it. Then he yanked back the barrel and slid it forward, clicking a cartridge into the chamber, adjusted the safety and shoved the weapon into his belt, six inches to the right of his navel.

"Okey," he said. "I'll get the revolvers."

HALF AN HOUR later Jules shifted his weight from the right to the left foot in the shadow of the apartment building and peered once more along Seventy-sixth Street, West. He straightened away from the wall and stared at a small man just rounding the distant corner from Amsterdam. The man passed through the light of a drugstore window and turned his head in a furtive side glance.

Jules walked to the curb and looked both ways along the street before he crossed under the Elevated and moved along Seventy-sixth on the same side with the man. Most of the houses were old, with brownstone fronts and high stairs. A quarter way down the block an apartment house nudged a saucy false brick front up to the building line. Near its top was a black oblong on which block white letters, reading vertically *2, 3, 5, RMS,* were illuminated by hooded Mazdas.

The clop of the small man's heels echoed briskly against still buildings where only dim lights showed. Back behind Jules the Elevated slashed and banged through the night. Tremaine increased his stride and the two men converged on the apartment house at almost equal pace. They still had fifty feet to go when a low, black car slid around the corner from Amsterdam Avenue and droned up the street.

In the full light of the apartment doorway, Tremaine halted. He crouched and pointed at the swiftly nearing car.

"Look out there!" he shouted.

The little man wrenched his chin around on his right shoulder, saw the savage sweep of the car, and a tiny smothered squeal rose in his throat. He darted for the basement entrance of the apartment building. Jules dived after him and together they slid down a short flight of cement steps.

Gun explosions racketed against the houses, then the hum of the motor increased and faded out. On Amsterdam Avenue a police whistle became excited.

"Let's get out of here," Jules muttered.

The other man's breath rasped in his throat. "Mother in Heaven! Mother in Heaven!"

He whimpered as he edged out of the stairway and into the door of the apartment house. Jules kept at his side and in the crass brilliance of the modernistic lobby the man halted and stared into his face.

"Who are you?" he demanded.

Tremaine's face was expressionless, his eyes hard.

"I haven't asked you that," he pointed out.

The man blinked at him. The muscles of his upper lip and the left side of his nose quivered like a rabbit's.

"I know you ain't," he mumbled. "I know you ain't."

His eyes slid off over Jules' left shoulder, crossed the floor back to his own feet, glanced momentarily at Tremaine's unchanging face, then slid off into distance again.

"What do you want?" the man asked.

"I did you a favor," Jules said. "Those hoods shot only because they saw you were taking to cover… with somebody to help you. They were going to invite you for a little ride. Maybe you know what they do on those… little rides?"

The muscles quivered in the man's face again. He leaned his shoulders against the wall. His arms were straight at his sides and his palms pressed against the mottled lightning bolts of the wall's decorations. A fine beading of sweat broke out on his upper lip.

"Mother in Heaven! Mother in Heaven!" His eyes were small and black. They slid again across Jules' face. "What do you want?"

"Let me park in your place tonight."

The man's eyes forgot to be furtive. Dilated pupils fixed on Jules'.

"What d'ye want to do that for?"

Jules leaned towards him so that their faces were only inches apart. He whispered: "I want a crack at those Catrini! Do I guess right?"

The man licked the pale pink point of his tongue over his upper lip. He swallowed, opened his mouth, gulped it shut again. "Who are you? Who—"

Jules sliced the air with the side of his hand.

"Do I stay—or do I stay?"

The man stared, blinked and looked down, pressed himself away from the wall with his hands, and stepped falteringly to a metal door painted in the semblance of mustard yellow oak. He pushed a large black button with his thumb and another button below it glowed with yellow light. Behind the door, machinery clicked and presently light descended across a round window in its middle, a row of vertical round bars contracted to the right and the man pulled open the door.

Jules followed him into the elevator and the man pressed a black button on which was painted a white six. The grating slid shut and the cage quivered upward. The sixth floor had a dingy, half-lighted hall. When the apartment door labeled C had been opened, Jules saw at the end of a narrow hall an expanse of rose window drapes and an imitation Oriental rug. He smelled scented powder and cheap perfume, and a girl's voice said: "Is that you, Bunny?"

The man answered hoarsely: "Yeah." Jules was at his heels as he stumbled down the hall. A girl was sprawled on a davenport. When she saw Jules she swung her feet sharply to the floor and pulled a kimono of washed-out blue across bony knees. Her voice rose in a shrill complaint: "It's a wonder you wouldn't say you had somebody with you."

Bunny stood looking at her, saying nothing. Jules moved across the room, eased aside a corner of the drawn shade and peered out. He turned back to the two.

"Cripes," the girl's voice drooped. "What's the matter, Bunny?"

She stood up. She was taller than Bunny, a fraction taller than Jules. The sharply demarked crimson of her lips made a small ellipse. "Bunny," she pleaded. "Bunny!"

She took him by the shoulders and shook him, forgetting to hold her kimono.

Bunny pushed a weary hand into her face and spilled her on the davenport.

"Shut up!" he said dully.

The girl said nothing. She lay awkwardly straggled along the couch and stared up at the little man. Jules sank into an upholstered chair and draped a knee over the right arm. He leaned his head back and said comfortably: "Those Catrini ought to be back in a little while."

Bunny whirled and his voice rasped in his throat. "Why are you so happy about it?"

Tremaine raised eyebrows. The girl screwed to a sitting position, bounced to her feet.

"Your number's up!" she screamed at Bunny.

The little man spun towards her.

"Shut up!" he howled. "Shut up!"

The girl crouched. Blonde, frowsy hair straggled about her face. Her mouth was a writhing circle of red. "I told you you'd get in trouble going to that psalm-singer!" she spat out.

Her left hand clutched the kimono tightly across her breasts. The fingernails were as red as her lips.

"Shut up!" Bunny said again, his voice a whining whisper.

The girl's mouth opened in a choking scream, she plunged to her left with out-flung arms, let out another whispered shriek and fled through a dark doorway with the blue tails of her kimono fluttering.

Bunny straightened slowly and turned to Jules, the muscles of his lip quivering. "Molls are all lice," he said disgustedly.

He dragged the back of his hand across his mouth. Jules swung the foot he had draped over the chair arm.

"What are you going to do?" he demanded.

Bunny looked about the room with furtive eyes.

"I'm going to get out of here," he said.

"And go where?"

The man blinked. "I dunno. I dunno."

Jules looked at him unwaveringly. The girl showed in the doorway again, blonde hair stringing out from under a big black hat, a bright green coat about her and a brown suit-case held in both hands before her. Bunny turned on rigid legs.

"Where you going?" he asked.

"I ain't gonna stay here and get murdered!" she whimpered. "I told you to leave that priest alone. *They* found out about—"

"Will—you—shut—up?" Bunny's voice again had a hunted, high note.

"Don't, Bunny, for Gawd's sake, don't!" the girl babbled. She drew the suit-case up in front of her belly. "I still love you, Bunny, but—"

"Yeah, but—"

Jules broke in quietly. "Let her go, Bunny. She's just in the way."

Bunny turned his head sidewise and stared at Tremaine.

"Women," said Jules, "are lice."

"Yeah, they are." Bunny turned towards the girl. "You're a louse! Get out!"

The girl went with jerky, heavy-heeled steps, her face twisted back, a fading, pale luminance dimming into the hallway. She was outlined momentarily in faint yellow light as the door opened, then it closed, darkening the hall, and there was nothing there.

Jules got slowly out of the chair and stretched and went into the bathroom and drank two glasses of water. He returned and Bunny was standing in the middle of the room with slow tears tracing down his face.

"That tramp walked out with my last bottle of gin," he whimpered.

BUNNY RIGGS LET himself drop on to the davenport and leaned back with hands limp on the cushions.

"My last bottle of gin," he said.

Jules walked slowly down the hall towards the door. The tremulous whining of Bunny's voice stopped him cold. "You ain't goin' no place," it stated.

Tremaine glanced back over his shoulder. The little man was crouched in the middle of the room and his right hand was low at his side and held a gun.

"Just locking the door," Jules explained.

He did that and walked back and smiled at Bunny's twitching face.

"You can't take it, can you, Bunny?" he asked softly.

The little man straightened and looked sheepishly down at the gun. He hid it in his coat pocket.

"Sure," he said. "Sure."

"It looks like you're going to have to."

Bunny blinked into Jules' face, then his eyes slid beyond him to the wall.

"Not me," he said. "Not me."

Jules draped himself in the chair again.

"What are *they* after you for?" he asked.

"That's my business."

Jules raised eyebrows and pursed lips, thrusting forward the points of his mustache. He shrugged slowly and slumped farther down into the chair.

"I'm glad it is," he said.

"I thought you wanted to tangle with those Catrini?"

Jules' eyes nearly closed, he let his lips smile a very little.

"I aim to do a little shooting, maybe," he admitted. "But they wouldn't *shoot* you."

The man flung out two words like bullets. "—— you!"

Jules continued to smile. He looked quite sleepy. Bunny's body lost its tension gradually. His eyes flitted about the room.

"That tramp took my gin," he muttered finally.

"Getting drunk won't keep you from taking it," Jules said.

The man's eyes shot more rapidly about the room, flew about like imprisoned birds. Jules laughed softly.

"The door's behind you," he said.

"Damn you!" Bunny shrilled. "Damn you!"

Jules laughed again, throwing his head far back and opening his mouth, with little sound. When he had finished, he said: "I told you you couldn't take it."

The man exclaimed: "Cripes!" and again: "Cripes!" He knotted his fingers and ground the palms together. "Cripes!"

Jules eased up in his chair and leaned forward, thrusting the black hat up off his brows.

"Those Catrini can do a rather nice job on occasion, can't they, Bunny?" he asked. His eyes never left the other man's face. He went on: "I saw Louis Ricci in the morgue. They did a nice job on him."

Bunny's hands became frantic in their massaging. He thrust them rigidly before him, tottered two steps and slumped on the davenport and gripped his skull with tight fingers.

"Cripes!" he whispered. "I wish I had that gin."

A metallic rattle from the door, a key in the lock jerked Bunny to the middle of the room. Jules sat and regarded the hallway curiously. The door swung inward and admitted a narrow line of light, then checked on the safety chain Jules had fastened. Bunny's gun was in his hand.

A hoarse whisper: "Let me in, Bunny."

Bunny quick-footed down the hall. The infiltration of light outlined his eager crouch.

"You bring the gin back, honey?" he asked.

"I killed it this morning… Let me in. Oh, let me in!" The girl was frantic.

"Get out!" Bunny snarled.

"No, no! Please! *Their* auto is out front. I can't—"

"Get out!"

"Oh, please—"

"Get—*out!*"

The light went out of the hall and the door clapped shut. Woman's hands beat dully a few times on the heavy barrier. Silence, then more beating.

"Bunny!"

Jules heard a few caught sobs, followed by more waiting silence, then sobs fading into distance. Bunny returned slowly. The man's face was drawn, his hands kneaded.

"She killed the gin! She killed the gin!"

Jules put his elbows on his knees, gaze still fixed on the little man, and tapped his fingertips together in sequence, little finger to thumb, little finger to thumb.

"And *their* auto is parked at the door?" he asked politely.

"Yeah."

Bunny's hands quieted and drooped at his sides, his body drooped, shoulders bent, head bowed and he was utterly still except that his upper lip twitched now and then.

"I gotta take it," he mumbled. "I gotta take it."

He began to button his coat with fumbling, tapered fingers. The nails had a pink, freshly manicured sheen. He looked around vaguely and finally centered his beady, black eyes on Jules and nodded his head once with a little jerk.

"I can take it," he declared clearly.

Jules continued to tap the tips of his fingers together in sequence, his gaze discomforting the other's small eyes.

"Listen," Jules' voice was portentous. "I don't owe that bunch anything. If I can pay them off I'm going to."

The little man unbuttoned his coat and patted his vest pockets, found a green and red package of cigarettes and hung one on his lower lip. He started feeling for matches. Jules leaned far forward and slowly shook the forefinger of his right hand in a ninety-degree vertical plane.

"I'll bet we can fix it so you don't have to take it... not *their* way."

"Yeah? How?"

Their eyes were locked. Jules spoke with heavy emphasis. "You got to play ball."

Bunny's upper lip twitched. He jerked his head in a single quick affirmative. The cigarette still dangled unlighted from his lower lip. Jules stretched out his right hand, took a paper of matches from the table, struck one and held it up. The little man sucked in the flame and Jules snapped the match across the room. It threaded an arc of smoke.

"I'll play ball," the man said.

Jules said: "Okey, then spill it."

Bunny's face flinched. He puffed jaggedly at the cigarette. It wiggled up and down twice when he asked: "Spill what?"

"Why are those Catrini after you?"

Bunny's eyes wandered. He took the cigarette between the first two fingers of his right hand and looked at it, put it back in his mouth with the ash still on it.

"They think I'm gonna squeal," he said.

"What about?"

Bunny threw the cigarette violently into a corner. He began buttoning his coat.

"Hell, I gotta take it!"

Bunny finished buttoning, stared down at the floor between his feet. He shoved his right hand into the pocket with the gun, turned heavily towards the door. He picked up each foot deliberately and put it down the same way.

"Why don't you squeal?" Jules asked softly.

A hoarse cry smothered itself in Bunny's throat. He whirled, his eyes gone wide.

"I ain't gonna squeal," he said violently.

Jules' mouth was tight. He opened it a quarter inch and said: "How about the girl?"

"She wouldn't squeal!"

"You kicked her out."

Jules leaned forward, staring into his eyes.

"Why not tell what you know," he urged softly. "Those Catrini would have to take the rap. You'd get off easy. And you wouldn't have to take it… their way."

Bunny's eyes darted around the room again. "There's no way out!"

Jules jabbed the left palm of his hand with a rigidly held forefinger.

"I'll get you out," he said. "If the deal is on."

Bunny looked at him for a full thirty seconds. He opened his mouth, then closed it again, breathed out noisily through his nose. He jerked a little nod and said hoarsely:

"Okey, pal."

TREMAINE WALKED BUNNY down two flights of stairs to the superintendent's quarters and used his phone.

"Mr. Bogan in? ... Do you know where I can reach him? ... Yes, I know. Will you phone him to prepare there to take an important statement before witnesses? ... At once, yes... Thanks."

Jules forked the receiver and turned to Bunny with a queer tight smile. His eyes were heavy lidded. He dropped a quarter into the brown-pink palm of the superintendent, a tall West Indian negro, and the man bowed them out.

"Now where?" asked Bunny.

Jules still wore that tight smile. He jerked his head towards the stairs. They walked up three flights and shoved out into damp, chill air. Bunny shivered slightly. The sky was thick with clouds.

Jules ducked under the radio aerials and led Bunny to the fire-escape ladder. Its cold rungs let them down two stories to the roof of a brownstone lodging house. There were six of those in a row towards Amsterdam Avenue, and on the last they found a scuttle that could be opened. Jules, leading Bunny, padded down carpeted stairs through light-housekeeping smells to the basement, slid out through a hinged grating and shot a furtive glance up the street.

Dim light from the apartment doorway made dull glints on the glossy low body of a limousine parked across the street from it. The hood was pointed the other way.

Jules took a tight grip on Bunny's arm and barged out on the pavement towards Amsterdam, without a backward look. The little gangster twisted his head, a furtive glance at the lurking car.

"You fool!" snapped Jules.

Up the street the mutter of an engine broke the silence. The limousine scooted backward down the street. Its drone deepened and swelled. Jules sprinted, Bunny pounding flat-footed beside him.

They pivoted at the corner of Amsterdam! Jules shoved Bunny ahead of him into a Ford coupé parked there, swung around its hood and jumped in. He kicked the starter and above its whine heard the deep-throated roar of the limousine spinning backward out of Seventy-sixth Street. The Ford motor belched and coughed and Jules threw the coupé in a tight left whirl out from the curb and across the nose of the trailing machine. A taxi squealed brakes, swerved, and tangled with the pursuing car and Jules, racing down Amsterdam, won a block's lead.

He kept that to Columbus Circle, shot through into Eighth Avenue, jerked east on Fifty-seventh and hit a red light at Sixth Avenue. When he whirled right, the limousine shoved its pointed hood alongside. The window at Jules' left cracked and dribbled glass dust into his lap. There was a twin hole starred with radiating cracks in the windshield and a jet of cold air fanned his face.

Bunny, gun in hand, twisted in his seat and there was a crash and tinkle of smashed glass behind Jules.

"Hold it," he ordered.

He slammed on brakes with a whine of hot rubber, ripped

into reverse and shot the Ford back ten feet. Raucous horns and shouts bellowed at him, but the black limousine had passed. Jules cut across behind it and wriggled through traffic towards Fifty-second Street.

A taxi, all cream paint and chromium plate, shot at him from his right. Jules stamped on the accelerator. There was a blare of horns, a crashing concussion and the Ford's rear skated three feet to the left, slowed up on two wheels.

Jules spun the steering gear towards the left, the gas took hold and the coupé flopped bouncing back on all fours, bumped over the curb and drummed with wide open throttle east on Fifty-second.

Bunny breathed hoarsely on Jules' neck. "They'll cut… cut through on Fiftieth. Smash into us."

Jules grunted, swung left on Fifth, dodged north a square and cut west again on Fifty-fifth, shot across Seventh Avenue and Broadway with a lucky break on lights and sped on to Tenth Avenue. He dodged shifting trains for a score of squares south, turned east until he spotted a taxi, signaled it and left the coupé.

The taxi sped them across to Fourth Avenue where it becomes Park, twisted over the viaduct through Grand Central and drifted northward up the double-laned avenue. The broad steps of the *Clinton Club* marched upward across the street. The taxi spun at the next corner and swung to the curb before the club.

The meter read .75. Jules tossed a dollar bill to the driver and hit the pavement running. He still gripped Bunny by the arm. A belching snarl of gunfire tore out of the night. He took the steps in bounding leaps, dragging Bunny. At their head, Jimson, the doorman, toed about and heaved his body towards the twin glass doors. Jules was just behind him. He caught Jimson by the left elbow and braced. The doorman whirled, his right arm and coat-tails flying wide, bumped head-on against the stone pillar and collapsed. Jules stepped over his body, shoved Bunny ahead through the doors. Behind them a gun crashed again and then again.

Across the red and gilt lobby a fat man with a ruddy face and big-toed shoes stumbled towards them, his hand groping under his coat.

Jules glanced at Bunny and said: "Quit it!" He seized Bunny's gun wrist.

"It's all right," he soothed. "It's all right."

Bunny's voice was a whine. "That guy's a hood."

"He's a special cop."

The fat man had his gun out now, a nickel-plated .38 that showed a black throat to Jules at close range.

"Stick 'em up!" the man wheezed.

JULES TREMAINE TURNED towards him with supercilious eyebrows and nodded briefly.

"I'm pleased at your efficiency," he said. "I shall see that the board hears of it."

The man went back on his heels and blinked blue eyes in a puzzled face. A page boy bustled forward, saw Jules and stopped ten feet away.

"What is it you wish, sir?" he stammered.

Tremaine turned towards him.

"Tell Mr. Carl Bogan that the gentleman who called him about a statement is here."

A stubby, brisk man pushed through the grouped formality

in the high white arch of the door. He had a ruff of black curly hair, shot with gray at the temples. He stiff-legged it towards them. The page boy did a right about face, spotted him and started a set phrase. The stubby man waved a decisive hand.

"I'm Carl Bogan," he said. "You—" he stopped and blinked behind the thick lenses of Oxford glasses from which a black riband looped to his neck; he finished uncertainly: "—Jules Tremaine!"

Jules bowed deeply with his black hat pressed against his stomach, his blue eyes bland and his lips oddly twisted.

"Mr. Bogan."

The man frowned importantly, "Did you have my secretary phone me?"

"Yes; are you ready?"

Bogan took the Oxford glasses off his beaked nose, held them in his right hand and tapped them lightly against the palm of his left. He said: "Yes."

"Are your witnesses reputable?"

Bogan's head went up with a jerk. "They are club members."

Jules' eyes were veiled.

"Are your witnesses reputable?" he asked again.

Bogan's attempt to stare at Tremaine down his nose was not very successful. He tapped more rapidly with his glasses.

"Tremaine," he said, "I am in no mood for jest."

"Excellent," said Jules. He turned to Bunny. The little man's stomach was caved, his shoulders drooped and his eyes dodged over the gilt and crimson of the lobby, the high white arches, and the ranks of men in black and white twinhood. Jules took him by the arm.

"Okey, Bunny. Let's go."

Bogan gestured with his glasses towards a stairway that swept upward from the lobby, and marched towards it, his back stiff, his head thrown far back. Jules shoved Bunny ahead of him. As he passed the puzzled, red-faced policeman he winked slowly.

His heels clicked on the white marble of the stairs, but were muffled by thick green carpets on the second floor. Bogan led the way through a high door into a small card room. A man in a blue serge business suit sat at a small square table with a notebook and a mottled green pen upon it. There were two other men seated on yellow satin chairs.

Bogan said: "Mr. Nichols," and the man with black brows beneath smooth white hair arose and bowed. When Bogan said: "Judge Perry," the one with a grizzled full beard did the same. Jules nodded shortly once and thrust Bunny forward.

"This man is Bunny Riggs," he said, "a gunman for the Catrini gang. They tried to kill him three times tonight, even firing at us as we entered the club. They are afraid Mr. Riggs will confess about certain matters of which he shares knowledge with the Catrini. So Mr. Riggs has determined to throw himself on the mercy of the authorities and ask protection, rather than on the mercies of the Catrini with which he is well acquainted."

Jules' smile was mocking. He turned to the little man.

"Bunny," he said. "Mr. Bogan is the District Attorney. You may not like him but he has a reputation for honesty. These other two gentlemen are witnesses. They're as nearly incorruptible as could be obtained on short notice."

Bogan cleared his throat heavily. "Mr. Tremaine!" he said sharply.

Jules waved an impatient hand at him and went on: "So,

Bunny, you can tell your story, knowing the Catrini will get theirs and you—" he paused, staring full into the little man's shifty eyes "—you won't have to take it *their way.*"

"What's your name!" Bogan shot out, lunging forward, with an out-thrust forefinger, from his chair.

Bunny cringed away, his mouth twitching.

"Just a minute, Bogan," Tremaine put in quietly. "I don't believe the court room manner is called for here. Suppose you let me do the questioning for a while."

The District Attorney cleared his throat twice and put his glasses on his nose. He cleared his throat again, mumbled something and sat down slowly. Jules turned away from him.

"Now, Bunny," he said, "suppose we begin this way. You're called Bunny Riggs, eh?"

"That's right," the little man's voice was small.

"But your real name is Ricci?"

Bunny slid a side glance at the three men grouped about the stenographer whose pen made four more little hooks and paused. The man did not look up. Bunny jerked his eyes to Jules and licked his lips.

"Yeah, my name's Ricci," he said.

"You're a gunman for those Catrini?"

"Yeah."

"And you came here of your own free will to make a statement?"

Bunny said: "That's right," and unbuttoned his coat and began groping for cigarettes. Jules lighted one for him.

"Now, Bunny," he asked, "why did those Catrini try to kill you?"

"They thought I'd squeal."

"About what?"

Bunny took two quick drags at the cigarette, hiding his face momentarily in gray smoke. He drew a deep breath, nodded his head with a jerk and said rapidly: "The murder of Louis Ricci."

"The murder of Louis Ricci, eh?"

Bunny nodded. "Yeah."

"Your brother?"

"Yeah."

Bogan took off his glasses and let them hang by their riband. He leaned forward on his chair and ran his hand through his black long hair.

"Do you know who murdered Louis Ricci?" he demanded eagerly.

Bunny glanced at the District Attorney, then at Jules and nodded again, saying "Yeah."

"Who did it?" Bogan rapped out.

Bunny took his cigarette out of his mouth with the first two fingers of his right hand. He looked at the ash. His hand shook a little and a thin line of gray smoke threaded up from it.

"Well," he said, "there was four of us...."

Jules moved slowly back. He was smiling a queer small smile and his eyes were masked.

"There was Joe Catrini," Bunny spoke almost inaudibly, "and there was Slim and Turkey, and... and there...."

"There was you," said Jules softly.

Bunny swallowed, his lips and the base of his nose quivered like that of a rabbit which smells the dogs near and hot-tongued. He took another drag at the cigarette.

"Yeah," he articulated hoarsely.

JULES TREMAINE STEPPED close to Bunny and asked: "You confessed this murder to Father Boniface, didn't you, Bunny?"

Bunny Riggs' head went up, his mouth gaping, his eyes wide. He shook his head violently, but the words "No! No!" were lost in his tightened throat.

"You're lying, Bunny!"

"No! No!"

"You might as well admit it."

Bunny swallowed loudly again. "If you know—"

"I do," said Jules.

"Yeah, I told him."

Jules' hands were tight fists at his sides. He leaned forward a little, his eyes bright and commanding.

"Father Boniface tried to make you go to the police, didn't he, Bunny?"

"Yes!"

"And you stabbed him tonight, fearing—"

Bunny trembled. His mouth became lax and the jerking of the muscles of his upper lip was continuous. The cigarette fell from his fingers and smoldered unnoticed in the deep pile of the yellow rug.

"I… I… never did!" he cried out. "I wouldn't kill a priest, I didn't do it! It was—"

Bunny broke off suddenly and Jules whispered piercingly: "Who killed Father Boniface, Bunny?"

The little man crouched suddenly and his gun was in his hand.

"You're trying to frame me!" he whined. A hunted fright screwed his face into a white knot. "You're trying to frame me!"

Jules retreated two slow steps from Bunny's gun covering the five men. The stenographer was on his feet, his white face thrust forward over the table, his pen spilling a blot on his notebook. Bogan, Perry, Nichols sat stiffly, bright eyes fixed in panic amazement on the gun. Out of the tail of his eye, Jules caught a movement in the doorway behind Bunny. The little gangster whined on:

"I helped kill Louis, sure I did, but not the priest. Louis was a sneaking thief and he was selling us out. I killed my own brother, but I—"

"Turn around, animal," came a cool voice from the doorway.

Bunny whirled, gun poised, but it was another pistol, farther away than his, that barked first, and Bunny, after standing there a moment with a twitching, surprised face, bent his right knee and slumped down on the yellow rug. A red stain blotted out from under him and a hand flung wide. The fingers were bent and the nails had a pink, freshly manicured sheen.

Bogan took two steps forward and dropped on one knee by Bunny.

"Quick," he said. "You killed the priest, didn't you?"

Jules' heavy-lidded gaze was not fixed on Bogan and Bunny, but on the lean, tall figure in the doorway, a man in faultless evening dress, a man with a high dome of a bald forehead and parenthetical creases deep about a sardonically curving mouth. The man lifted his right hand and thrust an automatic pistol out of sight under his left coat lapel. He bowed grandiloquently to Jules.

"My charming brother," he said.

Jules bowed with equal grace, sweeping the floor with his black hat.

"My dear brother," he said, straightening, "that was an excellent shot with which you shut the mouth of this witness against... the Catrini. Were you driven to shoot by your abhorrence of a man who would *kill his own brother?*"

Bogan, still kneeling, reared aloft from beside the man whom his body almost concealed from the others. Erect on the yellow carpet, his eyeglasses dangling by their riband, his black ruff of hair a triumphant crest, he cried out:

"Reporter, add to that confession that Bunny Riggs, with his dying breath, admitted he had murdered Father Boniface!"

Jules Tremaine stared at Bogan's flushed face with narrowed, glittering eyes, then he threw back his head, his arms hanging limply at his sides, and laughed and laughed.

A TAXI DROPPED Jules Tremaine in Eighty-fifth Street where he groped his way to a basement grating and pressed a button. The door opened almost immediately and Jules followed Frank down to the room with its opposed gun and sword above a hooded fireplace. He tossed his hat to the desk.

"How'd you come out?" asked Frank.

"Lousy," said Jules.

He dropped to the brown davenport, leaned forward and put his elbows on his knees.

"Hell," said Frank. "I thought I did a swell job. Finding you at the club when I was parking the car to leave it was positively a masterpiece. I opened up again before I beat it."

Jules nodded, his eyes focused beyond the cold black hearth.

"That bullet through the windshield came close. Seems to me you were going to use blanks."

"I forgot to take more than a dozen blanks along," Frank said.

"Nerts."

"Honest, I didn't have more than a dozen blanks."

"No doubt. You *said* you wanted to try out Ruby."

Frank looked down and grinned again, patting the right side of his waistband where it showed a slight bulge. "Ruby's a nice girl. That test barrel puts a bullet where I point her."

Jules said absently: "Yeah, you're a good shot," and continued to stare into the fireplace. He grimaced, twitching the ends of his black mustache. "So is my brother," he added.

"Yeah?"

"Yeah. I was leading Bunny Riggs up to the point where he'd accuse Andrew of having the priest stopped and Andrew walked in and shot Bunny, who had his gun out. I had to let him keep his gun to bolster his courage up to the confessing point."

"Andrew? The hell he did!"

Jules shrugged. "And then Bogan pulled the prize. Bogan got down on his knees by Bunny and then looked up brightly and said Riggs had confessed murdering the priest."

"Good Lord!" Frank grated. "And you let the big yum get away with that!"

Jules leaned back on the davenport. He touched his mustache with his thumbnail.

"I did," he declared shortly.

Frank narrowed his left eye and looked at Jules and said nothing. Presently Jules said: "After Bunny was dead I didn't have any choice. When I found Father Boniface dead I left my fingerprints all over the dagger that killed him."

He threw back his head and laughed with little sound.

"When dear Andrew and Bogan find out *that,*" he said with

a twisted, wry mouth, "find out what a chance they've lost to frame me for the priest's murder, they'll be sorry about that false confession Bogan got from Bunny Riggs!"

Black Harvest

Jules Tremaine sings in the streets of Little Italy and sees an old Italian game

JULES TREMAINE SAID: "No, no, Caterina, you keep the penny and I will sing for you again."

He bent gravely over the little girl and stroked the even, square-cut blackness of her hair. She looked up with eyes that were very large and very black and presently she answered Jules' smile, showing small white even teeth.

"I like you to sing," she said.

Jules plucked a soft chord from his guitar and the child took the penny in her right hand to put it into the pocket of her bright red sweater and Jules saw that the first and second fingers had been chopped off close against the hand.

Tremaine muted the strings with the flat of his palm and stared at the jagged scar, his round blue eyes hard.

"In heaven's name, Caterina," he asked, "how did that happen?"

The smile tightened off the child's mouth. She jerked the hand behind her and turned and flat-footed up the street, small stockinged legs flickering black under a stiff-starched dress.

Jules frowned after her.

Scanty winter sunlight was cold on Cornelia Street and made the red brick buildings appear dirtier than ever. The fire-escapes were a mussy disorder, draped with stiff frozen rags.

In such surroundings, in such an occupation, Jules was a figure of incongruity, with his expensive gray top coat that fitted his square shoulders like a uniform, with his look of a man of comfortable ease. He sang well, to be sure; but he never accepted money for his songs. Rather, he seemed bent upon making friends with these poor people of Little Italy, as he drifted from street to street, pausing for a song that drew them around him, stopping to chat with one or another, and always, always peering from face to face with studied carelessness.

Perhaps his singing was an excuse for frequent appearances in the quarter, a reason that would not be questioned too closely; for in spite of his air of indolence, he seemed a man with a purpose, one he was not sharing with the world.

It was indolence that was dominant in Jules now as he stood singing on the curb, an erect man just under middle height. About him a few children scampered. Two doors away a girl in a black sweater sat back outward in a second-story window with the frame resting in her lap and moved a white cloth rhythmically over the glass. Her arms, bare to the elbows, were plump and tapered. She smiled down at Tremaine.

Up near the corner a young man in a long, pinch-waisted blue overcoat entered a tenement doorway. Jules had nearly finished his song when the man emerged and swaggered to the next door. He repeated that down the street. Watching him with curious, heavy-lidded eyes, Tremaine sang on softly, plucking the strings.

Jules glanced up at the girl in the window. Her right hand pressed the cloth against the glass, but she was not washing it. She was staring with strained stiffness at the man in the tight blue coat. She jerked her head around, slammed up the window and ducked inside. "Madre! I..." Jules heard, then the window guillotined her sentence.

Jules realized that the children had disappeared, that the street was cold and empty except for himself—and the young

man in the tight-waisted coat. He was drawing near and a chill wind whipped ahead of him, flopped the long coat against his calves. He shot a thin glance at Tremaine and entered the doorway nearest at hand. Still singing, Jules strolled along until he could see into the building's hallway.

The man stood in the light of an open door, and an Italian woman, with tight mouth and small dark eyes, stared into his face. Jules could not hear what was said, but the man's shoulders were hunched and his arms swung slowly forward and back at his sides, the fingers slightly curled. The woman thrust out her hand. The man's fingers met it slowly, extracted green money, then closed about the wrist and wrenched it savagely. The woman's mouth opened, but no sound came forth. The man shoved his face close to hers and his lips moved over tight words.

As Jules bit off his song and bounded to the steps, the man pushed the woman away and without a backward glance, patted quick, shiny shoes up the stairs, vanishing towards the second floor. The door closed slowly.

JULES TREMAINE COMPELLED himself to relax and moved slowly back and down the street until he stood before the next house. He twitched little resonances from his guitar and began a sombre phrase from *Faust*. Presently the man came out of the building and advanced on light feet.

Tremaine met his eyes indifferently. They were small, brown and sharp and were nearly hidden beneath the snapped-down brim of a fedora of that pale, flashy gray called white. He did not slow in his stride, or glance a second time at Jules as he turned smartly up the steps of the tenement.

When he had entered, Tremaine strode quickly back to the next house and knocked at the door where the woman had given money. It opened an inch and an eye peered through the slit.

The eye blinked and the woman said: "I got no money."

Jules smiled. "I don't want money."

The eye looked at him a moment longer, then the door opened so the woman's entire face was visible. The rims of her eyes were red. Her mouth was a hard line. A boy with a pale, precocious face peered from behind her severe dress. The woman thrust him back and asked:

"What you want?"

"I saw a man twist your arm."

The woman's eyes became flat and dull like dusty grapes.

"No man twisted my arm."

"That young man in the blue coat and the white hat. I saw him twist your arm. You gave him money."

The woman shook her head, her face stiff as a wooden mask. Jules frowned.

"I'm Jules Tremaine," he said gently. "Everyone in Little Italy knows Jules Tremaine, the street singer."

The woman's eyes were sly. She put her left hand on the edge of the door and stepped back. Tremaine jammed his right foot against the door.

"Listen," he said with quick words. "I want to...."

The woman strained her shoulder against the door, panting.

"I don't... don't know nothing."

The woman continued to push, the color draining slowly from her face. Jules lifted his right shoulder in a slight shrug, took his foot away and the door slapped loudly shut. He stared at it a moment, looked down at his hat and put it on his head and walked out.

The young man in the blue coat was just coming out next door. He stopped halfway down the steps. Jules kept deliberately on until he stood a yard from him. Their eyes met and the man eased down the three remaining steps to the pavement. He was two inches taller than Tremaine.

He said: "Were you looking for me?"

Jules slid his guitar under his right arm and up on his back. He smiled with a slow lift of his lips that moved his mustache.

He said: "Yes, louse."

The man's head jerked up. His brows were arched and his eyes very wide. Then they narrowed and the thin lips sneered down at the corners.

"I don't know who you are..." he began.

Jules bowed, still smiling, but did not take his eyes away. "Your most obedient servant, Jules Tremaine."

"Jules Tremaine!"

He slipped his right hand to his pocket.

"Yes, louse."

Jules stepped up close to him, his blue eyes round and hard. The man retreated a step, striking his heel against the step. His right hand thrust forward his pocket and Jules rocked his body, clipping a straight right to the chin. The man arched his back and flopped down on the steps. His white hat rolled off and he slumped so that he squatted on his heels, then his legs straightened and he sat on the pavement, lolling against the steps with his mouth open.

Tremaine scooped a pistol out of the man's coat pocket and tossed it into a cellar doorway. He caught the man's coat collar close up under his chin and hauled him to his feet. Up the street, a police whistle spluttered and Jules twisted his head sharply about. A man in a blue uniform was pounding towards him from Bleecker.

Jules deliberately picked up the white hat and crushed it down on the man's head, drew the right arm across his shoulders and dragged the still inert gunman towards the policeman. The man's feet began to move limply, toes stumbling and scraping. His head lifted, drooped, came up again with the quick over-controlled movements of a drunk.

The cop stopped in the middle of the sidewalk, straddle-legged, fists on his hips, lower lip thrust out. Jules smiled up at him and there was mockery in his eyes.

"Well, well," he said. "It's Mr. O'Reilly."

The policeman's lips barely moved. "I saw you slug this gent."

Jules raised polite eyebrows. The gunman was trying feebly to pull away. Jules' left arm was about his waist, his hand gripping the left wrist. He had the right arm across his shoulders and held that wrist. The man's breath came sharply.

"Damn you," he panted. "Damn you, let me go."

"I don't think you can stand alone yet, louse," Jules said.

"Turn the man loose," said O'Reilly.

Jules released his grip on the right wrist and yanked sharply on the left. The man reeled away and struck the wall of the tenement with his shoulder. He leaned there, breathing hard, then squirmed around and set his back against the wall and stood, eyes wide, crushed dirty hat on the back of his head.

"I was afraid he was too weak," said Jules mildly.

O'Reilly toed his two hundred pounds of beef lightly forward, his nightstick in a tight fist. Jules looked directly into his eyes and said: "O'Reilly, I want this man kept out of this neighborhood."

"Do you, now?" the policeman asked softly.

"I do and you'll keep him out."

"Will I now?"

Jules quit smiling and said: "I'm sorry to cut in on the racket...."

A sharp curse from the man against the wall snapped O'Reilly's eyes that way. "What's the matter?"

"I've been robbed!"

The man was feeling his right-hand coat pocket. O'Reilly looked back to Tremaine with small, happy eyes.

"Turned heist man, eh, Tremaine?" he bit off the words.

Tremaine's eyes became sleepy. His knees bent slightly.

"So, O'Reilly, you're in on the racket? That means those Catrini are running it. You were close to a murder rap once, O'Reilly. Don't forget I can close down on you if I want to."

O'Reilly's happiness spread to his face. His smile showed yellow, irregular teeth. He jerked up the club and sprang. He shouted: "Resist arrest, will you?"

Jules slid out from under the nightstick, took two quick steps past the officer and pivoted lightly. O'Reilly spun about and now metal gleamed in his hand. A pistol.

"Try to escape, will you?"

A choked cry tore out of Tremaine. He jerked his body sidewise at the waist. The gun deafened him. He felt the guitar jerk on his back.

"O'Reilly, you damned...."

He darted to the policeman's left. The gun came up again. Tremaine jerked to the left, seized the wrist and wrenched down. O'Reilly cried "Ow!" and the pistol clattered to the pavement. Tremaine twisted the arm savagely and with an upward heave sent the cop plunging head first against the tenement wall.

His shoulders caved, he whirled half around and slumped down and his feet shot out straight.

Jules stood, his chest rising and falling quickly, his lips tight. He kicked the gun into the gutter and looked around. A frightened face jerked back from a window. The man in the dirty white hat was running without a backward glance, his blue coat flapping. He rounded the corner into Fourth without slowing.

Jules walked over to O'Reilly and bent down and slapped his face. He hit him four times, hard, before the cop's eyelids lifted. His eyes focused with difficulty, blinked and abruptly glittered hate. His arms flexed.

Jules said coldly: "Don't move, O'Reilly!" and the arms went limp.

Tremaine stared directly into his eyes and said: "O'Reilly, when you stalled around and let those Catrini gunmen get away after killing Angela, I rubbed the guns out and let you get away. I thought you were a young cop and might snap out of it, but you tried to get me then and now a second time—and that's once too many, O'Reilly. You're going to pay!"

He slapped the cop again, deliberately, heavily.

"If you want me for this, you know where to come."

He threw back his head and laughed softly.

"I don't think you'll want me, O'Reilly," he said and walked away.

JULES TREMAINE, SINGING, paced slowly up and down Cornelia, waiting. O'Reilly had walked heavily away with backward scowls, and soon children popped out again. The little girl in a red sweater, black-stockinged legs, nimble beneath a starched white dress, romped down towards Bleecker.

Jules stopped his song, thrust his guitar up on his back and called "Caterina."

The child turned big eyes, black in the whiteness of a face chopped off square at the top by black bangs. She moved slowly to meet him and Tremaine stooped and looked directly into her face.

"Caterina," he said, "I saw the loveliest doll down around the corner!"

The girl's eyes regarded him gravely.

"It is for you."

The eyes widened. "For *me?*"

Jules nodded. He led her by the hand to Bleecker and in a crowded shop window full of baby clothes and accessories pointed out a big doll that reclined with closed eyes.

"See," he said, "her eyes close!"

"Oooh, yes!"

Jules bought the doll and placed it in Caterina's arms. She cuddled it, patting its hair, and Jules squatted on his heels and looked at it.

"She's nice," he said. He took the doll's right hand in his.

"You won't let anything happen to *her* hand, will you, Caterina?" he asked, and pointed to the doll's fingers that corresponded to the two that had been sliced from Caterina's own hand.

The girl shook her head quietly. "No," she said. "I'll pay the man so he won't carry my dolly off."

Jules' lips tightened so that his words were clipped. "The way your father pays the man so he won't take you, again?"

Caterina nodded, then her mouth opened and she jerked out: "Oh, daddy told me...."

"Not to tell? He won't mind your telling me, child. Was the man here this afternoon the one who hurt your hand?"

A quick, frightened nod.

Jules stood abruptly erect, his right hand gripping the end of his guitar keyboard until his knuckles were white. His eyes were heavy-lidded, his mouth tightened so that the sword points of his black mustache thrust forward.

The little girl called up to him and he stroked her hair, looking down without seeing her. She jerked away and patted flat-running feet around the corner into Cornelia.

Jules Tremaine stood for a long moment staring after her,

then paced deliberately along Bleecker towards Seventh Avenue. In the middle of the next block he spotted a blue-uniformed back. He lengthened his stride and overtook the back at the corner of Jones.

He said softly: "O'Reilly."

The policeman spun, left forearm raised on guard, right hand groping through the slit of his overcoat pocket for his gun. Jules looked into his eyes with a smile as thin as a knife and asked gently: "What's the matter, O'Reilly?"

The policeman dropped his arm, stalked towards him and his bulk loomed above Tremaine.

"What the hell do you mean...."

"Shut up, O'Reilly."

"I'll...."

"Shut—up—O'Reilly, *or I'll tell Joe.*"

The policeman stammered and no words came out. He fell back a pace and frowned at a spot below Jules' chin.

"What are you talking about?" he muttered.

The street singer's eyes were veiled mockery. He jerked his head to the left.

"Come over here."

He moved to the extreme edge of the curb at the corner. The nearest pushcart was ten feet away. The passing shoppers would be three feet distant. O'Reilly hesitated, then heaved his weight over beside him.

"What do you want?" he grumbled.

Tremaine ignored him, his alert gaze searching the crowd.

O'Reilly asked sharply: "What do you want?"

Jules looked up blandly and said: "I want you to tell Joe this Black Hand racket has got to stop. Tell him I say so."

O'Reilly inspected an overripe orange in the gutter and said: "I don't know what you're talking about."

Jules raised his eyebrows. "Too bad. Then I'll have to communicate with Joe personally." He nodded pleasantly and swung briskly off with the crowd.

"Hey!" O'Reilly called.

Jules stopped and waited while the policeman broke through the ranks of shoppers to his side. The cop fixed wide anxious eyes on those of the street singer.

He said: "Tell me what you know about this Black Hand racket and I'll stop it."

Jules showed his white teeth. "Thanks, no. I wouldn't think of asking you to endanger yourself. Just tell Joe."

"Joe who?"

Jules threw back his head and laughed. He turned his back. A hand, heavy on his shoulder, halted him. Jules pivoted and his eyes were like the point of light on a rapier.

He said softly: "Take your hand off my shoulder."

O'Reilly jerked away as from fire. The street singer smiled with his mouth. The cop shifted his weight from his left to his right foot. He growled: "I ought to run you in for what you did."

"Certainly."

The policeman's eyes came up sharply and his face was ugly. He said: "Damn you! The next time I will."

Jules laughed and said: "I'll give you a chance if you'll drop in at Joe's around seven tonight."

"Where is Joe's?"

Tremaine shook his head slowly. "On second thought, I don't believe Joe's is the place for an honest young policeman. I'll take my own message."

O'Reilly looked at the pavement between his feet and muttered: "If Joe runs a gang joint, you'd better keep out of it."

"Yes?"

"Yeah. You can't go around telling gangsters to lay off a racket."

"So you just don't try, eh, O'Reilly?"

O'Reilly looked at Tremaine with wide eyes that were utterly guileless, perhaps too guileless.

"Listen, Tremaine," he urged. "If you get in trouble, your brother will raise the devil with the police. Take...."

Jules laughed into the policeman's face, laughed twice, then threw back his head and laughed long but with little sound. "Andrew worry if *I* get in trouble?" he gasped. "O'Reilly, you'll kill me with your little jokes."

He walked off, still laughing.

JULES TOOK UP the telephone. It had tobacco breath. Tremaine wrinkled his nose and dropped a nickel in the slot and said: "Hello, Frank?" He waited a moment until he heard the private detective's bored "Yeah!," and then said: "I wonder if you'd like to take Ruby out for an airing tonight? Yes... Well, I'm calling on one of those Catrini, Antonio to be exact, and I'd like you to hang around outside just in case... I'm pretty certain the case will materialize.... About half-past six, and better rent a Ford.... Yes. Bye."

Jules found a taxi on Sixth Avenue and gave an address off Central Park West. He held his guitar in his lap and idly fingered the hole O'Reilly's bullet had ripped in it. His eyes were nearly shut.

The meter ticked on and the cab swung across Columbus Circle, past groups of men about soap-box orators, scooted four blocks farther north, cut into a side street and squealed to a halt at a canopied entrance. A blue-coated *chausseur* swung open the door and blinked fat-squeezed eyes when Jules got out with the guitar and deliberately swung it across his shoulder before he paid the driver.

The taxi pulled off and Tremaine saw that a man, with wide shoulders hunched high, sat on a bench in Central Park and that a Ford coupé was parked a half block away. Frank was on time and waiting. Jules walked up to double doors and waited while the attendant opened them.

Another man in uniform asked: "Whom did you wish to see, sir?"

"Catrini. The name is Jules Tremaine."

The man repeated this into a telephone against the wall and turned and said: "Mr. Catrini wall see you, sir. Suite seventeen K. The elevator is to your left, sir."

Jules was lofted sixteen floors very gently and the gate opened. He walked out and the gate closed, and two men with their right hands in their pockets stepped up to him. Tremaine said: "I'm not armed."

One man, peering up with pale eyes through thick brows from a downward-looking face, jerked his head sidewise and the other man slid along the wall until he was behind Jules. He patted over his clothing and said finally: "He ain't got no rod."

The man jerked his head at Jules and stepped aside and shoved open a door with his foot. Tremaine slipped the guitar down under his right arm and up on his back and walked through the portal first. The foyer was large and a five pointed glass star dropped blue illumination from a gold-leaf ceiling.

The guard behind said: "Go on," in a dry, expressionless voice, and Jules walked on and saw a man standing with his back to a fireplace. Between the man's legs he saw the blue flames of a gas log.

Jules showed his white teeth and bowed and said: "Hello, Tony."

The man in front of the fireplace looked beyond Tremaine, and the guard's dry voice said: "Clean." The man clasped his hands behind him and nodded shortly. Jules heard a door behind him opened and closed, and the man looked at Jules calmly and said: "So what?"

Tremaine laid his guitar on a chair that had spindly golden legs.

"You don't mind if I make myself at home?"

The man said: "You ain't going to stay here that long."

Jules laughed easily and placed his top coat on the back of the chair and turned to face the man. They were of a size and both had wide, erect shoulders. Tremaine looked about and rubbed his palms together and said:

"Charming little place you have here, Tony."

The man said: "Quit stalling, Tremaine."

When he spoke his upper lip slid back from buck teeth. He had too many teeth. They crowded his mouth and smothered his words so that his speech issued with a faint whisper of hissing.

Jules stopped rubbing his palms together and stopped smiling and his round blue eyes fixed those of Tony.

"Catrini," he said, "you've got to cut out your Black Hand racket."

The man frowned and said: "Come again?"

Jules let his hands hang and repeated: "Cut out your Black Hand racket."

"My Black Hand racket?"

"Precisely."

Tony Catrini jerked his shoulders up quickly, threw his white hand out with spread, long fingers.

"Sorry, I can't oblige you." It was a sneer. "I have no Black Hand racket."

Jules' smile warped his mouth. "Now I'll tell one."

Catrini looked at him in mild contempt. "You are alone in my house. If I wish it, you never leave alive. I do not think your brother would seriously object and you cannot hurt me. Why should I lie to you?"

Jules jerked his head impatiently. "Why bring my brother and his politics into this affair? I never have used his filthy influence yet."

Catrini clasped his hands behind him again, still warming his back before the dancing blue flames. His eyes were wide and the pupils distended. He kept them focused on Tremaine and said nothing. Jules took a step forward and a dry voice from behind said: "Now take one step back."

Tremaine obeyed and laughed. "You are prone to misinterpret my intentions."

Catrini, frowning, got words past his teeth: "Cut the comedy. Why did you come here?"

"I've told you why."

Tony teetered on his toes, raising on them, lowering his heels again soundlessly. The carpet was a thick, silky Sarouk.

Jules nodded at his feet. "That's good for the calf muscles."

Catrini's frown drew his close-clipped black hair towards his brows.

"Why did you come here?"

"To tell you to cut out the Black Hand racket," Tremaine insisted. "Listen, Catrini, it's a lousy racket. Those poor wops can't pay your collectors more than a few dollars a week to protect their children. And every now and then you'll have to kidnap some kid and do him like your man did Caterina Scioni, cut off a finger or two. Sooner or later some of those wops are going to talk and you'll have a tough time beating the rap. The papers would hop all over you, the police couldn't help you. Nothing can get the public so stirred up as hurting a kid."

He drew a breath and finished: "It's too small a racket for the Catrini, Tony."

Catrini, his crowded voice very soft, said: "It's nice of you to take such a friendly interest."

Jules' mouth was very tight, but his eyes were oddly wide and round.

"I don't give a damn if you boil in oil, you lousy dago, you and your brothers and all your gang," he rapped out. "But I'm giving you some good advice so you'll cut the racket and leave the honest wops and their kids alone.

"They're good people down there. They've been kind to me ever since I got tight and went street singing among them on a bet. I'm glad to do something to help them…."

Catrini was staring at Tremaine with dilated but expressionless eyes. There seemed to be no iris around the pupil and no light in them.

He said: "Okey. Now that you've got that off your chest,

suppose you tell me the real reason you're here. Did your brother...."

Jules' voice rose slightly. He slapped his right fist against his left palm.

"Damn it, Catrini...."

The man nodded slightly and hands vised on Tremaine's shoulders, seized his wrists. Catrini walked over on careful feet and looked at him without smiling. Their eyes were on a dead level and neither blinked, but the gang leader's narrowed very slowly and an ugly light was in their depths.

He asked thinly: "Why did you come here?"

Jules Tremaine answered without expression, "I've told you the truth."

CATRINI RAISED HIS right hand slowly to his waist and Jules shifted his gaze to watch his fingers slide under the flap of his vest and withdraw with a thread of steel glittering between the curved forefinger and the down-pressing thumb. Catrini kept his elbow snug to his side and drew the forearm back and to the right and bent the hand gripping the blade back at the wrist.

"You have seen what I can do with this little toy?" he asked.

Jules swallowed hard. His stomach muscles contracted. He looked at the stiletto and swallowed again. He whispered: "Yes."

Catrini leaned forward and thrust his face very close to Tremaine's.

"Perhaps," he said, "you will tell me now why you came here."

Jules closed his eyes to hide from Catrini the hard smile he knew must lurk in them. He swallowed again and said in a weak voice: "Let me sit down."

He was slammed into a chair and the grip on his arms did not relax. He said: "Put that —— damned knife away," and opened his eyes and watched Tony's lips smile away from his buck teeth.

"I am sorry," the man said, "that you do not like my little toy."

He came a step nearer and poised the dagger a few inches from Tremaine's throat. Jules opened his eyes very wide and strained them downward, so he could just see the point. No eye in that position could reveal anything.

"I'll... I'll talk."

Catrini grunted and Jules swallowed and looked directly into his gaze. Tony toyed with his stiletto and looked at it. Jules spoke rapidly. "I was down in Cornelia Street this morning and saw a collector making the rounds. He was about two inches taller than I and young and wore a white hat and a tight-waisted blue coat."

Catrini said with whispered sibilance: "A white hat...."

Jules continued: "Yes. He took money from everybody in the block that had kids, and I stopped him and O'Reilly came along and put a bullet in my guitar trying to shoot me."

"O'Reil-ly," Catrini lingered over each separate syllable.

"And so I thought," Jules went on, "since O'Reilly tried to help out this bird that you knew all about it and it was your racket and I wanted to stop it to help those poor wops. Even if it did mean telling your gang something for its own good. That racket will make trouble, Tony."

Catrini said: "Yes, it would."

He met Tremaine's eyes for a flash and then looked back to the three-cornered sliver of steel in his hand and Jules gulped and said: "For —— sake, Catrini, I told the truth!"

Catrini stared down at him and the hands tightened on Jules' arms, and the street singer said: "I can prove it, Catrini. You may be telling the truth about not having a hand in it, but O'Reilly and this other man have. I told O'Reilly I was going to tell your brother, Joe, tonight to quit the racket. I told him I'd be there at seven.

"If it's O'Reilly's private racket and he's holding out on you, he'll be at Joe's tonight to keep me from telling, and that other man, the one with the white hat, probably will be with him."

Catrini, fingering the blade, said: "So what?"

"So, if you take me down there, you can find out whether I'm telling the truth and whether these two are doublecrossing you."

Catrini, looking not at Jules' face, but at his throat, said: "That's a lot of trouble." He moved the dagger point from side to side by flexing his wrist.

Jules licked his lips and said: "If these two are holding out on you, you ought to thank me for the tip-off. And you ought to stop the racket, Tony. Hurting kids is bad business for any gang." Catrini looked back to his dagger and did not speak.

Tremaine said slowly: "It's ten minutes of seven, Tony." He smiled stiffly. "And seeing it's my party, I'll pay the taxi fare."

The dry voice of the guard said: "It's just as easy to take three for a ride." Catrini raised his gaze from the stiletto to Jules' eyes and said: "That clock is five minutes fast."

IT WAS TWO minutes later that Catrini, Jules Tremaine and the guard got into the taxi and headed south. Tremaine put his guitar between his knees and slid his hand up and down its neck absently. Catrini was at his right and the other man straddled a small seat backwards, his pale upward-looking eyes unwavering on Jules' face.

None of them spoke and Tremaine watched traffic slide past, spotted finally the high apartment-like bulk of Women's Prison and knew the cab was on Tenth Street. After they crossed Fifth Avenue, there were many parked cars.

Catrini raised his voice: "By that fire plug to your left."

The driver's head nodded. He glanced back and swerved to the curb at a point where the light was faint. The man straddling the seat opened the door, slid out and folded down the seat. The light in the roof of the taxi glinted on a gun in his fist. His pale eyes were cold as they met Jules' and he said: "You're next."

Jules got out slowly, holding the guitar high before him, and Catrini was just behind him. Jules lowered the guitar and proffered it to Tony. "It's my party, you know," he said, and the left corner of his lip twitched upward. "Would you mind holding this while I pay the driver?"

Catrini's mirthless smile showed bulging teeth and he took the guitar and Jules stepped towards the driver.

The guard said dryly: "Careful, bo."

Jules nodded, slipped the taxi man a five-dollar bill and whispered: "Get away from here fast!"

The taxi did. The diminuendo thunder of its exhaust was broken by a series of sharper, barking explosions. Jules dropped flat. An automobile without lights pulled out from the opposite curb. Spears of red flame jetted from it, one source in the front, the other in the back. A man gasped out a curse. Jules twitched over on his back and peered at Catrini under half-closed lids.

Catrini was stumbling on slow feet towards the basement

entrance of Joe's, leaning on the guitar as on a cane, gripping the keyboard's end in his right fist, resting the base on the pavement. His teeth were bared by pulled-back lips. The other gangster crouched against the iron fence. A gun racketed in his fist.

Catrini's head jerked forward as from an invisible blow. His chin hit his chest and his chest buckled, his stomach caved. He tumbled down the stairway leading into Joe's like a kid turtle-diving off a raft. The guitar teetered a moment, then flopped flat on the sidewalk and the vibration of its strings sliced oddly through the crash of guns.

Jules rolled his head over and saw that one gun in the auto had been silenced, but the driver's still spurted red fire. As he watched, the crouched guard loosed a fresh clip of bullets and the car darted ahead like a deer mortally wounded, yawed wildly, recovered, swerved again and hurdled the curb. It nose-dived against a building, bounced back. Its horn rasped out. A woman screamed behind walls somewhere, and the horn kept on blowing and blowing, on and on and on.

Tremaine drew up his feet to scramble erect, then saw the gangster against the fence and decided not to. He lay still with his eyes closed, watching through his lashes. The man couldn't get out of his crouch. He was bent forward at the waist but he was on his feet and he dragged them as if they weighed a hundred pounds each and pushed one ahead of the other slowly. His gun dangled from his hand.

Three, four, five feet, ten feet he crept towards Tremaine, that gun dangling but ready. Jules dared not move. The man's mouth was open and he was breathing through it with slow, hoarse sounds. His eyes were fixed on Jules. He coughed tearingly but did not stop staring at Jules. He cursed in a strangled voice.

Up the street an automobile engine roared through two gear shifts. Tremaine sent his slitted gaze hopefully through the dark. A Ford coupé was racketing up the street. Lights behind it silhouetted the driver's high, wide shoulders. That would be Frank—and Ruby. Then the gangster's slowly moved legs blocked Jules' line of vision.

From under his lids Tremaine stared up into the thin, distorted face looming over him, its lips drawn back tightly from the gums. The dangling gun rose slowly, began to reach out a hungry muzzle, enlarging, shoving nearer, nearer to Jules' narrowly alert eyes. He clenched his jaws, forcing himself to wait with muscles tensed to roll....

The shot came from yards away, crashed through the Ford motor's drone. The gangster's gun jabbed nearer and gouged Tremaine's forehead and a weight collapsed on Tremaine's chest. He heaved, rolled and slid out from under the body, bounded across the walk and sprawled down the steps on top of Catrini.

Auto brakes squealed at the curb and Frank shouted: "Get in! Get in!"

Jules blew breath out of his lungs, grabbed the guitar and sprang across the pavement, swung around the back of the Ford coupé at the curb. The car, its door swinging, was already in motion. Jules leaped in, slammed the door and the motor ground to a high whine in second. The continuous rasp of the horn in the wrecked gang car came nearer. The body of a man with white hat lay inertly over the wheel. In the back something dark was huddled and Tremaine caught a flash of a beefy face with an open mouth.

Above the throb of the Ford and the horn, the mounting shriek of police sirens penetrated to his ears, but they were still blocks away. The coupé crossed Broadway in a bound, swung north into Fourth and slowed to the pace of other traffic. Two blocks north the coupé turned east and the shadowed stilts of the Third Avenue Elevated began flashing by.

Jules leaned back in his corner of the seat and took deep breaths. His round blue eyes were fixed on his guitar, resting upright against the windshield. There was blood on it. He twisted his head about.

"That was O'Reilly in that car. O'Reilly and the lad I bumped into today. They were waiting to ambush me and hopped Catrini and got shot." He breathed deeply again. "Tony Catrini's dead. He was going to take me for a ride with those other two and I gave him the guitar when I got out of the taxi and O'Reilly thought he was I. We're the same build."

The driver turned a ruddy face queerly shadowed by a reddish brush of a mustache in the dim light of the dash.

"Where would you have been without Ruby?" he asked.

"Or without you, Frank," Jules chuckled. He said affectionately: "I wouldn't be alive now if it hadn't been for you two rubbing out that hood. He had his gun almost against my head."

"I'll put it in my bill," said Frank, "Here, shake Ruby's hand about it. And keep an eye out behind for some of Joe Catrini's boys." He reached under his coat and took out an automatic pistol. Jules hefted it comfortably and grinned down at it, a flash of white teeth beneath his mustache points. "Nice girl, Ruby," he said.

He twisted about and watched the shadows behind them.

The Murder in the Tunnel

JULES TREMAINE KICKED a rock fragment and listened to the echoes clacking along the tunnel.

He said: "You pick out the damnedest localities for your cases, Frank. This aqueduct is eleven hundred feet under the city."

Frank walked along with his rolling swagger and turned the beam of his flashlight up towards the ceiling.

"It's a nice tight aqueduct," he said. "There's not a drop of seepage water coming through here."

They turned a sweeping curve, and a huddle of men in a yellow circle of radiance came into view.

"There's your murder, I guess, Frank," said Jules.

Frank grunted: "Yeah."

They walked up to a group of six men in charge or a sergeant of police. On the floor of the aqueduct, a short way from the group, a man lay stretched out on his face, with the point of a pickaxe buried in his skull. The handle slanted backward over his body. The handle of the pick was wet. Unlike elsewhere in the aqueduct, water dripped slowly from the ceiling, and struck on it—splash—splash—splash—and left a brownish stain.

Frank turned to the sergeant. "Are these all the men who were in the tunnel," he asked, "at the time this man was murdered?"

The sergeant said: "Yes. I have verified it."

Jules stared at the corpse, while Frank went through some routine investigation work. Jules suddenly smiled.

"Sergeant," he asked, "have any of these men been near the body since it was discovered?"

“Naw,” said the sergeant. “The foreman, there, who called me, saw it from a distance. The others wouldn’t come this close until I made ’em. They’re a sullen, dumb bunch. Can’t get anything out of ’em.”

Jules’ smile widened. He said: “Frank, you can pick out the murderer very simply. If you don’t know how, I’ll show you.”

WHEN THE MEN had turned their backs, Jules Tremaine picked out one who had a brownish stain on the back of his collar.

“It’s quite simple,” Jules said in answer to Frank’s question. “You notice that there’s water dropping on the pick handle, and the rest of the aqueduct is tight, no seepage at all, so that this man who has brown water stains on the back of his collar must have got them while committing the murder.”

The Green Death

The keen brain of King Landers could not pierce the insidious secret of the power-mad Ch'ien Feng. For Ch'ien Feng could not die! In his taloned fingers were the lives of the mighty. And the mighty cowered under the horrible menace of having their skin turned green, their bodies shriveled to old age, and their minds robbed of sanity. Ch'ien Feng ruled—and his decoy was a bewitching, glamorous woman.

1

The Veiled Chinese

IT WAS A sleek car, black and low and long, and it slid over the rutted streets of Chinatown as if they were velvet. The greasy yellow fog opened before its pointed hood and swirled shut again behind its sloping back. The shops, only a few feet distant through the night, showed as dim blurs of yellow light.

Henry P. Nicholas turned toward his companion, seen vaguely in the opacity of the interior, half revealed by the reflection from the dash lights before the chauffeur. Nicholas felt uncomfortable, felt all at once terribly alone, felt that an imminent and invisible horror pressed about the polished black body of his car.

"Damn it, Thais," he grumbled with the petulant, half cajoling complaint which is the only tone of protest a man, fat and forty, dare use to a slim darling of a girl. "Damn it, we don't have to go places like this to get dinner. Mouquin's, Pierre's, the Brevoort. I don't like this."

Thais was a vague shadow at his side, a bewitching half-seen shadow. He could make out the glimmer of her white face and her white, white throat. He imagined he could see the dark fire of her almond eyes, the masked smile about her thin, bitter lips. Her voice was soft and low with a quality of seduction in each slow syllable, syllables that were slightly slurred, tinged by an accent of the East at once indefinable and alluring. She spoke now out of the dusk beside him.

The girl moved quickly.

"It is not that my Harry is afraid of this so dark Chinatown?" she murmured.

"Certainly not," Nicholas grumbled.

He wasn't actually afraid. A man who builds and holds on to millions doesn't shrink from shadows. Such a man does not believe in shadows. A boo in the dark, a cold touch in a black room wouldn't feaze him, not in his Park Avenue duplex. But this was Chinatown. And in Chinatown the East that is old and can be very evil thrusts a damp occult hand into the breast of a white man and closes with slow, cruel fingers about his heart.

"Most certainly not," grumbled Nicholas. He wasn't afraid—but he should have been.

Silence closed in on the car. An elevated train threshing along a block away seemed an alien, unknown sound. The soft purr of the Duesenberg's motor should have been reassuring, but somehow wasn't. The fog pressed against the windows.

"Is this place much farther, Thais?" Nicholas asked fretfully.

Thais' pale arm glimmered as she reached out and picked up the speaking tube.

"Turn right at thee next cor-ner," she said, "and stop when you see a green light over a door on your right."

Nicholas chuckled. "You aren't taking me to a police station, stopping like that at a green light, are you, Thais?" he asked.

"No," she said. "I am not taking you to a police station."

Thais did not laugh. She did not seem amused. Nicholas stared at the obscurity beside him and fell silent. The sleek car turned its pointed nose to the right and drew to a purring halt. A green blur threw ghastly radiance through the fog. The chauffeur alighted, threw open the door. A light under a ground glass dome in the ceiling flooded the tonneau.

"This is thee place," Thais murmured.

Nicholas turned and looked at her. The almond eyes were dark and half-veiled by smooth, heavy lids. He could read nothing in them. Nicholas shrugged, mumbled to himself, stepped down on the wet, narrow pavement and held a hand to help Thais alight.

The green made his slightly florid face hideous under the high gleam of his silk hat, but it only heightened the pallor of Thais.

"How long will we be here, Thais?" he asked.

The girl was taller than ordinary. She moved with lithe grace. Moving toward the green light she raised one shoulder delicately.

"I am hungry, Harry," her low voice drifted back. "We shall probably be here—a while."

There was an edge in Nicholas' voice as he spoke to his chauffeur.

"You may go. We'll use a taxi."

"I could wait, sir," the man said.

Nicholas shook his head. He walked through the black door beneath the green light. The door closed behind him. Up near the ceiling, small green luminescences began to glow. Their brilliance increased slowly and revealed that the two stood in a square space perhaps twelve feet across which was draped all around with black curtains. There was an absolute silence about them.

"This is darned silly," rumbled Nicholas. The edge in his voice had increased. Thais did not speak, but abruptly the black curtains ahead of them parted and a thin Chinese, dressed in the same sombre black of the curtains, bowed with his hands in his sleeves.

"Fong Wu," he said in a sing-song voice, "welcomes the *mei kuo jen,* the honorables, to his humble place."

His face was bland. His eyes were inscrutable.

THAIS MADE A slight gesture with her left hand as if she brushed an unworthy thing from her path and they moved forward. Behind them the black curtains fell heavily into place. Nicholas stood very erectly and peered at small tables set about the room. Abruptly he smiled.

"Look, Thais," his voice showed absolute pleasure. "There is King Landers."

Thais turned slowly. A black cloak edged in smoky blue fur drooped from her white shoulders.

"King Lan-ders?" she asked. Her voice lingered curiously over the name.

"Yeah."

Nicholas was himself once more, as if just the glimpse of this man had restored all his flagging enthusiasm, as if this man's presence had knifed through all the fog of Orientalism that had depressed him.

"Yeah, King Landers. Come on over here, Thais."

As Nicholas strode across the room with the girl moving more leisurely behind him, a tall man rose from a corner table. In contrast to the sleek evening dress of Nicholas, he wore, and wore nonchalantly, a suit of excellently cut brown tweeds. His face was thin and long, his forehead thrust high up in peaks amid dark, dull hair. His lips did not smile.

"King Landers," again repeated Nicholas. "I don't know when I ever was so glad to see a man!"

Landers bowed, waved his hand negligently as if brushing aside the compliment. He said nothing.

"Let me present," said Nicholas, pride rising in his voice. "Miss Thais L'Hai." He pronounced it "Lahigh."

"Miss L'Hai," murmured Landers and pronounced it with that almost imperceptible roughening of the "h" that few Occidentals master.

Thais allowed herself to nod slightly. She let her head hang forward so, almost staring with her dark almond eyes into the frosty blue gaze of the man before her, staring from under the delicately drawn line of her black brows.

"You are," she hesitated, "King Landers, the detective?"

Landers bowed again. His lean, long face was expressionless, his blue eyes unwinking.

"You will forgive me," he murmured. "I was just leaving."

He left with another bow, his tall, muscular figure moving lightly across the dim room. And with him went Nicholas' buoyancy.

He sat down in the chair Landers had quitted and Thais stood looking at him for a moment. A fleeting shadow crossed the calm dark depths of her eyes, a trace of—was it pity? But it was gone instantly. She, too, sat. The black silk of her dress molded itself about the supple length of her thighs. Her hands were slim and narrow. She clapped them twice softly and a Chinese appeared beside the table.

"We desire soup, of birds' nests, and *ching g'or,* succulent shrimp baked in rolls, and *ch'ang,* tortoise meat stewed in honey," she paused, her eyes swept over, but did not see the Chinese who bowed obsequiously at her elbow. "And afterward," she continued, "you may bring us *'ng po li,* liquor of the Tiger."

Once more her eyes swept over the Chinese, then she placed her elbows on the table and leaned the point of her chin upon her hands. Nicholas looked up but for a moment his eyes did not see the pale oval of the face before him.

"Why did Landers walk out like that?" he demanded.

Thais' left shoulder raised perhaps a quarter inch, discarding the lean cold strength of Landers like a bunch of withered flowers.

"You are not polite tonight, Harry," she said.

Nicholas shook himself physically. The waiter slid dexterous service on the table between them, the meal moved through its courses and the fiery *'ng po li* was before them in little thimble glasses. Nicholas stared at it suspiciously, sipped it and gulped water. Thais drank hers slowly, with apparent enjoyment and presently Nicholas sipped again and again and again....

"SO YOU ARE fully awake, Mr. Nicholas?" a voice sing-songed its way into the man's consciousness.

Nicholas opened his eyes and found he was staring at a ceiling, a ceiling that sagged weightily here and there and was caught up with balls of light that glowed with a venomous green. It was black velvet, that ceiling. The man allowed his head to turn to the side and his gaze met more of those ebon drapes.

"I am over here, Mr. Nicholas," the voice came again.

The voice was low. It was soft. But it had an edge like razor steel in the night. It pierced through the muddle of Nicholas' returning senses. He flopped his head over the other way.

A figure in black robes stood there. Nicholas' eyes roamed from the thick, felt soles of the shoes, up the voluminous skirts, past the folded arms, the hands hidden in wide sleeves, then jerked suddenly to the face. There was no face! A black hat like a mitre sat on the head. But there was no face to be seen. From the edge of that black hat to the shoulders hung a green veil. It was opaque and formless. Through it Nicholas could make out absolutely nothing of the features of the man.

Nicholas sat up suddenly. Good Lord! Where were his clothes? He was nearly naked. Anger surged through Nicholas.

"What in hell does this mean?" he shouted. "I've enough of this Chink mummery. Give me my clothes, bring the young lady I was escorting here and let us out. You'll pay for this!"

He paused, breathing heavily through his nose. He rose to his feet. The man in black did not move. The green veil that covered his face did not move. Only Nicholas felt that eyes were boring through that veil.

"Get my clothes!" Nicholas thundered.

Suddenly Nicholas felt himself grasped by two pair of hands. They held his arms. He tried to turn. His legs were seized, and a moment later he lay flat on his back on the couch again, spreadeagled by six Chinese, helpless. He raved curses. His face grew purple with anger.

The man with the green veil appeared beside him. Slowly he drew up the wide sleeves and revealed yellowy muscular arms. In one hand he held a hypodermic needle filled with a sparkling green liquid, in the other he held a swab of cotton.

"As for your clothes," the soft, edgy voice came from behind the veil. "You shall have them in a moment and you shall leave also when you have dressed. The young lady was slightly indisposed and has been sent home."

Nicholas writhed in an effort to escape. The grip of his captors' hands became painful. The man in the green veil leaned over him, swabbed his side With the cotton and thrust the needle into him. While the prisoner panted out curses in a voice hoarsely intelligible and squirmed futilely, the masked Chinese slowly squeezed the hypodermic plunger down, driving the green liquid into the helpless man.

"You dog!" Nicholas gasped hoarsely. "You dog, what are you doing to me?"

The Chinese finished, snicked the hypodermic out and stepped back with his hands folded into his sleeves. Suddenly Nicholas was released. He sat up, glanced about him. The black curtains swayed a little. That was all. His six captors had disappeared. And before him, just out of reach, stood the preposterous figure in black with that imponderable green veil.

"You dog!" panted Nicholas.

"The name," again the singsong voice. "The name, my friend, is Ch'ien Feng. I will tell you what I did. I just injected the germs of Fu Lung."

Nicholas sat staring at the green veil. He breathed harshly, but said nothing. The Chinese paused a moment.

"I am sorry the name of the illustrious scholar Fu Lung means nothing to you," he went on, "but I can easily explain.

"The germs of Fu Lung are very insidious little animals and quite unique. The first thing they cause is small ulcers in the mouth. They are slightly uncomfortable, of course, but that is the only really uncomfortable reaction of the germs.

"A few days after the ulcers you will notice a slight greenish tinge to the skin under your eyes. In two days this will deepen and widen. In four days your face will be the color of a lime that is not quite ripe and in a week your entire body will be emerald."

"Dog! Yellow dog!" gasped Nicholas. "You're lying. There isn't any such germ!"

Ch'ien let his breath hiss through his teeth in amusement.

"You will discover that there is, my friend," he said tolerantly. "This green skin you will have is not unpleasant. You will have to stand a bit of joking at the club. Perhaps your sweetheart will not understand the joke. That is all.

"In the next week the germs of Fu Lung really begin to work. You will notice deepening wrinkles about your eyes. Your voice will develop a little quaver after the manner of the aged. But here is a curious thing, though your body will gradually become as decrepit as that of a man of ninety, you will not mind. In fact you won't know anything about it.

"At the end of the third month, thanks to the insidious little germs of Fu Lung, you will have lost your mind completely, *you will be insane!*"

2

Slave of Fear

KING LANDERS SAT erect in a chair at his desk and stared at the French phone cradled on its base at his elbow. Over it Nicholas' panic-stricken voice had quavered, promising one hundred thousand dollars to Landers to rid him of the germs of Fu Lung, to rid him of the curse of the green-veiled Chinese. The Chinese whose singsong voice had knifed into Nicholas' mind and ripped aside the strength of his will, left him a trembling, terror-ridden man. For Ch'ien Feng had given no hint of his purpose in injecting the germs into Nicholas' system.

Landers' door opened abruptly and a man slouched in. He was pale. He had a beak of a nose and under it a mouth with a short upper lip that showed perpetually his narrow long teeth. His eyes were heavy-lidded and intelligent. He hauled a chair from the wall and draped himself on it. From his inside pocket he pulled a letter which he tossed on Landers' desk.

The detective ran his hand slowly over his high forehead, ran his fingers up the peaks of it into his dull dark hair. His lean face was without expression.

"What you after, Mallory?" he asked. "There's no news in me nowadays."

Mallory grunted. "I'm news myself now," he said in a strangely bored voice.

Landers continued to look at the reporter. The man's shoulders were drooped. The circles under his eyes, ever present, were darker and deeper, were greenish! They looked as if they had been blackened by a hard-swung fist and the bruised blood was just getting back into circulation again, leaving this greenish blue mark. The detective's blue gaze narrowed. Mallory slowly drew a package of cigarettes from his pocket, lighted one and tossed the pack on the desk. Landers shook his head slightly. He said nothing. Mallory smiled wearily.

"So you're not interested in my news?" he asked.

"I know your news," said Landers softly. "You're going to tell me that a Chinese in a green veil shanghaied you, and did things with a hypodermic needle."

Mallory sat up very straight in the chair. The short upper lip that never quite met the lower was wrinkled in astonishment, showing the full length of his narrow teeth.

"Marvelous, my dear Holmes!" he exclaimed, but the mockery he intended wasn't in his voice. "But go on. What happened next?"

Landers shrugged his high, broad shoulders, ran his hand again over that peaked forehead of his.

"You know the rest well enough," he said shortly.

Mallory leaned forward, his elbows on his knees and talked smoke out of his nose and mouth.

"Yeah," he said, and lassitude crept back into his voice, "Yeah. I know the rest right enough."

He looked up, shoving a sloppy gray felt hat to the back of his head, showing a few strands of lank blond hair under its brim.

"It's about ten days since I got my dose of germs," he said, "and things are moving just like the Chink said they would. I got ulcers in my mouth and you see the green starting under my eyes."

Landers nodded.

The reporter waved his hand toward the letter on the desk. "Ch'ien Feng says if I come get his antidote tomorrow it will knock out the green and stop the germs from working on the old brain."

Landers reached out and picked up the letter. He looked at the paper. It was ordinary bond, not cheap, not expensive, the kind that could be bought in any one of a dozen stores. The letter was typewritten. He screwed a small magnifying glass into his eye, studied the type and grunted.

"Royal, number ten," he said, "Pica type. You've probably got fifteen machines like it in your office."

Mallory nodded glumly, his eyes on the cigarette in his hand, watching the twisting spirals of gray smoke. Landers skimmed through the letter. It stated that unless Mallory obeyed future orders, the nature of which was not specified, the doses of the antidote would be withheld and senile debility of mind and body would set in. It further explained that each dose of the antidote was made individually for the person for whom it was intended, that no surplus supply was kept on hand, and that the formula lived in the brain of one man only, that of Ch'ien Feng.

"Try and beat that combination," Mallory said heavily. "I might as well go jump in the river."

One of Landers' rare smiles twisted his mouth corners and it didn't look as if he were amused.

"I'm going to beat that combination," he said.

Mallory looked up at him with awakening eyes. He flicked his cigarette butt out the window and massaged the palms of his hands together.

"You wouldn't fool me, would you, mister," he asked, life creeping back into his voice.

Landers' face was expressionless, his frosty blue eyes slightly narrowed. He reached slowly forward and took a cigarette, struck a match. Holding the burning pasteboard, he looked across the flame at Mallory.

"I don't know," he said slowly, and lighted his cigarette, snapping the match out with his finger.

Mallory stood up briskly, yanked the brim of the shapeless fedora down. He sighed deeply. "Thanks, Landers. I think I'll take my medicine." He made a wry face, "And wait awhile before jumping in the river."

Landers said, "Good-bye, Mallory."

The newspaper man jerked his chin upward in salute, his long, narrow teeth revealed, in a small grin. He sauntered out the doorway, his shoulders jaunty.

Landers stood up. He didn't put his hands on the arms of his chair. He didn't touch the desk. He just stood by straightening his legs. Few men stand that way. It takes strength. The detective puffed at the cigarette twice more, staring down at the phone through the smoke, then he snapped the butt out the window. He walked over to a water cooler in a corner, drank a glass and crossed to the window. Mallory was just crossing the street. There was no slouch in his shoulders at all. He skipped in front of a taxi, poised in a hairbreadth stop as a truck charged by, then walked calmly on to the opposite sidewalk.

The man's figure wavered in Landers' vision. He peered more narrowly, his blue eyes squinting. The entire street was vague. The detective whirled, taking wooden steps toward the telephone cradled on his desk. His hands stretched toward it.

He said clearly, "I've been doped."

He slumped to the floor.

LANDERS OPENED HIS eyes and stared at a black-draped ceiling dotted with green globes of light. He closed them again and thought swiftly. There was no doubt, and little surprise in his mind. He was on the operating table of Ch'ien Feng. If the opening of his eyes had not been detected, he might stave off for a time the injection of the germs of the green madness. He might get a chance to dash out of the Chinese trap.

Abruptly hands closed on his wrists and legs. Landers tensed into instant action. He jerked his arm and leg on the right side and rolled to the left. When the men were straining violently to resist this surge, he suddenly reversed the movement, then jerked. His right hand came free. In the same movement, he swung it across his body, balled it into a fist and crashed it into the yellow, distorted face of a huge Chinese who gripped his left hand. The man went back and down.

Landers jack-knifed, caught the necks of the two men who held his feet and cracked their skulls together. Twenty seconds after those hands had seized him, Landers crouched, free of his attackers, on the black couch in the midst of the green-lighted room. He whirled to his right where the man he first had wrenched free from had dropped. There was no one there. He spun toward the bodies of the men he had knocked out. They, too, were gone. He peered about him tensely, his lean face grim.

The black curtains around the walls did not even sway. The detective straightened slowly. He was nearly naked. He stepped off the couch and swept his eyes completely around the room again. Then abruptly he looked up. Either his eyes had flickered momentarily or those ghastly lamps were fainter. Staring upward he discovered his eyes had not flickered.

As the light deepened into a green dusk, Landers started a slow circuit of the couch, moving on his toes, alert for the first hint of an attack. The dusk deepened, and abruptly the room was black. The detective took six silent steps backward, two sideways and halted, listening, straining his keen eyes to pierce the darkness.

Off to his right through the blackness he detected a faint rustle, something moving furtively across the floor. He flexed his knees, waiting, waiting. On the sound pushed, until it had nearly achieved the centre of the room. Then it halted. Landers held his breath, listening. He heard nothing further. Nothing breathed over there by the couch. Of that he was certain. There was no rustle in the black curtains to betray a human presence. *What was that?*

Landers strained his ears. The noise was a faint hissing!

Good Lord! Had Ch'ien loosed some venomous snake in the room to do what his six men had been unable to accomplish? The detective fought down an almost overwhelming impulse to dash madly against the walls. The primal fear of things reptilian merged with the dread of darkness in his breast. He took deep breaths, calming himself, crouched to listen for the inescapable sound of sliding, chill coils. He knew the sound, like a feather brushing a lead. As faint as that.

The hissing continued, but its position had not changed. It was still over there in the middle of the room. Landers drew another breath. A dull pain stabbed his lungs. His clenched hands tingled. Then suddenly he knew.

There was no snake in the room. That hiss was gas escaping from a tube, some odorless gas that was sapping his strength, that was sending that blood spinning, humming in his brain.

He held his breath, moved swiftly toward the sound, found the tube. He held his breath as long as possible, pressing his hand over the end of the gas jet. The hiss stopped. He groped with his hand to find something to plug it with.

He bumped his head against the couch, but felt only the jar, the shock, no pain. He lay flat on the floor, seeking fresher air, then unconsciousness closed in on him again.

"YOU ARE A most troublesome prisoner, Mr. Landers," drawled a voice. It was soft, and low, but it knifed through into the detective's mind, tore aside the anesthetic veil that obscured his senses. He tried to raise his hand to his head, but bands caught his wrist, held it to his side. Then slowly, experimentally, he moved each limb, with the same result. He was tied down, hand and foot.

"A most troublesome prisoner, Mr. Landers," the voice repeated.

Landers gave up pretense of coma and opened his eyes, seeing again the green globes of light and black, draped velvet.

"I'm going to become even more troublesome," Landers spoke clearly, without haste or apparent heat, "unless I am instantly released."

The piercing voice hissed in amusement.

"It is a curious thing, Mr. Landers," it said, "but every man who awakes on that table says something like that. As a student of psychology, Mr. Landers, how would you explain the motivation of that remark?"

Psychology? This Chinese was a curious monster, Landers thought, his head now entirely clear from the gas. Well, he would play along with this Ch'ien Feng.

"It is written, Oh, master," he said, his voice lapsing into the singsong intonation of an oriental, "that whatsoever a man least has, it is that he shall most desire."

Once more the hissing breath of Ch'ien Feng. "It is really quite elementary after all, is it not, Mr. Landers?" the Chinese went on. "I agree, of course. You are helpless, so you bolster your courage with thoughts of power. But where did you read the learned wisdom of Fu Lung?"

Landers swung his head slowly to the left and regarded his interrogator. A figure garbed in black robes, a green veil draped from a black mitre cap.

"The wisdom of the wise," he intoned in the same singsong the Chinese used, "the wisdom of the wise is as fruit in the wilderness. It is there for everyone, but only he may eat with impunity who knows that this skin brews a poison while that other hath a seed will heal a sore."

He could thank Carter Mallory that he had read Fu Lung's psychology and analogues, Landers thought. The newspaper man knew many recondite works of the East. He stared at the veiled man. The green mask contemplated him impersonally. Suddenly the hands slid out of the black sleeves and the robes swayed forward. In the right hand was a nickel-gleaming hypodermic needle. In the left a swab of cotton. And Landers could not move.

A slight nausea twitched at his stomach as the green liquid was pressed slowly into his body. A shudder swept over Landers, twitched at his whipcord muscles, but he listened to the Chinese recite the merits of the injection with well-feigned horror. It would be just as well if Ch'ien Feng did not know that he had previous acquaintance with the details of his enslavement.

"There is this difference," said he of the green veil, "between the way I treat you and the others. You I shall keep with me instead of turning loose. First, King Landers, I had planned to kill you. But I like your mind. It would be a shame to wipe it out, or to sponge it clean with madness. So, Mr. Landers, you will turn that brain to protecting me from the police, who presently will be thrusting their noses into this business transaction of mine."

Landers cut in on him.

"Would you have any objection to me dressing now?" he asked in an expressionless voice.

"But certainly not," said Ch'ien. He drew a knife from those wide black sleeves of his, leaned toward Landers and prepared to cut his bonds. He paused a moment.

"It would be well for you always to remember, Mr. Landers," he said, "that if I am captured, there will be no antidotes, and the green madness will creep on you, not too swiftly, Mr. Landers."

HE SLICED THROUGH the bonds then and the detective sat up slowly, rubbed his wrists until the blood tingled in his hands again, bent over and massaged his ankles. The Chinese clapped his hands softly twice and a servant brought Landers' clothing. Five minutes later he was clothed.

Ceremoniously then Ch'ien Feng ushered him from the black chamber into a room of imperial yellow. A throne chair on a dais stood at one side of the room, cushioned in yellow satin. The walls were hung with weapons of the ancient East, Chinese swords, Japanese daggers, and the huge curved executioner's blade.

"Your first duty," said Ch'ien Feng in his dry, penetrating voice. "Shall be to write a letter to your friend Carter Mallory. Tell him that I shall depend on his spreading pacifist propaganda, that he must ridicule the idea of the yellow peril at every opportunity, that his paper must preach disarmament, reduction of armies and navies. He has profound influence on the editorial writers and owners. He can accomplish this."

Landers stopped and faced the Chinese, peered at the green veil that made the black-robed figure seem more like a stuffed dummy than a human being.

"I don't get you," he said, his blue eyes glittering. "What's behind this?"

Ch'ien Feng's breath hissed inward in laughter.

"I have," he said, "the names of fifty of the country's leading industrialists, inventors, millionaires. Many of them have been inoculated with the germs of madness. All shall taste the needle and bow to the slavery of the green madness.

"Then," he paused, his body seemed to swell, to grow visibly larger. "Then I shall use these men to establish China's dominion over the world! These fifty leaders shall finance her rule, they shall supply the genius, the inventions we need. China shall rule the world. I—" his long-nailed hand barely touched his chest. "I shall rule the world!"

Landers' breath was hissing between his teeth. His lean jaw was clenched.

"You fiend!" he burst out. "I'll kill you!"

He whirled to the wall. His hand grasped and unsheathed a dagger. He spun, plunging the dagger in a strong, upward thrust toward the heart of the Chinese. And Ch'ien Feng laughed! Two monosyllabic explosions of mirth. That was all, but it checked the dagger in mid-thrust. Landers held it poised, ready to thrust home.

"Do you think I am afraid of your green madness?" he asked calmly. "Do you think I love my life more than my country, my race?"

Behind the green mask, the man's breath hissed again in laughter.

"Do not forget," he said gently, "The germs of Fu Lung. Even if you do not fear the green madness, there are already twenty of the leading men of your nation who have been inoculated. If you kill me, they die by the same stroke!"

One long hand drew forth a fan, opened it with a click and gently agitated the air beneath the pendant veil so that it bellowed out as if Ch'ien's face had suddenly swollen.

"Think, Landers," he went on slowly, "what it would mean to your nation to lose them all. My plan can go on without me. Your nation, deprived of its leaders, would fall easy prey, and—" he paused, "—only I know the antidote which will stop the creeping green madness." He clicked the fan, thrust it into his sleeve, lifted a hand and pointed a single finger toward his head, its long nail protected by a jade guard. "Only I know it and I keep the formula in my brain."

Slowly Landers' arm relaxed until the dagger hung at his side. His fingers opened and the blade fell with a soft thump into the deep piled rug beneath his feet. The detective ran a slow hand over his peeked forehead, pushed lean fingers through the dull dark hair, wearily.

He said, "I guess you win."

3

The Slave Thais

CH'IEN FENG DISAPPEARED through ebon drapes. A short time later, he sent for Landers. The detective followed the Chinese who served him through a maze of corridors and draped chambers to the yellow throne room. He stopped against the wall, just inside the swishing imperial silk.

A small table had been placed in the middle of the room. Beside it stood Ch'ien Feng, his long black robes seeming slightly dusty in the brighter lighting of this hall. Beside it also stood a woman, Thais L'Hai. At Landers' entrance she turned slightly so that she faced him. Her dress was garnet silk, heavy and long and simple, sleeveless so that her slender arms became pale exclamation points against the dark beauty of the garment. Black gloves, long and costly, were crumpled on her forearms. A small hat of dark green sat upon the blue blackness of her hair. She did not smile at Landers.

Ch'ien's hissing voice broke the silence of the room, issued mocking from behind the green veil.

"May I introduce another slave of the green madness, my dear Landers?" he pronounced. "This is Thais L'Hai. She has come for her weekly treatment."

As he spoke his long-nailed hand, with its intricately carved jade guards, waved toward the table and Landers noticed for the first time that a glass beaker there held a liquid that gathered green fire in its midst. Landers' eyes narrowed on it, but his high, peaked forehead was smooth. He moved his tall, lean body slowly across the room and took the hand the girl offered, bowed low over it, looking up into the still blackness of her eyes. Her thin, pale lips did not smile. Landers wondered if she ever smiled.

"I called you, Landers," broke in Ch'ien's slutted speech, "that you might see the antidote. Yours is not due for a while and I mix it only in individual doses. But you know that already, don't you, Landers?" He poured from the beaker a small cup full of the bright green liquid.

The girl shuddered but took it eagerly. Her eyes were strangely stirred. She drained the cup greedily, held it out again, and again, and again. Six times was the cup filled and six times emptied before the beaker stood empty on the table.

"Now, for another week, Thais," his singsong reached them clearly. "Your soft white skin will be safely white. It would look quite odd green, don't you think?"

THE YELLOW SILK lifted and fell and Landers was alone in the room with Thais. He turned slowly toward her, his blue eyes as inscrutable as the dark, veiled depths of her own. He regarded her unwaveringly. She raised her chin slightly, making a melting line of her throat. A faint bitter smile crossed the paleness of her lips.

"It is too bad," came her soft, slurring speech, "that you dislike me."

Landers thought of Nicholas, terror-ridden, half mad already with fear of the green madness because with this woman he had come to this place. He thought of the hate in her eyes when Ch'ien Feng had touched her. He permitted one of those rare smiles of his to cross his face, lighting his entire countenance. It was a kindly smile. He said nothing.

Thais looked at him from under her heavy lids, looked at him steadily and with studied purpose, analyzing the thin long nose, the squarely set eyes, the intelligence of that peaked long face. When she spoke next her lips did not move. Six feet away you could not have understood what she said, ten feet away you would not have known she had spoken.

"We share a common lot," she said. "If we can help each other, we should. Is there some message you wish to send outside?"

Landers' eyes flickered with amusement. This was all too pat for it to be accidental, he and the girl being left alone in the room.

"I am well paid," he said softly. "I am not dissatisfied."

He took a step nearer her, lifted her slim, narrow hand to his and looked into her eyes, so nearly on a level with his own.

"If you were to remain here," he went on, his voice gentle, "I think I might say even more. I think I might say I would be happy."

The flicker of amusement that had been in Landers' eyes was in hers now. The half-smile briefly disturbed again the serenity of her pale lips, and her lids drooped a little. But her head did not go back in token of her woman's surrender. The bitter lips did not part in offering. On the contrary she dropped her chin a little, regarding their two hands still clasped between them.

"One of my grandfathers was Irish, too," she said. "I know blarney when I hear it."

She released her hand gently and turned away with a little tinkle of laughter and Landers really grinned this time. This was beginning to be the sort of game he liked. If there were only his own life at stake—but the smile faded. That, unfortunately, was not the case. Twenty of the nation's leading men were threatened with the green madness, twenty of the nation's leading men would be insane in three months if he were to kill this Chinese, willing to accept that fate himself.

His eyes were still on the graceful figure of the girl, remarking the slim strength of her body, the easy balance of her step. As she neared the yellow curtains, they lifted, and a Chinese stepped out with a green silken bandage for her eyes. Thais turned her left side toward the servant, stooped suddenly. There was a momentary gleam of black silk as she lifted her skirt, then the glint of a knife flashed in the corner where she and the Chinese stood. Her thrust upward from her garter was strong and true. The servant grunted, staggered back a step doubling up with his hands to his stomach. He grunted again and collapsed to the floor.

With a movement lithe as a panther, the girl whirled toward Landers. Her face was as inscrutable as ever, her eyes veiled so that they showed only as a gleam in the pale oval of her countenance. Her breath was quick. The soft slur of her voice reached him.

"Can you trust me now, King Landers?" she called. "Hur-ry."

Landers waited no longer. He snatched a sword from the wall and with the weapon in his hand, crossed to her side in long strides. The girl had already lifted the yellow silken curtains, revealing a dim opening. Into it they raced, swiftly, silently. From behind came no sound of pursuit, ahead they heard nothing, saw nothing dangerous.

"This is too easy," Landers said in a flat voice.

They entered a room that contained not a piece of furniture, that was all gray velvet and green small lights so that the whole room seemed green. Landers thrust the sword through the curtains and they walked swiftly through. Everywhere the blade rang on solid walls until they had nearly completed the circuit of the room, then it went through the gray drapes to its hilt and touched nothing.

Thais jerked aside the curtain and they ran on through another dim corridor. The girl's breath was rapid at Landers' side. He felt a racing excitement in his blood.

"We're not accomplishing a damned thing, you know," he said. "In a week you must return. I have a day less than that."

"What may we two not do in a week?" she whispered eagerly to him, "You are strong, brave, intelligent. And I—" the girl broke off with her tinkling laugh, "—I am Thais."

There were a thousand meanings in her words. Landers' senses were swept in a whirl, a drumming of swift blood. They hurried on.

"Look," Thais caught his arm. "There is daylight. There is the street."

Landers clasped his hand over hers on his arm and did not rush for the light, a narrow door opening into the street. He stood staring down at the girl. Her eyes swung up to his, heavy still, half-veiled with those languorous lids, the pale mouth twisted by its slightly bitter smile. Suddenly Landers swept the woman into his arms, crushing those thin lips with his. It was only a moment, then they were racing to the street again. In the doorway they paused while Landers probed the way with watchful eyes.

"Why did you do that?" asked Thais, her voice holding only curiosity.

Landers laughed sharply without mirth. "If you are leading me to death for Ch'ien," he said. "I've had my pay."

"But why should Ch'ien want you killed in the street?" she asked. "When up in those draped rooms you were in his power?"

Landers slid the hilt of the sword up under his armpit, masked the tip with his palm where it thrust from under his coat. He shrugged. "Bodies are troublesome things to dispose of," he muttered. "Come on."

He slid out of the doorway, turned left in the crooked Chinatown street and, keeping close to the building, eased along. His eyes darted about, over the opposing buildings, searching for danger. Suddenly, seeming to come from nowhere, and everywhere, a voice filled the street, the voice of Ch'ien Feng!

"Go, my children, my slaves," it intoned, soft and stabbing as always. "Go, but forget not to return for your—medicine. Thais, forget not your white skin. Forget not your so keen brain, Landers."

Ch'ien's monosyllabic laughter cut the air. Landers' sword glittered in his hand, then abruptly he cursed and threw the thing into the gutter, strode squarely in the middle of the walk with the girl on his arm.

Six days were his, six days to conquer the unbeatable.

4

The Slave Returns

WHEN THEY HAD found a taxi, Landers turned to Thais. "This was a fool's stunt," he said, "and you'll pay for knifing that Chink."

The girl shook her head slowly. She was too valuable to Ch'ien Feng for him to wax angry over a mere servant less. As for Landers' escape, that was his own affair, she told him. She leaned back in her corner of the cab and looked at him steadily under heavy lids.

"You have six days," she said, without emphasis.

Landers returned her regard unwaveringly, his blue eyes imponderable. "I'm going back tomorrow," he said.

The girl was startled into opening her eyes wide so that for a moment Landers stared into their depths. He found surprise there and a trace of fear. He shook his head slowly.

"I am not in Ch'ien's pay," he said. "I am, like yourself, a slave of the green madness."

He, too, leaned back in his seat and closed his eyes. It wasn't weariness, but he could think and talk better when he wasn't watching Thais, when the loveliness of her wasn't racing like fire in his blood. He asked her while they rode so, how the antidote had tasted.

"Sour, very sour," she said, "and bitter as gall."

He rode on for a while quietly, thinking of Thais, and their escape. Furlough, was a better word.

He said, "I do not trust you entirely, Thais. You hate Ch'ien too thoroughly. That stabbing might very well have been faked. I saw no blood. You may be trying to trap me, to find out what my plans are for attacking the Chinese and his conspiracy."

He opened his eyes suddenly. Thais was not looking at him. Her eyes were fixed straight ahead and her pale mouth twisted in her slight smile. She said nothing.

Landers went on. "You helped to trap Nicholas, got him into Ch'ien's power. I don't know how many other men you have taken to that den. I am not even sure that you have been injected with the germs of the green madness. In fact—" he leaned toward her, regarded the small lobe of an ear protruding from under the close green turban, from under the blue black hair, "—I am certain of nothing about you except that you are very—desirable, and very—dangerous."

Thais laughed tinklingly, but still did not look at him. Landers tapped on the glass behind the driver and the taxi swerved to the curb. The detective got out. Thais looked at him now and amusement was in her dark eyes.

"*Tsai t'ien,*" she said. That was all and the cab was gone.

Landers stood looking after the taxi as traffic swallowed it. Of course she would speak mandarin. "Good-bye," he muttered to himself.

He signaled another taxi and went to Nicholas' office. When he gave his name to the girl at the telephone, Nicholas came hurrying out to meet him. The man's voice was pitifully eager.

"Come quickly," he implored, and led the way into his private office, a room luxurious with rich mahogany and Persian rugs. "Have you got him, Landers?" he asked anxiously.

Landers carefully closed the door of the office behind them

before he spoke. "I have been a prisoner of Ch'ien Feng for eighteen hours," he said. "I got my dose of the germs last night."

Nicholas dropped heavily into his chair, the color draining from his face. He said dully, "I am lost."

"Don't be melodramatic," snapped Landers, irritated. A man had no business crumpling as easily as that.

Nicholas looked up at him, his full, usually jocular face flaccid. What Landers had said apparently had not registered on his brain.

"I've been ordered to take Ch'ien a quarter million dollars next Tuesday," he said. "If I don't take it, I don't get the antidote."

He moved his tongue around in his mouth, his eyes tightening in pain.

"I've already got the ulcers," he said, "but I can't see any green spots under my eyes yet."

He looked at Landers as a child might regard its father, searching for some hope there. The detective had not sat down. He returned Nicholas' gaze without expression.

"You'd better take the money next Tuesday unless you hear from me in the meantime," he said finally. "If I don't get in touch with you, I'll be on hand when you arrive to get the antidote."

LANDERS WENT OUT of the office and on the first floor entered a phone booth to make a call. Fifteen minutes later he was seated across a speakeasy table from Carter Mallory. The man's face had grown even thinner. His beaked nose stood out like a mountain on a plain, but the greenish traces had gone from under his eyes. He licked his short upper lip and his mouth parted, showing the narrow, long teeth. He tossed off whisky like water.

"I've met Ch'ien Feng," Landers told him. "I'm going back to his place tomorrow, perhaps later today."

"What are you going to do?" Mallory asked.

Landers' wide shoulders lifted a fraction of an inch, his blue eyes expressionless in his long, lean face.

"If I knew, it would save a lot of grief," he said. "I don't even know how to attack this deal. Usually it's a problem of finding a blackmailer. In this case there is no trouble finding the man, but you can't touch him when you do—or the victims die, and die so terribly that they are even anxious to do what the Chink orders."

He repeated the orders of the Chinese to Mallory, which the newspaper man had not yet had time to receive. The man grimaced, his tongue touching his short upper lip.

"And if I don't spread this pacifist propaganda he won't give me another dose of the antidote, eh?" he asked. Landers nodded shortly.

"Well, I won't do it!" Mallory stood up suddenly, striking the table loudly with the palm of his hand. "I won't do it."

Landers looked up calmly into the distorted face of the man. Determination was written largely upon it.

"I think you'd be wiser to play along with the thing for a while," he said. "Two or three weeks of that pacifist cry for disarmament wouldn't do any harm, and there's always a chance that we'll get a break and best the Chink."

"Such as which?" Mallory jeered.

Landers frowned, running his hand up over his forehead into his hair. He had a small plan. He wanted to get a sample of that antidote for analysis by a chemist. If he could learn what it was, the case immediately became simple. But Mallory was slightly hysterical now. There was no use in broadcasting his plans.

LANDERS DID NOT answer Mallory directly. He returned to his original attack as the newspaper man sat heavily down again and tossed off another drink.

"I can't see why this sudden patriotic ideal stirs you," he said. "I never knew you to be moved particularly by it before. You know and I know that newspapers are run for one purpose, the garnering of profits from the ads run in them. They campaign against corruption, but that's always proved good business in the end, you know. In other words most of this cant about the idealism of crusading newspapers is the bunk. They crusade, sure, but it's a good business proposition. Why should you allow yourself to go insane for any such thing as that?"

Mallory grinned sheepishly at his glass. He twirled it, empty, between his fingers.

"All right," he said. "Call it business, idealism, or any damned thing you please, but that goes!" His hand whacked down on the table again.

Landers stared at the hand in a detached way, his own hand running swiftly through his hair again.

"What are you planning to do?" he asked slowly.

Mallory's lips closed, despite the shortness of the upper, the pressure of those long squirrel teeth. It gave his face a drawn look.

"That's my business," he said shortly.

Landers nodded agreement. "Only," he warned. "Don't come gunning for Ch'ien Feng or I'll shoot you down. I don't want to die of the green madness."

The reporter stared at him without understanding.

"Get me?" Landers asked. He leaned forward against the table, both his hands outlined on its top.

Mallory's tongue dabbed at his lip. "Sure," he said. "Sure, I get you."

Landers left. He called next at the library where he looked up Fu Lung. He found many learned psychological treatises by the man, many of which he had already read, thanks to Carter Mallory. But he could locate no medical works. Fu Lung had founded a secret society in old China, it appeared, which had accomplished marvels with the power of mind over matter. Landers gave it up, visited a chemist and made arrangements for a speedy analysis of the antidote of Ch'ien Feng if he should obtain it.

Then he bought a heavy hammer which he slung with a little loop under his armpit. He went to a stationery store and bought a large-barreled fountain pen which he refused to let the sales girl test in ink for him. He put it carefully in an inside pocket, walked out and hailed a taxi.

Back in Chinatown he walked quietly along the twisted, rutted lanes until he came to the side street where he and Thais had fled a few hours before. He searched in vain for the exit they had used. Presently he shrugged and went into a curio shop where an old Chinese bowed to him.

Landers said quietly, "Take me to Ch'ien Feng."

The old Chinese wagged his head, shrugged his shoulders.

"I'll wait here," the detective said. "You go tell Ch'ien Feng that King Landers wants to come back to him and it will be all right."

Almost inaudible in the distance a bell tinkled faintly, was silent a moment and tinkled again. Abruptly the Chinese bowed to Landers.

"It is well," he said. "You come with me."

He blindfolded Landers and led him through a maze of evil-smelling corridors. Finally the blindfold was removed and he stood before Ch'ien Feng in the golden yellow of the throne room. On the dais sat Ch'ien behind his green veil.

"I am so sorry," he intoned, the voice stabbing into Landers, "to tell you that your friend, Mr. Mallory, decided he would not wait for the green madness. He jumped into the river a little while ago and was drowned."

5

The Revolt

KING LANDERS BLINKED and looked squarely, unwaveringly at the green veil, stared as if trying to pierce that inscrutable mask and gaze into the eyes of the Chinese. Carter Mallory dead, a suicide, he had said.

"I am so sorry," Ch'ien Feng said softly, "to bring you this sad news. Now I must ask you to find me another newspaper man who has the influence to accomplish what I desire."

Landers felt there was some trap in these slow words. He ran his hand up over his peaked forehead, through his dull hair and still did not speak. He looked at the man in the green veil again, then he shrugged, turned and walked across the room.

Ch'ien Feng's voice suddenly rapped out.

"The audience is not yet finished, slave!"

Landers turned beside the silken drapes, his head inclined slightly forward, his mouth corners drawn down tightly. His blue eyes were frosty.

"I do not desire to talk further with you," he said slowly, almost gently.

"But I wish to talk with you!" The Chinese bit out the words, showing anger for the first time since Landers had been in his power.

Landers bowed stiffly, very slightly, his expression unchanged. "That," he said, "is unfortunate."

He turned, thrust aside the yellow silk and stepped into the corridor. The Chinese voice followed him, stopped him, so that he stood, his back to the man, still holding up the yellow drape. Silkiness had returned to the slurred syllables.

"Do you think it is wise, King Landers," the voice asked, "to ignore the fact that I hold the fate of—shall we say others—in my hands?"

Landers' mouth tightened but he made no reply. Instead he allowed the yellow silk to slip from his hand so that it bellied and swayed and fell shut behind him, cutting off the sight of that sinister figure in black with its masked face. But it did not stop that slow, soft voice, that persisted, thrust at him through the folds of the drapery.

"And yet," it went on, "these—others—have done much for you, Landers."

The detective stood there, behind the yellow silk of the drape, his back turned toward where the Chinese sat on his yellow satin throne. His fingers slowly clenched.

"Perhaps," Ch'ien continued, "you would prefer that these—others—also pay for the folly of helping you?"

Landers swung about with a low oath, swept aside the silk so that it fluttered as if in a furious wind. He strode up to the throne so that he faced the Chinese at no more than three feet distant.

"Today," he said, "I saw three men. One is a coward, one is now dead, but the other—" Landers paused, smiling crookedly. "The other will bring about your safe destruction, so that you will not long be able to threaten these—others."

He checked then, his glare unwavering on the green veil.

"You notice I hope, that I said destruction, not death?" he went on. "But perhaps you are not familiar with the customs of our American newspapers. They always, when they refer to humans, say death. They use destruction to apply to animals.

"I do not think that animals, about to be destroyed, should threaten humans, do you, *chien,* dog?"

He spun on his heel this time with finality and strode from the room. And this time no angry voice rasped after him. No anger, but Ch'ien Feng's thin, monosyllabic laughter cracked out, deadened by the draped walls.

LANDERS IGNORED THE laughter, went deliberately to his room where he sat on the side of his blue-covered couch, his eyes fixed on the opposite wall. Presently he clapped his hands and ordered the servant, who appeared instantly, to prepare his bath. The Chinese parted the blue curtains and went through into the bath, starting the rush of the shower.

As soon as he disappeared, Landers crossed the room and slid the heavy hammer from beneath his coat. He gripped it by the handle, raised it and waited. Presently the curtains stirred, the man stepped into view. The hammer swished down, cracked on the man's skull. A cry was snuffed in his throat and he slumped to the floor. But Landers had pulled the blow. He had no intention of killing unnecessarily. He bound the man swiftly with strips torn from the curtains, gagged him with the same material, then turned off the lights and the shower and lay down to wait.

An hour later, he put the Chinese in his own bed, covered him with the blue silken coverlet and, hammer in hand, crept back to the room where the yellow satin throne stood vacant. He crossed the hall to where the day before two servants had whisked out the table after the girl had drunk the antidote.

Behind the yellow curtains was a sizable corridor, but it ran nowhere. It ended, within ten feet, in a blank wall.

Landers crouched there and pressed his ear against the surface. He heard nothing there. Suddenly he straightened. Far off within the interior of the building, muffled by the draped walls, came a faint cry. A deep gong was struck thrice and its vibrations beat through the still air. The detective's mouth closed in a straight line. There was but one explanation of that. The bound Chinese had been discovered!

Landers darted back to the yellow room and concealed himself behind the drapes just at the edge of the corridor. A moment later, yellow light flung down the hallway from that dead end, and he heard the knife-like tones of Ch'ien Feng calling sharply in mandarin, asking questions. The Chinese advanced swiftly, flung aside the yellow curtains, almost uncovering Landers and stalked on into the throne room. Landers peered furtively back down the corridor. The end of the hall now showed an open door. Swiftly the detective slipped down the passageway, and entered. He closed the portal quietly behind him.

Here was a room showing a strange mixture of the Orient and the West. The walls were hung with silks and exotic paintings, but the furniture was American, heavy overstuffed chairs, an end table by one, a desk, and a wall safe—open! Before starting to search that, the detective looked over the place carefully. On the end table by the chair was a bottle of gin, half emptied, a siphon of soda and a beaker of green liquid that seemed to gather to itself all the light in the room so that it glowed with emerald fire. The antidote!

From his pocket Landers drew out the fountain pen he had

purchased that day and which was innocent of ink. He rapidly filled it with the green liquid, then he crossed to the safe. There was a book, green and leather bound, several thousand dollars in large bills, a box of capsules marked quinine and a bottle of the clear green antidote!

Landers' eyes were narrow in concentration. For once this Chinese had made up a larger batch than necessary of the antidote. But he did not touch it. He already had a sample. Instead he opened the green bound book and ran hurriedly through its pages. It listed about fifty names of the nation's wealthiest and most powerful men. Landers thrust the book into his pocket, returned to the door by which he had entered and pressed lightly against it. It did not budge!

Landers pressed harder. No movement at all. In a burst of desperation he hurled all his weight and strength against it. Still it did not yield! He was trapped!

LANDERS WHIRLED THEN, put his back to the door and with frantic eyes studied the room in which he was imprisoned. He could see no other door. But had the entrance by which he had come in closed itself? Or had it been shut by one of the stealthy-footed Chinese who served Ch'ien Feng? Landers did not know. He wished now that he had bought a pistol instead of this hammer which he had intended to use to crack the safe he had guessed must exist somewhere in this elaborate den.

For an instant panic seized him. A wild urge almost drove him to dash about the room and seek another outlet. Resolutely he fought it down, his hands clenched at his sides. He conquered after a while, but his palms were wet, and the marks of his nails were on them. Slowly he steadied. He stood erect then and looked about him more carefully. There on the baseboard just to the right of the safe was a black box with wires running from it. Landers' tight lips relaxed. Of course Ch'ien Feng would have a telephone!

After a few moments' search, he located it, masked in a little alcove behind one of the paintings. He took it down, set it on the desk and drew up a chair. He lifted the instrument from its cradle, and called a number swiftly, his eyes on the locked door. A candle flickered in a death's head holder at his elbow beside some green sealing wax. Except for this and the green book, the desk was clear. Over the phone came the faint clicks and clashings of the connection being established, then the droning sound of the bell ringing came to him. It buzzed again. His eyes were glued on the door.

Was it his imagination, or *had that door moved?* Landers fixed his narrowed gaze on that narrow oblong of wood and waited. There was no mistake now, the door *had* moved. The detective twisted his long, lean face into a triumphant grin and spoke into the still vainly buzzing phone.

"Yes, Harry," he said again, "that's all the names. You will warn all these men about this crazy Chink and his germs and you'll send the antidote to those I told you already had gotten their dose of germs. Okay? All right, Harry."

The door swung open wide and Ch'ien Feng stood there. Landers could almost feel the Chinaman's eyes burning through the green veil. Over the wire finally came a voice, a woman's voice. It said:

"I'm sorry, sir, but the party does not answer."

"All right," said Landers. "That's fine."

He hung up the phone and looked at Ch'ien. The Chinese drew a gun from the depths of his sleeve, leveled it at Landers across the desk. The detective's smile tightened. He took his fountain pen from his pocket and made a check mark in the green-bound book, the book of green madness. The pen made only a slight wet trace which died quickly.

"Thoughtless of me to mark up your book, wasn't it, Ch'ien," he said. "But not so thoughtless as you in leaving your precious antidote lying around loose. I took some with me when I left this morning and a chemist friend of mine analyzed it. We've sent it to all of your victims."

Landers tore a piece of paper from the notebook and leaned toward the candle on the table. With it he lit the piece of paper, put a cigarette in his mouth and lit it with the paper. Instead of shaking it out at once he let it burn slowly, looking at it instead of at the Chinese who held the gun rigidly leveled at his heart. The paper burned down almost to his fingertips and where Landers' pen had traced an unseen mark, a slight brownish line appeared and was instantly consumed by flame. Landers laughed sharply once, then glanced up at Ch'ien Feng.

"I've found out your trick, oh, Ch'ien Feng!" he cried.

6

A Slave Dies

STILL CH'IEN FENG did not speak. Landers looked at the gun, saw the whiteness of the trigger finger and his lean face grew bleak. He leaned back in the chair and blew smoke at the ceiling.

"Well, Chink," he said, "what are you waiting for?"

He looked toward the open door and his frost blue eyes narrowed. There stood the girl Thais. Her dark red dress was a cry of danger against the blackness of the hall.

"Howdy, Thais," said Landers, "Won't you come in and witness my execution?"

"You talk too much, Landers," came finally the slow hissing voice of the Chinese. "And you do not usually talk too much, my friend. There is something here that is not just what it seems."

The detective swung his now sombre face toward the Chinese, the long, thin face with the small sinks in its cheeks, the blue cold eyes, the high forehead thrusting its peaks far up into the dull hair. He looked for a full minute at the Chinese before he spoke.

He said, "Yes, Ch'ien Feng, there are at least two things in this room that are not what they seem."

"What do you mean?" the Chinese asked swiftly.

Landers ignored the question, staring straight into the green veil, disregarding the thrust of that blue-barreled pistol leveled at him in a rocksteady hand a few feet away. Then he looked at the girl.

"Well, Thais," he said, "So you, too, came back sooner than you had expected, to see Ch'ien Feng. Or did you?"

She was looking at him with those heavy-lidded eyes of hers open very wide. There was tension about the bitterness of her pale mouth.

"What did you mean a minute ago?" she asked, her syllables so slurred, they seemed almost like some oriental language.

"I'm afraid I do not understand just what you mean, my dear," said Landers, his voice nonchalant.

"You said you'd found out Ch'ien Feng's trick. What did you mean?" she repeated.

The breath of the Chinese hissed in between his teeth, but he was not amused this time. He gestured with the pistol muzzle.

"Get up, my friend," he said softly.

Landers stood slowly, deliberately, his shoulders going back, his stomach muscles sucking in. Momentarily he expected that black muzzle to spit flame, to send lead plucking into his body, ripping through his vitals.

"I mean," he spoke to Thais, his lips tight against his teeth, "that this antidote—"

"If you please," Ch'ien spoke calmly. "If you will come into the other room I will permit you an opportunity of telling the young lady what you wish. I have work for my men to do in here."

Landers shrugged. If Ch'ien really believed he had telephoned for help, had given away the names of his victims over the phone, he was taking the entire affair very deliberately, without any fear at all, without panic. It was a weak hand the detective was forced to play in this game, its only strength lay in that the Chinese did not know just how weak it was, and so far had not been able to call the bluff.

Ch'ien Feng backed through the narrow doorway and beckoned Landers to follow. The girl remained in the small room, at his orders, and came out behind the detective. In this fashion they made their slow way into the brilliance of the yellow throne room.

Ch'ien stopped in its middle, the pistol leveled unwaveringly on Landers. The detective had stopped just inside the silken drapes. Back of him swords were crossed on the wall, short Japanese swords with heavy handles and slashing blades. If he could force the Chinese to look aside even for an instant, he might snatch one of these swords, and—Landers turned to the girl.

"I took some of the antidote with me this morning when I left here," he told her slowly. "My chemist analyzed it, has duplicated it and tonight I phoned him the names of all the victims, men and women, whom Ch'ien has inoculated with the germs of the green madness. In the morning the chemist will send them doses of the antidote."

Landers turned toward the Chinese who stood immovable. Once more he had the impression that this was no man before him but some dummy dressed in absurd dusty black robes with a green veil hiding the incompetently modeled face.

"So you see, Ch'ien," he said quietly, "Your hold over me, over this girl, over every person you have inoculated is at an end. And soon the police will be here to arrest you."

The Chinese drew in an amused breath. He raised his voice slightly in singsong mandarin and a gong boomed out, little yellow men hurried in and out of the room. Landers caught the name Nicholas and gathered that the Chinese was ordering him to bring the money at once, tonight. The Chinese had turned his head away, but there was no chance now to strike, with the servants moving constantly in and out.

The girl crossed swiftly to Landers' side, her deep dark eyes fixed on his, her pale mouth framing swift soft words.

"Is it true, King," she asked, "that you have found the medicine that cures this terrible disease?"

LANDERS LOOKED DOWN at her, deep into the mystery of her eyes. "I told the truth," he said slowly. "I know the cure."

For a moment longer the girl stared into his eyes, her swift searching pupils studying his face, then she swung away with an indrawn breath that was half a sigh. She moved slowly with her head down, back and forth across the room. Landers watched her lithe grace as she paced, heedless of the little yellow men who darted in and out carrying away loads of silks and furniture. Presently the yellow satin throne chair was carried out, the walls were stripped of weapons and nothing was left but the silken drapes and the soft, deep rug under foot.

"You see, my friend," said the Chinese softly, "I leave you a nice pretty room in which to die."

The girl was near Ch'ien now. She stood beside him, her back to Landers, a graceful figure in her garnet silks, sharp against the golden yellow curtains.

"But Ch'ien," she said in her soft slurring voice. "You will not hold it against me that I helped this man? I did not know he could harm so great a man as you. And he is handsome."

The Chinese did not swerve his head from staring at Landers as the detective had hoped. He answered the girl without movement.

"He has not harmed me," he said, "except that he forced me to move my quarters. His chemist will not find the secret ingredient of the antidote which alone will avert the green madness. I have had all of those whom I have inoculated so informed. But this Landers has done this. He has made himself very troublesome and so he must die."

"You won't hold it against me, Ch'ien?" she repeated.

Thais moved a little closer to the Chinese. Landers watched hopefully. The swords were gone from behind now, but the hammer still dangled under his armpit. If the Chinese would only look away for an instant. Thais leaned even closer. Steel glinted suddenly in her right hand! The dagger shot forward swiftly, strongly and struck Ch'ien fairly in the stomach. Even as he reeled backward he struck out viciously with the pistol. Thais ducked, but the steel caught her a glancing blow, hurled her staggering across the room. She reeled, tripped and dropped down on the floor, her shoulders striking heavily against the dais on which the throne had stood. She lay there, half dazed.

In the instant she was thrown clear, Landers leaped. He snatched the hammer from under his coat. Ch'ien raised his gun. The detective, straining forward, covering the floor with great bounds, struck savagely at it.

Crack!

The gun spat flame almost in his face. A weight struck his left leg. It collapsed under him, dropping him to the floor almost at the feet of the Chinese. The hammer was snatched from his hand, sent hurtling to a far corner of the room.

"Traitors! Dogs! Try to kill Ch'ien. Ch'ien who shall be emperor, ruler of the world!" The rasp of his words was like a file biting into metal. "I long have worn a steel vest against the treachery of your kind."

Landers raised himself slowly, with his arms thrusting him up from the floor. Blood was spreading on the thigh of his trousers where the man's bullet had pierced. He looked about for the girl. She was crouched against the dais, still grasping the dagger she had thrust in vain against the steel protector the Chinese wore.

Landers looked back to the girl. Her eyes were wide, her mouth a pale wound in a dead white face. Her body was taut with terror. Ch'ien spoke and the silkiness had returned to his voice.

"I had intended, Thais," he said softly. "To leave you dead beside this Landers. But now I have other plans for you. You must atone for that attack on me, atone in a way I shall very much enjoy, for you are very lovely, Thais. It is only afterward that you shall die."

Landers felt the muscles swell in his shoulders. His hands clenched at his side. There was an overtone to the man's voice that made horror crawl like a cold slug down his spine. He pulled his body away from Ch'ien, and painfully struggled to stand on his one good leg. He watched the girl.

Her dark eyes went even wider. Her mouth closed tightly, then twisted its bitter smile. Suddenly she turned the knife point toward her body, placed it just under her left breast and put both hands on the hilt.

"No," Landers shouted. "No." He scrambled up on his one

leg, hopped frantically toward her, the stabs of agony shooting through his wound. "No, Thais!"

Thais drew the knife toward her. The shining steel disappeared into her body and red, a brighter, gayer red spread over the garnet of her dress, well out on the silken yellow down of the carpet. Her breath came in painful gasps. The twisted smile on her mouth was distorted now, her dark eyes strained wider.

"There are limits," she panted, "to what a slave of the green madness will do." She stopped, her voice weakening. Suddenly it was strong again. "Carter Mallory did not drown himself. He—"

Crack!

There was, suddenly, a small black hole in the center of the girl's forehead. Her voice stopped and she slumped down on the dais, her body shuddering. Landers dropped down beside her, staring at the poor form.

"Mr. Landers," the voice of the Chinese was as unhurried, as soft as ever, "it is your turn now."

7

The Veil Lifts

KING LANDERS TURNED slowly about, slid himself up so that he sat on the edge of the dais, so that he was partly in front of Thais' crumpled body. He looked up at Ch'ien. A thin wisp of greasy smoke spiraled from the muzzle of his pistol. It was pointed at Landers' heart.

"It is too bad, Mr. Landers," he said, "that Thais cannot see you die."

Landers drew his one good leg up close under him. His right hand, apparently braced behind him, groped for and found the handle of the dagger that was buried in the girl's breast. The detective's long face grew haggard, his eyes wide, his jaw drooping and trembling with fear as death approached him. And now he quivered.

"Please," he begged. "I don't want to die."

Ch'ien laughed. He came even nearer, leveling the gun farther from him.

Landers groaned, his voice quavered.

"Please, please, Your Majesty," he said beseechingly, "I'll do whatever you say, I—"

Once more Ch'ien laughed. He was quite close now. Suddenly Landers thrust his body up on that one good leg of his, thrust himself up and toward the Chinese. The gun spat flame again, but this time Landers was quicker. The dagger he had snatched from the girl's body slashed the wrist of the

Chinese. Grimly Ch'ien held onto the pistol. Landers raising himself from the floor saw him struggle to pull the trigger again with his wounded hand, saw him fail. The man reached for the gun with his other hand.

Landers flung himself forward, snatching at the feet of the man with his hands. Ch'ien danced back. Once more, panting with the pain of his wound, the detective gathered his one sound leg under him and sprang forward to meet him. The Chinese raised the pistol in his left hand and stepped toward his enemy. Once more the knife flashed. The two men went down in a heap. The pistol spat flame into the air.

Landers rolled clear. He thrust himself up from the floor with his left hand and swept the dagger through the air, swept it in a short vicious arc that terminated just under the edge of Ch'ien's green veil, that ended when only the tip of the dagger's hilt protruded from under the bottom of that green veil. The Chinese shuddered, his hands beat the floor for a moment, then all was still.

For five minutes Landers lay panting on the floor, then slowly he dragged himself across the yellow room, up the little corridor to the room where the safe was. The phone stood on the floor. The detective called the police, telling them to trail Nicholas to the place. Then he crawled back to the room where the girl lay. He sat and looked at her poor crumpled body.

"Poor kid," he murmured, "Poor brave, pretty kid. What a tough way to die. At least it was your knife that killed Ch'ien."

It was twenty minutes later that police poured into the place, bringing Nicholas with them. There were also many others whose names had been in the little green book, called by Ch'ien that he might tell them Landers' story of a substitute antidote was false. Nicholas stared at the green veiled body on the floor.

"Good Lord, Landers," he groaned, his florid face pale, his fat body quivering. "You've killed the Chinese. Now I'll go crazy. My skin will turn green."

He whimpered and cringed. He began to grow hysterical. Others of the slaves cried out.

"Shut up!" Landers snapped. "Nicholas, go lift the veil of Ch'ien Feng."

Nicholas looked down at the figure gaunt in its dusty black robes, at the hilt of the dagger protruding from under the green veil. He drew back as if even in death, even the corpse of the Chinese might prove lethal. When Landers repeated his order he moved fearfully nearer, bent and suddenly snatched the veil from the face of the corpse.

"Good Lord!" he cried out. "It's a white man!"

Landers smiled grimly at the face disclosed, at the beaked nose, the short upper lip that could not quite cover the narrow, long squirrel's teeth of the man.

"Yes," he said. "A white man. Carter Mallory!"

"Mallory?" gasped Nicholas, "The newspaper man!"

Landers nodded slowly, his lean face tight with hate.

"I suspected him from the day of my capture by Ch'ien Feng," he said. "He came to my office and left a pack of cigarettes on my desk. I smoked one and in a few minutes I was unconscious from dope. That wasn't proof of course. It might have been something else that knocked me out, a glass of water from the cooler in my office.

"But today when I took him the orders of Ch'ien Feng, he refused to surrender on a rather minor matter, and professed an idealism I had never known him to show before. Then he committed suicide in such a way that his body couldn't be found. In other words he disappeared, and took entirely his other identity, that of the Chinese."

"And then, too, Ch'ien Feng called the germs the germs of Fu Lung. You remember, Nicholas?"

"Do I remember?" the man shuddered.

"Well, Carter Mallory a long time ago had introduced me to the books of a Chinese philosopher and psychologist of that name who had formed a secret society in China which did untold things simply by making the mental suggestion to its victims. But you understand, these Chinese did this only by the mind, not by germs. The night I saw you down here, Nicholas, I was checking up for Washington on a report that this society had established a branch here. It had, and Mallory was its head. That's how he got such obedience from these Chinks. I think he actually had promised to make China supreme."

Nicholas hadn't been listening to the last that Landers said. He was staring down at the body of Mallory. Suddenly he broke in.

"I'm not interested in this damned theorizing," he said. "What I want to know is what we can do to prevent these horrible germs from making us insane."

Landers laughed at him, laughed bitterly, thinking of the girl that had died that this man and others like him could survive. But they were the nation's leaders. They controlled its money, its inventions, its industries.

"Be easy, Nicholas," he said. "I was getting to that when I mentioned Fu Lung's society. The truth is, that Ch'ien Feng didn't inoculate you with germs. He made an injection of harmless acids and told you they were germs. He told you what the symptoms of these germs were. And because the first of these symptoms appeared, you believed the others would follow, and that the whole thing was true. When the ulcers came, you were tottering on the verge of a breakdown because you expected insanity to follow on its heels. Shall I tell you what these ulcers were? They were acidity, nothing else, induced by the injection he gave you.

"The antidote was more acid, to keep the ulcers there. It was nothing but lemon juice with quinine in it to make it taste bad!"

"Lemon juice!"

"Or lime juice. Ch'ien used the antidote minus the quinine to mix gin drinks with in his less active moments. When I discovered that and remembered what Thais had said about the taste, I suspected its contents. So I made a test. You remember that old trick you used in school to write secret letters to your girl? Disappearing ink? When you write with lemon juice, it just wets the paper, but when you heat it, brown lines show up."

"But why," asked Nicholas, grinning with relief now, "did Mallory want China to rule the world?"

Landers' laughter rang out frankly this time. He ran his lean hand up over his high peeked forehead, through his dull, dark hair.

"He didn't, Nicholas," he said. "He just wanted easy money, and he tricked the Chinese into helping him in a clever blackmail scheme. Green Madness." He laughed once more. "Green lime juice!"

Murder Undercover

THE AMBASSADOR'S MOUTH was fretful beneath his dyed, pointed mustache. "Haven't you finished with those Hutchinson papers yet, d'Albreti?"

Victor d'Albreti's face was blank, but his eyes were angry. He crossed to the ambassador's desk with a lithe, erect stride. "I told your Excellency twice that it would require at least another week to arrange the papers."

The ambassador jerked his spare, wiry figure erect behind his desk. "Now you are insolent as well as lazy."

D'Albreti stiffened. "Your Excellency!"

The ambassador fretted on: "The prominence of your family cannot excuse you. Millions hang on that deal."

Anger was in every rigid line of d'Albreti's tall, young body, faultless in evening attire. He struggled for calmness, but his voice was tight in his throat.

"Your Excellency forgets himself. I am your attaché, it is true. But I am not compelled to submit to such treatment."

For a moment the eyes of the two men locked bitterly across the desk. Then the ambassador shrugged a shoulder slightly, waved a graceful, exquisite hand.

"Perhaps I wrong you," he admitted grudgingly. "And I should take into consideration your uncle's most unfortunate demise. It must have been a terrific shock to you to have lost him when his living would have meant so much to you, motoring here to Washington as he was, to take over the embassy."

D'Albreti slashed in: "You know it is not the loss of my career

that pains me," and the ambassador waved a careless hand.

"...all because the steering knuckle chose precisely the wrong time to break. A what you call—bad break for you too, eh?"

There was an ugly light deep in d'Albreti's eyes.

"You are through with me for the evening?" he asked, his voice thin.

"Ah yes, you may go now, but get busy early tomorrow on those Hutchinson papers."

D'Albreti clicked his heels, snapped open the door.

"Rest well!" came the ambassador's fretful voice.

The door bisected the phrase, and the young attaché stood rigidly, fingers clenched on the knob. Out of the shadows of the high, dim hall, a man stepped alertly forward. He wore puttees, an olive green uniform.

"Sir?"

D'Albreti's lips lifted tightly, white teeth gleaming in a lean face. "Have the Lancia ready, Giorgio. I shall be down almost at once."

Giorgio ducked a swift, almost worshipful bow, and d'Albreti sprang up the broad stairs, three at a time. The room he entered was warm with color. A small parchment-shaded lamp over a chair revealed red drapes.

D'Albreti dismissed his valet brusquely and hurriedly stripped off the formal black and white. Muscles rippled lithely beneath browned skin as he donned dark tweed trousers, straightened to his full five feet eleven. He swiftly finished dressing and tapped a brown Borsalino jauntily on his smooth black head.

Without pause, he dipped into the top drawer of his chiffonier, pocketed a .38 automatic. He smiled briefly, tight-lipped, at himself in the mirror.

"Rest well, d'Albreti," he mimicked.

The hand that caught up a cane knotted into a hard fist.

THE LANCIA'S LONG nose swung off Pennsylvania Avenue into Eighth Street, its engine a soft bass drone, glided past a second-rate hotel into a region of cheap apartments and small houses and turned right after several blocks. The warm air of the summer night, a faint odor of asphalt still hot from the sun, flowed in. A mile away the needle point of Washington Monument was washed with white floodlights.

Victor d'Albreti sat silently, his poise alert.

Giorgio, profiled sharply against the dash lights, said softly: "Eight-sixteen should be in the next block."

"Drive past," d'Albreti ordered, a curious strain in his voice. "I'll walk back."

As the Lancia rolled by, he spotted number 816, black numbers on a lighted transom. A four story, narrow apartment building, squeezed between residences. Two blocks further on, Giorgio swerved to the curb and d'Albreti sprang out.

"I'll need you in the car, Giorgio," he said with swift tension. "Park on the other side of the apartment, be ready to pick me up—speedily."

Giorgio asked quickly, "There may be trouble, sir?"

D'Albreti laughed a single time, clearly, but with little gaiety. "It is to be hoped so, my Giorgio."

His cane tapped. He swung briskly up the street with his light, peculiarly ready step, a grimly purposeful figure against the soft night.

D'Albreti turned into the apartment, bent to peer at brass name plates, and pressed a button beside one that read, "Joseph Rochioccioli." There was presently a faint clicking of the door latch, and d'Albreti shoved in.

The third floor hall was empty, the air close. The white bell button of apartment 3B raised a dull clangor within. A slow thumping approached and the door eased open. A white glare of light from the opening outlined a man's head. The head peered around the door's edge, a shoulder hunched over a crutch. The cripple said nothing.

Leaning on his cane, d'Albreti asked quietly, "You are Joseph Rochioccioli?"

The man appeared to weigh his answer, then nodded slowly.

His coarse hair, sprouting in bristles, made his head appear enormous.

"The chauffeur of Victor Rascelli, who was killed last week?"

The man nodded again as before, still not speaking.

D'Albreti said, "I am Mr. Rascelli's nephew. I would like to ask you a few questions."

All of the cripple's movements were hesitant. He stood in silence a moment, then pulled the door wide and with hunched shoulders thumped awkwardly about on his crutches and swung his body slowly, heavily. His left leg was bandaged and thrust stiffly ahead.

The room was mussy with scattered newspapers. Unwashed dishes stood on the table and the air was close, smelling of stale, greasy cooking. The man maneuvered his crutches and dropped creakingly into a faded blue couch, propping his cast leg on a chair opposite.

D'Albreti stood so that shadows fell upon his face, but the single globe in the ceiling threw its white dazzle directly on Rochioccioli. D'Albreti said nothing, but slowly drew off his gloves, holding hat and cane beneath his left arm. Despite his ease, there was a tension in his movements.

The chauffeur had small, black eyes that grew sullen beneath a perpetually wrinkled forehead. The on-end hair was stiff with hair-oil. He broke out nervously, "You said you wanted to ask me something?"

"Why did you drive my uncle's car into the ravine?" d'Albreti demanded softly.

The man's head jerked up sharply. "I didn't drive it there," he said, "A steering knuckle broke, and—"

"Yes, yes, I understand perfectly," d'Albreti said. He stepped closer and bent forward, so that the sullen, black eyes were forced to meet his. "Nevertheless, Joseph, I ask you why you drove my uncle's car into the ravine."

The man's face worked; the frown tightened. "But sir—"

D'Albreti's pigskin gloves were in his right hand. He slapped them heavily into the contorted face.

"Animal! I ask you a question!"

A RED STAIN spread slowly where the gloves had struck. D'Albreti said softly, "It is true the steering knuckle broke, but I examined it. That knuckle had been filed, and you broke it with the wrench that threw the car into the ravine. That took courage, but then, your reward was to be high. And also, Joseph"—the man cowered as the gloves flicked forward again—"also, Joseph, it was you who set the car afire after you crawled out, making sure of—shall I say, *results?*"

The man's face was dead white except for the stain from the glove blows. His eyes started wide and his head jerked violently from side to side. "No! No!" he said, "It is not true, sir! You—"

The gloves caught him again, squarely on the mouth this time. Blood flecked his lip.

The nostrils of d'Albreti's aquiline nose were suddenly white-rimmed. "Animal!" he said. "I do not care about you. If I know anything of the underworld, and I should, Joseph, your colleagues won't let you survive long. But probably you know my family history? How long, Joseph, had you been with my uncle?"

The chauffeur was silent.

D'Albreti bent forward and his eyes were ugly. "It is my inheritance from my American mother which won't permit me to do as you deserve. Do you know that little chamber far underground beneath my uncle's castle, Joseph?"

The man shuddered and pressed back into the faded blue upholstery of the couch.

"Ah, I see you do know! I was very fond of my uncle, though I had not seen him for years. He was my godfather and sponsored my career. So you see, it is barely possible, Joseph, that for once my Latin blood might dominate. You understand?"

"Before God, I know nothing, sir!"

"Not even, for instance, the man who gave you the money? How much was it, animal? Fifty thousand? Surely you remember the man who treated you so well."

The gloves drew back again, and the little man cringed behind an upflung arm.

"Come, Joseph," d'Albreti urged softly, "tell me, so that I may match the fifty thousand with another fifty thousand. And this time you shall run no risk, Joseph. All you have to do is tell me who gave you the money."

The man's arm lowered slowly from before his white face. His eyes met the blazing ones of d'Albreti staringly.

"Sir! You offer me fifty thousand—"

D'Albreti straightened, his hand white on the head of his stick. "Yes. Fifty thousand for the name of the man who paid you. And you—go free."

"I go free, sir?"

"Yes."

"Then—I tell. I tell."

He studied d'Albreti's lean face anxiously, then something jerked his gaze to a point over d'Albreti's shoulder.

"Good God!" he gasped.

D'Albreti's movement was cat-swift. He whirled backward on his left heel, dodged aside. The door was ajar. A hand holding a gun jutted through the opening. It was prominent in the white glare, a dirty hand, with a knob-end thumb—the first joint had been torn off—a gun with the sight filed off.

D'Albreti took in all this flashingly. He was poised, cane in his right hand. His arm thrust out suddenly, his right leg, knee bent, shot forward, the weight of his leaning body with it. A fencer's lunge.

The ferrule of his cane clicked against the door, jamming it shut upon the hand with the revolver. The fingers closed convulsively. Powder-flame and gun-din filled the room. Still crouched, d'Albreti dropped his cane, snatched for his gun. The dirty hand jerked from sight; the door slammed.

D'Albreti sprang toward it, heard a coughing gasp behind him, whirled. Joseph was slumped on the couch, a hand clutching his breast, small eyes wide with fear. He coughed tearingly again, blood trickled from his mouth. Shaggy hair straggled across a white forehead. D'Albreti crossed to him in two strides.

He asked. "Who paid you?"

The man coughed again. Blood gushed. He seemed to collapse into himself, like a pricked bladder. D'Albreti's lips were grim; a smile lifted the corners.

He said lightly, "The freedom I promised you was even shorter than I had expected, Joseph."

He whirled, snatching up cane and hat, darted down the stairs.

He heard an excited voice muffled behind a door. "Police? Yes, yes, a shot! Yes—at eight—"

D'ALBRETI WAS DOWN the stairs, bursting out into the street. An automobile snorted through hurried gear shifts, darted away. As d'Albreti reached the curb, his own car hummed into life a half block away, spurted toward him. He sprang in, ordered swiftly, "That car ahead! Follow it!"

Giorgio nodded, a joyous smile on his sharp face.

The car ahead swirled into Second Street. The squeal of hot rubber floated back. Giorgio, with a jerk of brakes, skidded the tilting Lancia into Third, swished by the next corner in time for d'Albreti to glimpse their quarry. It was a Ford Eight, dark blue or black.

They continued to flash block for block with the Ford until it swung into Pennsylvania. D'Albreti, tense on the edge of his seat, cranked open the windshield, palmed his automatic and thumbed the safety. The car ahead weaved back and forth like a shuttlecock through the night-swollen traffic. The Lancia's long nose dove after if, scraped fenders with a taxi, skittered away from the cursing driver.

The Ford ahead, its tail light a drop of blood, raced on, began to pull away a little. D'Albreti's teeth were locked. His eyes strained to hold that dancing tail light among the crush of so many cars.

"Faster, Giorgio, faster!" he whipped out.

The Ford swept past Union Station, darted into the underpass, its horn sounding almost constantly as it flashed in and out among cruising cars. The mutter of the Lancia's engine became deeper. Pursuer and pursued streaked along the route to Arlington Bridge.

"Heading for Virginia," d'Albreti snapped.

Traffic had thinned some, the cars stringing out singly as they put on speed, and the Lancia began to stretch herself, circled at a furious pace. Tires whined. D'Albreti hefted his automatic with a grimly smiling mouth. Only three cars now between the Lancia and its prey. But a long, close line of machines was filing past in the opposite direction.

As the last whizzed by, the Lancia leaped forward under Giorgio's hand, swerved out and around the car ahead. Two more to go. The metal horses under the hood tightened the traces. Once more that swift, swerving circle, and now only one car to pass before they were squarely behind the Ford.

D'Albreti's eyes, intently narrowed, never wavered from the back of the fugitive auto. Black stretches of park wheeled back on either side of the road. The Lancia crowded the last intervening car, made blended music with its horn. A swift swing to the left, a cut back to the right, and the last barrier was gone. The Ford was just ahead, not fifty yards distant in the speeding line of machines.

The long, low lights of Arlington Bridge sprang up out of the trees, reaching across the Potomac. D'Albreti crouched forward, levelling the automatic. The driver ahead seemed suddenly to sense danger, like a hare scenting beagles. He spurted.

The Lancia sprang after it. The tail light that was like a drop of blood wavered from side to side in little zig-zagging, irregular jerks. D'Albreti took careful aim, hesitated. The red light danced like an erratic firefly.

"You'll have to take me closer, Giorgio," d'Albreti said. "I don't want to kill the man by mistake."

Giorgio, bending over the wheel, asked quietly, "Why not kill the vermin?"

D'Albreti said tightly, "He is only a small cog in the machine that snuffed out my uncle's life. Through him I hope to find others."

D'Albreti's lean young face was stern. The car ahead swung in a wide circle to the left, drummed out on the long, low-parapeted bridge. Water-freshened air fanned in from the Potomac, silvered by the summer moon. Ahead loomed the dark Virginia shore, racing toward them. No chance to shoot on the bridge, too many cars straight ahead to catch wild bullets. The Lancia pressed closer, shot down the ramp. Other cars swung into line between the Ford and the Lancia.

D'Albreti cursed under his breath, pocketed among crawling cars that would not let him crowd along side the Ford. But the fugitive, similarly impeded, could not pull away. Up the twisting, steep road into the black hills the trail ran and into Alexandria.

There the Ford swung suddenly out of line, roaring up a side road to the right. The Lancia was only a block behind, and charging swiftly in its wake. D'Albreti once more crouched forward with levelled gun. Now no more cars ahead enforced caution.

The automatic spat. The Ford answered with a yawning swerve and began to bounce erratically across the road. The Lancia inched closer. Bright light spilled across the road ahead, an arch of incandescents spelling "Colonial Hall."

ONCE MORE D'ALBRETI fired. The car ahead flinched aside, swung its tail light to the left, then to the right, rumbled to a shattering halt in the ditch. Instantly a door flung open and a man's squat, broad-shouldered body plunged to the road. Red gun-flame lanced from his hand.

The Lancia charged him. He ducked behind his car, floundered into the bushes. The roadhouse was fifty yards away on that side of the road. Giorgio braked to a halt near the Ford and knifed a beam from a fog search light into the shrubbery.

D'Albreti leaped out, gun holstered and dove into the woods. Ahead, the man crashed on and shouted.

"Help, Al! Joe, help!"

D'Albreti's long legs covered rough ground. He bored into the underbrush, twigs stinging his face. Once more powder flames felt for him in the darkness. He stooped, groped up a rock from the ground, and hurled it with the full swing of his arm at the spot. There was a sharp, low-pitched cry.

D'Albreti leaped ahead, thorned vines snagging his feet. He smashed into a man floundering in the bushes, seized him by the back of the neck and jammed a gun into his ribs. He fumbled for the man's pistol, wrested it away.

"All right," d'Albreti panted. "About face. Get back to the road!"

The light from the Lancia penetrated weakly, but it showed the man's white-faced glance. He looked only once into his captor's face and stumbled back toward the road. D'Albreti hustled him. Shouts came from the roadhouse now.

"Hey, Pete, where are you!"

D'Albreti seized the man called Pete by the collar, crowded him more swiftly toward the Lancia, guided by its yellow beam of light. Finally they crashed through to clear walking. The Lancia's motor purred, the door stood open.

D'Albreti boosted his prisoner bodily inside, sprang to the running board, gun still in hand. Giorgio backed swiftly, hummed the coupé in a fast turn. D'Albreti squeezed in.

Behind them gun explosions ripped the night. No lead plunked into the car.

The Lancia stretched its belly close to the ground, as it raced along the narrow road, whirled through Alexandria, and shot on toward Washington.

"Giorgio," said d'Albreti softly, "I'm afraid you're exceeding the speed limit."

The driver shot a quick glance at d'Albreti, glimpsed complete seriousness there despite the banter of his voice.

"Don't you think, my Giorgio," d'Albreti went on, "that it is discourteous for a host to run away from his guests? I am planning a little reception for Peter's friends."

Giorgio's teeth gleamed. "Where will this little reception be held?"

He eased the accelerator, and the Lancia lounged into the slow curving descent to the Potomac. Traffic had thinned. Moments later an automatic horn some distance behind them beeped and swelled nearer.

D'Albreti said softly, "I think our guests are arriving, Giorgio. They'll have no trouble identifying us.

Twisting in the seat he cranked down the coupé's rear window. A car whirled around a curve behind. To the right was a growth-cluttered ravine, seen dimly through tree tops.

A tongue of flame flickered and spurted to the right of the windshield of the following car. The Lancia's engine hummed a deeper song and d'Albreti twisted in his seat, levelled his automatic again.

Lead plunked into the back of the car near his hand. Headlights glared into his eyes. He laughed aloud, gaily, and his narrowed eyes sighted two feet above and a foot to his left of his pursuer's left light—and pumped five spaced shots into that area.

THE HEADLIGHTS YAWED widely, shot their beam to the left then swept across to the right, revealing a jumble of tree trunks like black specters, plunged toward them. Then the lights bored steeply downward, danced up and down wildly, executed a jagged somersault and went out. There were seconds of crashing wood and steel noise, then a red flare. Flames shot above the tree tops. The windows of the Lancia vibrated with blasting concussion.

Giorgio snubbed down the Lancia's nose with brakes, but d'Albreti, watching flames lick up over black wreckage, ordered harshly, "Drive on!"

"You think them dead, signor?"

D'Albreti threw back his head and laughed, and there was no gaiety in it. "I think my Latin blood reigns tonight, Giorgio. Flames," he said softly, reminiscently, "made sure of my uncle's death."

FAULTLESS IN MORNING-COAT and striped gray trousers, d'Albreti knocked lightly and entered the stiff formal chamber that was the ambassador's office. He bowed suavely. "Good morning, your Excellency. An official of the police to see you."

The ambassador tugged at his dyed mustache, frowning, "The police?"

"Yes, your Excellency."

The ambassador reared his short, spare figure behind the desk. "Let him come in; and d'Albreti—"

"Sir?"

"Remain here, please."

D'Albreti's face was expressionless as he bowed in a police lieutenant in dress uniform. The officer clicked his heels.

"Your Excellency!" he said in a sharp, formal voice. "I am instructed to tender the thanks of the police department for your capture of the murderer of Joseph Rochioccioli, the chauffeur of Prince Rascelli!"

The ambassador raised eyebrows at d'Albreti, standing behind the police lieutenant. D'Albreti looked beyond him.

"I am instructed to say," the police lieutenant went on, "that the gun found on this man, Pietro Scioli, corresponded with the bullets found in Rochioccioli's body as your call predicted. The police department wishes to extend its compliments for the cleverness of your work."

"Pietro Scioli?" The ambassador's slow voice was questioning, a little tense. He glanced down at his desk for a moment, then waved a long white hand. "Glad to have been of some small assistance, lieutenant. Thank you."

The policeman bowed, stalked out. D'Albreti closed the door and the ambassador asked very quietly: "Will you tell me what this is all about?"

D'Albreti's face was calm. "The morning papers, sir, say that the police captured this Scioli in a rooming house. A phone call, the source of which they did not reveal in the newspapers, told them Scioli would be found there, that his gun would match bullets in Rochioccioli's body."

The ambassador tugged again at his mustache, sat down and rustled some papers fretfully, glanced up sharply, "I trust you slept well, d'Albreti?"

D'Albreti's narrowed eyes burned. He stepped lightly, quickly to the desk and, stiffly erect, stared at the man seated behind it. "I did not sleep well last night, but tonight I think I shall."

"You choose to be mysterious," a faint sneer.

"And you are not sufficiently so!"

D'Albreti inserted fingers in a vest pocket, tossed a card, face up, on the gleaming mahogany. Crude penciling covered its face.

The ambassador continued to stare into d'Albreti's eyes for a full moment, then glanced down at the card.

"My name and address, eh?" he said. "Well, what of it?"

D'Albreti's weight was on his toes, his eyes alert.

"That is the one thing police did not find on Pietro Scioli," he said softly. "I took it from him before I gave him a narcotic and left him in a rooming house—and phoned police where to find him."

The ambassador's hands pressed whitely on the desk top, the tips of his exquisite fingers spreading.

"There is some trickery here," he bit out, his voice harsh, tense.

D'Albreti leaned across the desk. His right hand flicked out and the ambassador's cheek bore the red prints of his fingers. The man's mouth beneath his dyed mustache was a hard line. He reared to his feet, head thrown back, eyes fierce.

"The meaning of this?" he rasped.

D'Albreti's breath was quick. He said rapidly: "You had my uncle murdered by his chauffeur. It's that Hutchinson deal. If you could consummate it in the way you wished, it meant millions to you. My uncle's death would give you time to complete it before a new ambassador was sent.

"You bribed the chauffeur, then got frightened and had him killed. Scioli and two others have paid, as has Rochioccioli." He leaned forward tensely. "You, your Excellency, are next."

THE AMBASSADOR SMILED coldly, his face rigidly calm.

"You expect me to challenge you?"

"Unless you wish to go for a ride in the Lancia. It is true I've had a bit of trouble with a steering knuckle."

"You propose force?"

D'Albreti's exaggerated exclamation was shocked, his eyes mocking.

"Force, your Excellency?"

The ambassador's face lost its calm, contorted with hate burning in his face.

"Enough of this nonsense," he rasped. "It shall be as you wish." A sardonic expression veiled his eyes. "I propose that each of us write a suicide note to avoid odious explanations to the police."

He dipped a pen, shoved it with paper toward d'Albreti. The younger man smiled formally, demurring. After momentary resistance the ambassador shrugged quickly and wrote first, a hurried scrawl with his signature sprawling across the bottom of the page.

D'Albreti moved the pen deliberately on the white vellum. Under veiling lashes, his eyes skipped now and again toward the ambassador's exquisite hands.

The right retreated slowly, slid below the level of the desk top. D'Albreti deliberately attached his name. A gun jammed against his head.

The younger man flung sidewise. The ambassador did not fire, the wound would have to be at contact to simulate suicide.

A crouching stride took d'Albreti to the end of the desk. His hands leaped up and seized the ambassador's wrist. D'Albreti snapped erect. His shoulders hunched and swelled with strain, and the pistol's muzzle was deflected, pointed across their bodies.

The two men stood breast to breast, the pistol vised between them. D'Albreti stared coldly into the gleaming black hate of the ambassador's eyes. Neither spoke.

D'Albreti's lips tilted in a frigid smile. His shoulders rose a fraction of an inch, swelling with new effort. The ambassador gasped out explosive curses and struck wildly with his free hand. His wrist gave, the muzzle pivoted into his own breast.

The shot was muffled. The ambassador hissed between tight teeth, collapsed into his chair. The gun dangled an instant from his fingers, clattered to the floor. D'Albreti, chest heaving, snatched the pencilled card containing the ambassador's address and his own suicide note from the desk, glanced about the room. He had to destroy them, lest the police come too swiftly and search him. Ashes might cause questions. Grimacing, he shredded them....

After a moment, his eyes fixed on the ambassador. The man's face drained, blood spreading on the white bosom of his shirt.

D'Albreti swallowed with difficulty.

"I thought you'd shoot at me, animal, if I pressed you hard enough." His voice harshened. "I want you to know before you die that the card with which I trapped you was not on Scioli's body. I wrote it myself." He bowed with stiff mockery. "Rest well, your Excellency!"

Hard mirth in his eyes, d'Albreti crossed the room, leaned against the door, made his voice hoarse and panting.

"Help! Help! Call help! The ambassador has shot himself!" He fumbled open the door, reeled aside and supported himself weakly against the wall. Attendants rushed past him, and he panted out, "I struggled with him, turned one shot, but he broke away, killed himself."

Giorgio detached himself from the huddle about the body and paced calmly to d'Albreti's side. "He's dead," he said. "Permit me, sir, to help you to your room. It must have been a bitter experience…."

D'Albreti leaned on his arm, moved out into the dim, high hall. He screwed his lean dark face wryly, working his tongue in his mouth.

"Bitter is hardly the word for it, Giorgio. Did you ever eat paper, with nice fresh ink?"

Just Pals

Patrolman Berry Was Tired of Taking Guff From Crooks—And Determined to Upset Their Little Games!

PATROLMAN BERRY WATCHED a small hatless man stroll out from under the yellow lighted canopy of the "Russian Samovar." Berry shifted on his big, broad-toed shoes and restlessly waited until the man had passed him. He took a single stride forward then.

"Hold on there, Higgins," he said.

The small man called Higgins jerked his shiny black head about and spun his slight body slowly. His right hand was in the pocket of his tuxedo coat and the bosom of his shirt gleamed white through the darkness. He stared up into Patrolman Berry's heavy face insolently.

"When you speak to me, flattie, say mister," he mocked. Berry glared at Higgins under the drawn-down visor of his cap. He knew the man was a crook. He'd been arrested many times, but he always managed to get off. Somehow, somewhere, among the politicians, Higgins had pull. But this was a serious case they wanted to see him about now.

Crooks like him had it easy, while Berry, a hard-working cop, honest as they came, with a wife and three kids to support, had nothing but trouble and hard knocks. Berry pulled the corners of his mouth down angrily.

"Suppose you take a walk down to headquarters, runt," he growled.

Higgins snapped back at him, "Suppose you take a walk around the block, flattie."

BERRY HAD HIS club in his hand. He twirled it on its leather thong, down and back into his hand, down and back. He twirled it longingly. He'd like to bang into this crook with it, put him where all crooks, even slick ones with pull, belonged—behind the bars.

"Listen," he said deliberately, holding down his anger. "I'm passing word along to you like I got orders from headquarters to do. They want to talk to you down there."

Higgins stared up with flat, expressionless eyes. His right hand came slowly out of his coat pocket.

"Well, no cop is going to get hard with me," he said. "I don't have to take it and I won't. What's this all about, anyway?"

"The Cauley jewel hold-up."

Higgins shrugged.

"So what?"

Berry twirled the club a couple of extra times.

"So they want to talk to you down at headquarters," he said, and his eyes got hard. "I don't know where you get the pull, that I don't get orders to run you in like any other crook. I'd like to do that."

Higgins' upward stare continued inimical. "If they want me," he snapped, "they can come and get me."

"And that will be all right, too," Berry grumbled, his face carefully masking all expression. "There's ten grand reward. The robbers killed a cop." The little man threw back his smooth black head and laughed jeeringly. "And you want to cut in on that, eh? It will take more than a dumb flattie like you to get them crooks. You can't do nothing but go around shooting."

Berry's eyes narrowed on Higgins. "I shoot straight," he stated shortly, and their gazes locked.

There was a shot and he reeled, clutching his stomach

What Higgins said was true, all right. Lord, how Maggie and the kids could use a cut of that ten thousand dollars! But it would be a tough job to take those crooks. Cop killers, they would stop at nothing.

Higgins was talking straight up into Berry's heavy face, expressionless despite the rush of thoughts.

"I don't know a damned thing about the Cauley case," Higgins said. "And you can tell headquarters that."

He spun on his heel and stalked back toward the yellow gleaming entrance of the "Samovar," ducked down its basement entrance.

He almost bumped into a tall blond man sauntering leisurely out of the cabaret. The doorman, tall and fantastic in baggy brilliant dress, bowed more deferentially than usual to the emerging man.

BERRY, ADVANCING, SAID, "Good evening, Mr. Allen."

Allen's face was florid, his hair swept back smoothly from a bony forehead. He pulled his snap brim hat and said, "You seem to have riled Mr. Higgins."

Berry's voice was aggrieved. "They want to talk to him down at headquarters about that Cauley case. I tell him nice, and he calls me a dumb flattie."

Laughter lurked in Allen's eyes. He murmured, "That's too bad," and, "Well, I'll be seeing you," and strolled off down the street.

Berry swung his broad shoulders about and slapped heavy feet toward the entrance of the basement cabaret. The tall costumed doorman smiled. "We got to take guff off everybody."

Berry stood on braced feet. He said, "I may be a dumb flattie, but I'm not going to take laughs off your boss even if he does own a class dump like the 'Samovar'."

The doorman's smile faded. "You're a hard-boiled guy, aren't you?"

Berry grunted, turned his back and started to pace away. Hard-boiled! Sure he was hard-boiled, when he dealt with crooks—guys that took other people's hard-earned money, guys that could kill a cop like good old Pat Malone.

SUDDENLY BERRY JERKED about toward the yellow, down-slanting tunnel of the "Samovar's" doorway.

Two, three heavy explosions crashed within. Berry tugged out his gun and dived down into the night club, met an outward rush of white-faced men and screeching women. He threw both hands above his head, gun in one fist, club in the other and yelled, "Stay where you are."

His wide shoulders blocked the hallway and the crowd began to mill. He grabbed a waiter and rasped, "Keep these people here or you'll catch hell when the headquarters dicks come."

The waiter began soothing talk; and Berry hunched his shoulders, planted heavy feet and ploughed through the half hysterical mob.

He came out in a low, dim, table-cluttered room. An orchestra in baggy scarlet trousers and blue smocks were playing violently. On the far edge of a postage-stamp-size dance floor, a dark figure huddled.

Berry slapped across to the figure, lying with a knee doubled up, both hands clasped to its belly. The man on the floor had shiny black hair. Berry said softly, "So you got it, did you, Higgins?" and dropped on one knee beside the man.

Higgins was dead. Blood was widening in a dark sluggish pool beneath him.

BERRY HEAVED UP, moving on spring heeled feet across the room. A waiter trembled against the wall.

"Who did the shooting?" Berry demanded.

The waiter had a long beaked nose. Its end wiggled as he chattered, "I don't know."

Berry grunted, "Stop talking a minute, so I can hear. Listen, where was the guy when he was shot?"

The waiter jerked his head sideways at a door which framed blackness. "He walked out toward the doorway to see a guy who was waiting for him," he said. "And then there was some shots and he fell, holding his belly."

"Who was the guy waiting for him?"

The waiter shook his head frantically from side to side. Berry gripped him by the coat lapels with his left hand and jammed him against the wall with a fist on his throat. Trying to protect a killer, was he?

"Come on, who was the guy?"

The waiter would not meet Berry's demanding eyes as he gulped, "Honest, I don't know."

Berry slammed him up against the wall again. "Come across," he barked out meaningly, and the waiter mumbled, "All right, all right. It was Pat Dunn."

"Pat Dunn, eh?" Berry knew Dunn, too. A newcomer, but a crook for all that. Come to think of it, he'd heard some talk of Dunn living with Higgins. He shook the waiter again. "Where'd Dunn go?"

"He didn't come back in here."

Berry let go and the waiter darted away. The policeman turned small eyes on the doorway and blinked slowly. "So he didn't come back," he muttered.

He eased close to the door, crouched and dived through down low, rolling sharply to the left as he hit the floor. A gun belched red fire from the other end of the hall. Berry's .38 special spat back. He threw himself aside and two bullets smacked where his head had been.

Berry got cautiously to his knees, snapped another shot.

HE CROUCHED SILENTLY on the floor, trying to pierce the dim length of the hallway. Behind him the music had stopped. He could hear more screaming and shouts of men. Tables crashed to the floor. Then there was nothing but silence. It began to throb in his straining ears. Dim light from behind him showed dull gray side walls, but no end to the hall. And the silence throbbed.

Berry muttered to himself, "I wonder if I got that guy," and eased slowly up on his knees. Then he got up and put big feet down softly as he crept along.

Once more a gun ripped open the darkness. A hammer blow jerked Berry to the left, numbed his shoulder. Hit, damn it! He swore loudly, poured his last bullets into the blackness in a blast of sound and flame, then dropped again to the floor. He mouthed snarling curses, but no sound passed his lips.

One-handed, he swung open the gate of his revolver, thrust down the ejector, stuffed more bullets from his belt into the gun. He could feel slow, warm blood crawling down his left arm.

It made him feel weak, but there was no pain. Not now. Just deadness and that warm, slow trickle. Presently throbbing hell would begin. He had to move swiftly. He inched along, reloaded pistol leveled, wounded arm dragging. The end of the hall was black as the gun muzzle.

Berry wriggled on, stopped to strain his ears. He got to his knees with enormous effort. *Was that someone breathing?* He listened intently. No, no sound. His muscles were tight, set for the shock of lead, the gun flame he expected momentarily to lance out of the darkness. He closed his jaw tightly, small eyes narrow and ugly. He crept on.

The out-thrust barrel of his gun clinked dully. Berry froze in his tracks, straining eyes wide, ears tuned to whispers. There was no further sound, just that single dull clink of the gun muzzle. Berry frowned, moved his gun fractionally. It rasped against something hard.

HE CAUTIOUSLY THRUST the revolver into his belt, put out exploring fingers. They touched cold stone, circled, disclosed only an expanse of wall. He snaked out his flashlight, hesitated a moment, whispered a curse and squeezed the cylinder. Blank wall was six inches from his nose. He whirled. To his right was a closed door.

He planted his foot against it, thrust and lunged to one side. Nothing happened. The door thumped and shivered against the wall. He peered cautiously in, saw a small room empty except for a wooden table and a few chairs. A window high up let in fresh night air.

Berry climbed laboriously up on a chair and flashed his light outside. An alley ran to the front sidewalk. There was no one in it, nothing for anybody to hide behind. He climbed down off the chair and stood swaying. Pain gnawed at his shoulder now. It throbbed like dull waves of heat.

He groped his gun into its holster, took his left hand in solicitous lingers and eased it into his belt. Then he reeled out into the blackness of the hall, a hand against its side for support, and made his slow way back to the dimly lighted dining room.

It was deserted now except for Higgins' body and a tall blond man who straightened from beside it as Berry entered. The tall man's florid face was worried. He stared at Berry and his eyes widened.

"Good lord, man," he exclaimed, "you're wounded."

Berry's heavy face was pale, his eyes narrowed with pain.

"You're telling me," he muttered. "Listen, where does Pat Dunn live?"

THE CABARET OWNER jerked up a shoulder in a shrug, spread his hands. Berry swayed before him, hard-eyed. His head was strangely clear. He said, "You can find out where Dunn lives. Do it."

Allen's eyes narrowed. "Are you giving me orders, Berry?" he asked softly. "What would you think?" Berry snapped.

Allen ground out, "Why you—"

"—dumb flattie," supplied Berry. "Yeah, I know. Find Dunn's address, quick."

The two men glared at each other and finally Allen looked away and said, "I suppose you're not responsible—"

Berry's thick lips twisted in a nasty smile. "Yeah," he said, "I'm responsible. So are you. This shooting took place in your cabaret. How'd you get back so quick?"

"My employees called me," Allen shrugged.

Berry said, "Now you call your employees and get hold of Dunn's address."

Allen protested, "Honestly, they don't know."

Berry hunched his shoulders belligerently, winced with pain. He looked down at Higgins on the floor, at Higgins' rumpled coat lapel, back to Allen.

He rasped, "Give them to me."

Allen's eyes narrowed. "What?"

"You took papers off Higgins' body. I saw you do it. Now come across." Allen shook his head slowly. "There weren't any."

Berry got his gun balanced in his hand and his small blue eyes were flat. "Now—or afterward?"

"What do you mean?"

Berry raised the muzzle of his gun slowly. Allen's eyes went wide and he fell back a half step. "You—you wouldn't—"

"Oh, no?" Berry asked softly. "Remember, I saw you robbing Higgins' body and you might resist arrest."

The men's eyes looked grimly and Allen muttered, "Damned if I don't believe you would."

BERRY GRINNED WITHOUT mirth as Allen shrugged and dug a letter out of his pocket. The patrolman took it in the same hand that held the gun and glanced at it. It was addressed to Higgins on West 71st Street. And Dunn and Higgins lived together.

Berry grunted and weaved across the small dance floor. He slipped and would have fallen, but that Allen grabbed his arm and drew it across his own shoulders.

"Good lord, man, you can hardly walk. Better go to the hospital."

Berry mumbled, "I'm running this," and dragged heavy feet toward the doorway. It would be nice to be going home instead of—

"Where you heading?"

"Drugstore," Berry ground out; he made his way there on leaden feet, with Allen's help, and the druggist made a dressing for his shoulder. The bullet had gone through cleanly. Berry tugged his blue tunic on, adjusted the gun in its holster, and started wearily from the place.

The shoulder hurt like hell, but that weakness was gone. He only felt very tired.

Allen was at his side, supporting him. "You'd better go to the hospital, man," he reiterated. "You're all shot up."

Berry grunted and kept going. Radio patrol cars had moaned with whining sirens up to the "Samovar," and blue-coated figures were running in and out of the yellow-lighted door. "Some of these other men could go for you," Allen urged.

Berry grunted, "Yeah, and collect the ten grand."

HE HAD A clue now, a hot one, to the crooks. He had to keep on or the crooks might get away. He shut his teeth hard, made his slow way to a taxi, stumbled in and slumped down on the seat, giving the address he had got from Higgins' letter.

Allen climbed in beside him.

"I'm responsible for you since you got shot in my place," he told the cop stubbornly.

Berry's lips twisted. "My pal," he said.

He eased into a corner, resting with his eyes closed while the taxi honked through the traffic, scooting up Seventh Avenue.

The West 71st Street address was a four story brownstone, with steps that climbed steeply from the sidewalk. Dim lights sifted through the tall, old-fashioned doorway.

Berry, laboring up the steps, leaned hard on the bell and heard it jangle harshly in the dark interior. He rang three times more before a figure loomed against the glass and a stoop-shouldered hag of a woman opened the door. She began a nasal whine. Berry shoved past her, asking, "Where's Pat Dunn's room?"

The woman's whining expostulation rose shrilly.

Berry turned his heavy face toward her. It was hard. Everybody was always trying to protect crooks. He asked her again and his voice rasped. The woman blinked.

"Mr. Dunn's room is on the third floor back."

BERRY GRUNTED, "GUESSED right," and swung toward the broad stairs, lifting feet that weighed fifty pounds apiece, hauling himself upward along the smooth dark banister with his one good hand. Each step was colossal effort, and each flight of stairs that led from high-ceilinged floor to floor was a mile long.

Berry grouched at Allen's assistance, but it helped. On that third and last long flight of climb, it certainly helped. He came to a panting halt at the top, chest laboring.

Allen at his elbow spoke insistently. "Listen, Berry, if you're determined to go through with this thing, let me take your gun. You're about all in." He shook Berry's shoulder slightly. "I don't *want* any of the reward."

Berry swung his head heavily about and blinked into Allen's florid face. "So you're still with me."

"Lucky for you I am," Allen grunted. "Look, let me take your gun and go first. If Dunn sees your uniform he'll shoot. He won't shoot a man in civilian clothes."

Berry blinked and said, "I guess you're right," and dragged out his gun, giving it butt first to Allen.

Allen put it in his pocket and kept his hand with it, then eased ahead and knocked at the door. Berry moved out of the line of vision. The hall's light was dim and its corners shadowed.

There was a long wait. Allen knocked again lightly with his knuckles and the door opened a slit, letting out a bright gleam. Then the slit widened as the door was flung back.

Suddenly Allen fired through his pocket. He went into the room head down, jerking the revolver out of his pocket. Berry, galvanized into action, plunged behind him, snatched the gun and yelled, "What the hell did you shoot him for?"

Screams echoed behind doors and down on the first floor the landlady's police whistle got excited.

The man Berry had come for, Pat Dunn, was stretched out on the floor, beside a sagging white iron bed, dead with a bullet through his chest. A gun lay by his right hand.

BERRY'S FACE WAS hard, his eyes narrowed in an effort at concentration. The pain of his shoulder that his rush had aggravated was a throb in the back of his brain.

"What the hell happened?" he asked again.

Allen turned a face that had gone pale, shrugged and threw out his right hand in a small gesture. He said, "Dunn was going to shoot me. He had a gun in his hand."

Berry growled, "Yeah, I see."

Allen bent over the man's body and began to fumble in his pockets. Berry saw that a small round hole had been burned in the right sleeve of Allen's tuxedo.

Allen, on his knees, turned a flushed face and thrust out a hand, palm upward. A small diamond glittered in the palm. "There's part of that Cauley loot," he said.

Berry blinked stupidly down at it, the gun heavy in his right hand. "Yeah," he said, "I guess it is."

He stooped with enormous difficulty and picked up the dead man's gun, dropped it into a pocket. He dragged heavy feet over to the door and slouched against the jamb, leaning his head back so that the uniform cap tilted up off his forehead.

Heavy feet pounded on the stairs and a traffic cop burst in. He took in the body, glimpsed Berry.

Berry said dully, "Just shot a punk that was mixed up in that

Cauley diamond hold-up." There was a chair by him and he sank into it, gun on his knee.

"Listen, Cassidy," he said heavily, "you'll have to take charge of this prisoner."

Allen spun around and barked, "What?"

Berry was sagging forward in his chair. He looked up under his brows at the blond man and said, "You're under arrest, Allen, for the murder of Higgins and Dunn and for the Cauley jewel robbery."

Allen yelled, "Why you dumb flat-foot, I helped you here and tried to capture Dunn!"

Berry said, "Sure, I know I'm a dumb flattie. Can't do anything but go around shooting people, huh? Well, if you'll look at your right sleeve there, you'll find where one of my bullets ripped into it in the hallway of the 'Samovar' when you plugged me. And you were damned anxious to help me here, too.' That's what made me suspicious, first.

"IT'S EASY ENOUGH now to see you slipped down that alley by the 'Samovar', did your shooting, then slipped around to the front and in again. Higgins' murderer had to be somebody that knew the ground thoroughly, and that counted against you too."

Allen said clearly, "You're being a damned fool, Berry."

The big patrolman ignored him. "You must have been in it with these two guys, Higgins and Dunn. Dunn threw his door here wide open when he saw you, and he wouldn't have done that if he'd been trying to shoot you. When you found headquarters was after Higgins, you decided the safest thing to do was to get rid of him and take the stuff yourself, especially since it meant a cop murder rap.

"Dunn put Higgins on the spot for you, and you killed Dunn. Pretty smart, Allen, but you want to keep out of the way of dumb flatties who can't do anything but shoot. Sometimes they shoot straight."

Cassidy barged forward with hunched shoulders. "A double-crossing crook, eh?" he grunted. His hand went up under his coat-tail and handcuffs clinked.

Allen darted forward, shouldered into Cassidy. The traffic cop staggered toward Berry, and they both went down in a heap. Berry's wound stabbed him with pain, but he held on to his gun. As Allen flashed a flat automatic, Berry leveled his .38 special upward and squeezed the trigger.

Allen's head jerked back between his shoulders, a blue hole in his forehead, and a startled glare in his eyes. He took two wooden steps backwards and flopped heavily to the floor.

Cassidy sprang to his feet, pulled Berry up carefully. The big patrolman stood swaying on his feet, staring down at Allen. Well, Maggie would get that much needed money and there were three crooks less to rob people and kill cops like Pat Malone. He threw back his heavy head and laughed, a little lightheaded with pain.

"I'm just a dumb flattie, eh?" he mumbled. "Well, what does that make *you,* Allen?"

He peered with blurry eyes at the dead man's face and twisted his heavy mouth in a lopsided grin. "Just a real good pal."

Copper's Cross

1

Death on Demand

"BIG, BLOND AND beautiful," a newspaper woman had once dubbed Swede Larsen, and the damnable thing had stuck. Every guy who ever wrote a story about him after that—and they wrote plenty about him in the newspapers—called him the Beautiful Swede. Strangely, they did it in admiration rather than ridicule. But then it would be pretty hard to be audibly disrespectful toward six-feet-three of muscular Viking flesh. Larsen didn't mind any of it except the Swede part, and that was because he happened to be a Dane. But the rest he translated into his native Danish, and rather liked it. *Vakker,* beautiful. Yes, and fine, glorious. Well, tops....

Swede was that all right, the kingpin of the special force of Rangers that the Carson City police had built. Every man of them a one-man army, modeled on the immortal Rangers of Texas. Big men, of course, but more than that, hard, loyal, incorruptible, experts on guns and fists—and roughhouse; brown-faced, lean men with quick, glinting eyes.

"Private Larsen," the captain would say, "bring in Blackie Dilling and three or four of his top men."

And Larsen, very serious—not because Dilling was the town's biggest and most deadly crook, but because he was given a duty to perform—would answer, "Yes, Captain. Dead or alive?"

As simply as that, one man did it. The gold badge that was

shaped like a star and worn proudly on the breast of their coats was their whole uniform, but they had a reputation like the Canadian Mounties. Everywhere they went men stared respectfully—or scuttled for cover. And women cooed. A fine organization, a thing to be proud of, its gold badge the ultimate accolade of honor... until the day politics sneaked in and bounced Captain James Boone Dalton right out of the saddle.

Captain Dalton had to almost fight the Beautiful Swede to keep him from quitting the Rangers, too. Dalton and Larsen had begun this thing together and fought side by side through its toughest battles. It had been Captain Dalton who ran down the Bradley kidnapers and been bundled up by a ten-man gang for torture and death. It had been Swede who crashed through and scattered them in a berserk rage that could not be stopped. And the time Swede had gone to his knees with a bullet in his chest, facing a roomful of killers, it had been Dalton who stepped in front of him and made a shield with his own body while he shot it out with the gang.

They were like that together, so when Dalton put it up to the Swede that the prestige of the Carson City Rangers depended on his staying, Swede stayed. Dalton took his money and his reputation and opened the *Red Eye Club.* It was being done these days. Heavyweight champions were opening cabarets as were retired home-run kings and public enemies who had made a graceful retreat before the G-men.

That was all right until Carson City went on one of its periodical reform sprees and began shutting down the night-life—and Swede Larsen got a call from Hemingway, the new captain of the Rangers.

You wouldn't have thought Hemingway tough to look at

The Beautiful Swede could save his friend or do his duty. And because they wouldn't mix, Larsen began tearing things—and men—apart, indiscriminately.

him. He was a sleek man, rosy-cheeked, young-faced beneath a smooth cap of hair that was frosty white. He was a chubby, genial, smiling man. But Swede knew him from way back. There was steel under the padded fat, and there was steel, too, behind the beaming of his blue eyes.

Hemingway nodded, smiling. "Go down and close the Red Eye Club," he said negligently. "Bring Jim Dalton here."

LARSEN'S HAND HAD already started up in an assenting salute. His face had the serious look he always wore when he received orders. But his hand stopped, whipped back to his side. His face suddenly became wooden.

Hemingway leaned forward. "I've got a special reason for sending you, Larsen," he said. "You and Dalton are friends. There won't be any trouble if you go."

Larsen's mouth shut and angry color began to creep up from his throat. "Assignment refused, sir," he said curtly. He about-faced and had his hand on the doorknob before Hemingway spoke.

"Larsen, the order comes from Van Houtten," Hemingway's voice was oleaginous. "I know that the Rangers have a right to refuse assignments because of the danger of their type of work. Yet it seems to me they make a point of never refusing. Am I wrong?"

Larsen's face was washed with red. Hemingway wasn't a Ranger. He had been captain of detectives before this new régime of politics. He had brought with him to this new post the acerbity which tinged the pride which all the uniform men felt in the picked squad of Rangers. Furthermore, Hemingway had had the knife in Larsen from the first. He knew the Rangers thought the captaincy should have gone to Larsen. He would like, very much, to blacken Larsen's name, to kick him off the force. His refusal of an assignment would be broadcast and Hemingway wouldn't explain to the gossips what the assignment had been.

"I wish you'd take this assignment, Larsen," Hemingway urged, still smiling, his eyelids heavy.

Larsen's jaw began to grow stubborn. To hell with it. Let Hemingway say what he liked. His record.... But it wasn't his record. It was the whole squad's, all the Rangers. *A Ranger had refused an assignment.* Their prestige would suffer, and if once that broke down.... But, damn it, he couldn't take Dalton! He could feel the muscles swelling in his shoulders. He wanted to strike out, to hit some one, any one.

"No!" he said thickly.

He opened the door and stepped back respectfully as the Commissioner came in. William Van Houtten was small, wiry. His movements were abrupt, as if wires jerked his limbs. He bobbed his head to Larsen's salute.

"Dalton?" he hurled at Hemingway. "Good. Good. Just the man for the job. But alive, Larsen. Bring Dalton in alive." His grin flashed and was gone. "Don't often bring them in alive, eh, Larsen?"

Hemingway said sorrowfully: "Larsen has refused the assignment."

Van Houtten reached up and thumped Larsen on the chest. "Don't be an ass, Larsen. Dalton would toss anybody but you out on an ear. Start hell of a row. Listen, Larsen.... You do it. See?"

Larsen stared over the head of the Commissioner and his jaw grew more stubborn. Van Houtten thumped him again and his voice rose.

"Bring in Dalton or you're through. See?" He jerked out of the office.

Swede Larsen faced Hemingway again. He couldn't think clearly for the anger that boiled in his brain, but he was remembering. Dalton had warned him that the new mayor and his appointees, of whom Houtten was one, would try to break the spirit of the Rangers. For among the Rangers, there was no such thing as "going easy" on the boys of the political power transiently in office. And in Carson City, the sinister alliance of crime and politics had not died with prohibition. The Rangers were a potent threat to both. If Larsen were fired from the force for refusing an assignment....

Larsen's lips clipped out the words, "I'll bring in Dalton!"

2

When Friends Meet

SWEDE LARSEN HAD a habit of stopping for a drink at Angelo's whenever he left headquarters and he went there now, not because he needed a drink before he faced the job ahead, but because he was preoccupied and habit took control. He went in blindly, not answering the hails from all sides, the golden star on his breast catching the light gleams richly. He elbowed the bar and the barkeep set *brændevin* before him without a word. Larsen had downed two shots when the girl took hold of his arm.

"Swede," she cried. "Swede, you've got to help me!"

Larsen turned his big blond head slowly. The liquor was burning through his veins and impatience rose in him. He had explained to so many people, so many times. "I am no *svensk,* no Swede. I am from *Danmark,* and…."

He stopped then, looking into eyes that were as blue as his own—pleading eyes.

"Larsen you've got to help me!"

Larsen rolled his thick shoulders. "Later. Now, I have work." He turned away.

The girl tagged along and Larsen came belly-to-belly with a man he knew. A man almost as big as Larsen, big in the shoulders and in the paunch. He held up his hand. "Wait now, Swede…."

It was not often that this Swede business really got under

Larsen's skin, but tonight.... The *brændevin,* the burning wine, was in his veins. He felt blood in his throat. His head pulled down an inch. "Quinn," he said thickly, "I am no...."

Quinn lifted both hands. "Wait, Swede, it's about Dalton!"

Larsen swayed back, but there was a trembling in his limbs. Anger in him was a mighty force. To check it now.... The adrenalin made his nerves quiver. He couldn't stand still. He swung toward a booth against the wall, the girl still beside him, and Quinn dropped into an opposite seat. Larsen looked at Quinn, Rocks Quinn, one of the crooks the police knew about but couldn't touch. There was never anything on him, and he had "protection."

"You," said Larsen, and his mouth corners pulled down. "What have you to do with Dalton?"

Quinn was not a soft man, but his voice was pleasant under that scorn. "I have a tip," he said, "that Dalton's place is going to be closed down. I thought maybe you could do something to prevent that."

"You are Dalton's friend!" A deep laughter rumbled in Larsen's chest.

"Oh, please," the girl whispered. She took hold of Larsen's right arm and he looked down at the hand. His muscles swelled at her touch and there was no reason for it. No reason at all. He looked into her eyes that were as blue as his own, and now he saw other things about her, how golden her hair was, how white her skin.

"You are Norwegian," he said.

"I'm in Mr. Dalton's floor show," she told him rapidly, "and I asked Mr. Quinn for help. I know he has—influence."

The sardonic curve of Larsen's lips increased. "He should

then use his influence!" He got to his feet and he was imprisoned by the booth and the two about him. He felt trapped in that small space. He lifted the table, walked out and set the table back in place again. He looked at Quinn, at the girl a little longer. He laughed a single deep note. Swede Larsen stalked out of the bar room.

Outside the door, he did not hesitate, but turned right and stretched out his long thick legs. It was a dozen blocks to Dalton's cabaret. Larsen preferred to walk it. His forehead was knotted in a frown. The girl should beg him to help Jim! He stopped thinking. The thing he had to do, he must do. For the Rangers....

The doorman of the Red Eye hailed him joyously and Larsen moved his head an inch in acknowledgment. Inside the door, he looked up into the great red eye of neon lights at the head of the steps. It winked at him three times solemnly while he made his way up. He went directly to Dalton's office and it was empty except for a girl who was Dalton's secretary.

"I want Jim," he told her.

She gazed up into his eyes. "Oh, yes, Mr. Larsen," she breathed.

Larsen snorted through his nose and went to the window. He looked out on the garden behind the Red Eye. It was festooned with lanterns that kept winking suggestively. Larsen's shoulders swelled with muscle. He ground out a curse and wheeled from the window. It wasn't Dalton who had come in. It was the same blond girl who had been with Quinn at the bar room. She came towards Larsen, running. She put her hands on his chest.

"You can't do this," she said rapidly. "You can't take Mr. Dalton in."

He stared into her face. Hers was not a rosebud mouth, not a child's.... It was wide, full-lipped, a woman's mouth.... He reflected that Quinn undoubtedly had influence since he had learned so quickly that Larsen had been assigned to close Dalton's place. He shook his head. His stubborn lips smiled at the girl.

"What's your name?" he asked softly. "It should be Freya, for you are lovely. A goddess of love."

The girl flushed and stepped back, put her hands behind her. "Helga," she stammered. "Helga Eiricksdatter.... I mean Helga Ericsen."

Larsen laughed. Dalton opened the door and came in with a small smile on his thin, hard-boned face. Dalton didn't smile much, but he always greeted Larsen that way. He came forward with his hand thrust out, a man heavy in body, but tall and clean. Larsen forgot the girl. He shook his head at the outstretched hand.

"No, Jim," he said, almost sullenly. "I come not in friendship, but in duty. I must close your place, take you to headquarters."

DALTON'S HAND STAYED out for a moment. The smile dwindled to his mouth corners, pinched out there. He asked "What?"

Larsen didn't repeat and Dalton shook his head. "You're serious, Lars?"

Larsen nodded and Helga came close to him again. "You can't do this, Lars," she whispered.

Over her head, the eyes of the two men met and the mouth of Jim Dalton compressed.

"Nothing doing, Larsen," he said curtly. "This is a put-up job. I'm running this place straight and clean and there's no reason to close it. There are plenty of crooked places in town, and… say, Van Houtten is behind this! He's got a piece of a lot of crooked places in this town, gyp places, and he's afraid me being straight will ruin him. Look here, Lars…."

"You can prove that maybe when it comes in court," Larsen said doubtfully. "Jim, close your place."

Dalton said, deliberately, "Go to hell!"

Helga sobbed. "Oh, can't you see, this is what Van Houtten is trying to do! He's crooked and he knows he can't beat the two of you together. You're dangerous to him and to the politicians. If he can destroy you, the Rangers will fall to pieces. So he fixed it up so you two would quarrel!"

Larsen felt Helga's hands on his chest. He could feel each separate finger, and one of them was over his heart. It throbbed five times heavily while he looked into Dalton's eyes.

"Orders, Jim," he said thickly. "I refused the assignment, but…." Hell, he couldn't talk. Jim should understand. It was duty. The words choked him. "Close up, Jim!" His voice rang out hard and challenging.

Helga beat on Larsen's chest. She shouted at him. She ran to Dalton, pleading, and neither man heeded her. They just kept staring into each other's eyes. They couldn't talk. They weren't talking men. Friends, but hard men.

Dalton was smiling again and this was a smile Larsen knew. It had been on Dalton's face that time Dalton had stepped in front of him to take the bullets, to shoot it out with the men who had dropped him….

Dalton whispered, "Go to hell!"

Helga ran whimpering to the door. "Oh, somebody stop them, stop them…!"

Out of the tail of his eye, Larsen watched her go. He was so aware of her!… In front of him was Dalton's hard grin. He wouldn't yield. He wouldn't!… Larsen realized that he would have to hammer Dalton into insensibility if he were to take him captive, hammer him with his fists. His friend…. To hell with it! No job was worth that. The whole damned Rangers wasn't worth it. He….

The door opened and the girl let out a choked scream, pitched floorward. Larsen, out of the corners of his eyes, glimpsed that—and the reason. There was a man in the doorway with a gun in his fist and he had slapped Helga down. Just a flash in the edge of his vision, all that, and Larsen looking straight at Dalton all the while. He saw Dalton's hand dart toward his belt, and he knew that movement. Dalton carried his gun there, tucked into his waistband on the left-hand side, butt foremost. His draw was greased lightning. Dalton's eyes were glaring into his own….

A frame-up, a trap! Dalton had framed him with that hood in the hallway ready to burn him down! Dalton had known that the close-down order was coming. The girl had known, must have told…. A great shout rose in Larsen's throat, his hand clawed toward his gun. He couldn't avoid the bullets, but by—

3

Cop Killer

LARSEN'S THOUGHTS OF treachery were a flash across the screen of his brain. His hand moved with the same speed, darting across his body to the gun he carried as Dalton did, thrust into his belt. Dalton had taught him, trained him in that draw, and now they were matching their speed against death, against murder.... But first that killer in the doorway!

Larsen doubled forward as he drew and fired across his body at the doorway. He shot by pointing. There wasn't time to turn his head, not with Dalton ready.... A shot across his body, whip the gun about and down on Dalton.... The forward lunge of his body had pulled him out of the line of the ambusher's gun, his muzzle was pointed toward Dalton—and he couldn't shoot. He couldn't! Even now that he knew his friend had rigged a murder trap to destroy him, he couldn't shoot.

With a curse, he pulled his gun back to strike and heard the deafening crash of Dalton's gun. An instant later, he drove against Dalton, slapped with the barrel of his revolver, and the two men hit the floor together. The windows rattled with the jar of their fall and a picture crashed from the wall, but Dalton had taken most of the impact. Larsen rolled free, came up on his knees with his gun pointed.... There was nothing to shoot. The doorway was empty!

Instantly Larsen was on his feet, racing across the room. In the hall he stopped dead. The lifeless body of the gunman lay against the opposite wall, where heavy lead had hurled him. The bullet had drilled through the heart and Larsen cursed under his breath in surprise. That was damned accurate for a snapshot. Damned good! The girl was on the floor, too, rolled over on her back with her arms thrown up like a baby asleep. Larsen cursed again and felt the heat of his anger creep over his body. So pretty. Just like a baby. Footsteps were pounding toward him down the hall, but he ignored them. He kept on cursing and the heat washed over his face and concentrated in his brain.

Rocks Quinn hurried up, his heavy brows pulled down in a scowl. He dropped on his knees beside the dead man and flipped back his coat to feel for the heart. A badge glittered there....

"Hey!" Quinn shouted. "The man's a cop. Dalton.... Golly, Dalton killed a cop!"

Larsen stared at Quinn, swaying a little. His eyes were wide and he took a slow step forward. Quinn's mouth flew open. He scrambled to his feet and ran a few steps down the hall. Larsen walked after him, gun at his hip. As he passed a doorway, two men jumped out and tried to slug him with blackjacks. One blow landed on Larsen's arm and his mouth came open in a shout that turned into a roar. He forgot his gun. He seized the man who had hit him by his right arm and jerked him off his feet. Using his great weight, Larsen pivoted on his heel, whirled the man once in a complete circle and let him fly, legs-foremost, against his companion. There was a mingled scream, then silence. Without a second look Larsen stalked along the hall. Men shouted and ran before him. In the arched entrance of the dining hall, he stopped.

On a platform across the room, a jazz band poured out hot stuff. Larsen fired a shot into the ceiling and the music ended on a discord.

"This place is closed by order of the police," Larsen said, and felt the harshness of his own voice. "You will all leave at once."

Five minutes later, the hall was a cluttered, empty mess. Larsen had stood there all that time, gun shoved back into his belt. The heat receded slowly from his brain and he began to think again. He hoped he hadn't killed either of those two thugs who jumped on him. They had only used blackjacks. He fingered his left arm where one of the blows had landed. It hurt.

He walked across the dining hall to the outer entrance and the doorman was standing at the foot of the steps.

"Lock the door, John," Larsen said. "Keep it locked."

He turned on his heel and went back to Dalton's office. He saw the two thugs lay where they had fallen, but they breathed. He didn't know them. Rocks Quinn had revived Helga—had her in a chair in the office. Dalton was still sprawled where Larsen's charge had hurled him. Methodically, Larsen went about restoring Dalton to consciousness. He left off once to go out in the hall and stare down at the face of the dead man. He stooped and stared at the badge Quinn had discovered. Carson City all right, *X-517*. That *X* meant he was a member of the undercover squad, and as such, wouldn't be known to Larsen, yet to his trained eye the face was familiar. Larsen went back to Dalton and squatted on his heels beside him.

"Want me to call the wagon, Larsen?" Quinn asked. "The dirty cop killer!"

Larsen stared up at Quinn steadily. "I killed the man in the hall," he said. "Thought he was trying to gun me."

HE LOOKED BACK at Dalton, who was beginning to stir. This was going to be pretty serious for Larsen, killing a fellow officer. But, damn it, the man's gun had been pointed at him! What a fool he had been to think that Dalton would plant a murder trap like that—Jim Dalton, his friend. His lips tightened grimly....

Quinn laughed. "That's just what anybody would expect you to do, Larsen," he said, "take the blame that way. You're a white guy. But it won't do. That was Dalton's forty-five that laid him out, if I know anything about guns. You use a thirty-eight...."

Larsen sprang furiously to his feet. He shouted: "I killed him! I did it!" He said it three times, beating his chest, walking toward Quinn. Larsen shook both his fists. "I did it!"

Dalton's voice, coming suddenly behind him, wasn't quite steady. "Don't be a fool, Lars. You didn't come within a foot of him. You were snap-shooting and I took my time. I put a pill right through his heart!"

Larsen faced him abruptly, but understanding came slowly. Dalton said he had killed the *X*-man and Larsen was realizing there couldn't be any doubt about it. Dalton knew where the bullet had hit, and the body lay out there in the hall where he couldn't see it. So Dalton had shot him. Dalton.... *Jim?*

"Why?" Larsen whispered. "Why, Jim?"

Dalton pushed himself up from the floor, gripped his head, swayed for a moment. But he looked Larsen in the eye. "He was shooting at you, punk."

Quinn strode forward angrily. "Listen, if you two think you can frame this between you!... Listen, why would a cop try to plug Larsen?"

Dalton cried hoarsely, "A cop! That gunnie a cop!"

Larsen drew in a slow, deep breath. "He's got an *X* badge, Jim. Looks like headquarters didn't trust me to carry through and sent him to check up." He sucked in another. "And they're right! I won't carry through!" He caught the golden star on his coat and tore the pin through the cloth. Before he could hurl it to the floor, Dalton's fist closed over his.

"Don't, Lars," he said swiftly.

"To hell with it!"

"Don't, Lars!" Dalton repeated. "Listen, if you're doing it to help me, you can do a lot more on the force than off."

Quinn laughed harshly. "Golly, I'm going to get out of here before you two frame me with the murder!" He strode to the door. "A swell cop you are, Larsen! Duty doesn't mean a damned thing to you...."

Helga pushed in between Larsen and Dalton. "Did you know, Mr. Dalton, that this punk closed the place while you were out cold? He's trying to pull a phony on you now so that you'll take the rap for him. Don't do it, Mr. Dalton. You know he killed that man...."

Dalton stared over Helga's head into Larsen's eyes and read there the truth of what the girl had said. His lips tightened. "You sneaking dog!" he bit out. "You did behind my back what you couldn't ever have done otherwise! And I thought you were a friend!" He whipped back his hand and hurled the star badge, which had come loose in his hand, into Larsen's face. It cut his cheek, clung there for a minute and dropped to the floor. Larsen did not flinch, but presently he stooped and picked up the pin. He fastened it back in his coat.

"All right, Jim," Larsen said woodenly. "I'm taking you to headquarters.... Right now."

4

A Challenge

THROUGH A LONG minute, the eyes of the two men held unswervingly, then Dalton laughed. It was a single, sardonic snort. He threw back his head and laughed until Larsen's ears ached with it. Dalton held out his arms.

"Handcuffs, please, officer," he panted.

Larsen stared at him a moment longer, then he methodically unhooked handcuffs from his belt and clicked them shut about the wrists of his friend. His lips were pressed in upon themselves. There was a heavy thudding in his breast that was his heart. Dalton had killed a man to save Larsen's life, and he must take him in for it. But that wasn't possible, was it, that the *X*-man had tried to kill a brother officer?

Helga jeered at him. Her face was flushed and she was terribly angry. It wasn't because she was in love with Dalton. Larsen was pretty sure of that. She didn't pay any attention to Dalton. She just called Swede names; she slapped his face. He smiled at her and led Dalton out of the door, through the long halls to the street. He got a taxi and left Helga behind, shouting at him from the curb. He turned slowly to Dalton.

"Helga is not... is not your *kjæreste,* your loved one?" he said.

Dalton stared at him, laughed shortly. "If you're doing this to get rid of me on account of her...."

Larsen smiled a little. "Now, Jim, you know me better than that. The captain told me I should bring you in. I bring you in, that is all. I thank you for saving my life, Jim. That was a fine shot."

Neither man spoke after that. Larsen was frowning again. It was funny. He could not doubt the *X*-man had pointed a gun at him, had knocked down Helga.... He felt the heat rush to his brain. It was good that he had been killed, this man who had hit Helga.... At headquarters, Larsen took Dalton before the sergeant and swore out a short affidavit.

"Operating a cabaret contrary to ordinance," he said. "James Dalton, proprietor of the Red Eye club. I'm taking the prisoner to the captain and will be responsible."

The sergeant stared curiously at these two who were such famous friends. "That's all right," he said. Newspaper men whooped and raced for the telephone. News all right. One of them lingered.

"Office phoned me a man had been killed at the Red Eye," he said. "You know anything about it?"

"Very little," Larsen told him seriously. "I never saw him before. He was shot through the heart." He led Dalton up the broad wooden steps to the captain's office on the second floor and felt Dalton eye him curiously.

"What the hell did you use the cabaret charge for?" Dalton demanded. "You might as well charge me with the murder right now. You know Quinn.... Hell, ballistics will show...."

Larsen went directly to Hemingway's office and was admitted. Hemingway rose behind his desk, smiling. "Sorry about this, Dalton," he said smoothly. "But orders are orders."

Larsen stood at attention before Hemingway and made a full and complete report. Hemingway had sunk back into his chair when it was finished. His lips tightened. "I'll see that you burn for that, Dalton," he said sharply, "if it's the last thing I do! Killing an undercover man!"

Larsen interrupted, "Sir, I think I should tell you before you begin action that the undercover man shot at me, and that Dalton shot to save my life. He had no way of telling he was an *X*-man. I will testify like that when he's tried."

Hemingway exploded, "Nonsense! An undercover man shoot at you! That's ridiculous. Let me tell you, Larsen, it will do you no good to lie for your friend. I won't have it. I.... *Larsen!*"

Larsen was bending over the desk, his blue eyes wide. "You take that back, Captain. I do not lie!"

Hemingway said hurriedly. "No, no, of course not. But you are mistaken. Why should a fellow officer shoot at you?"

Larsen did not answer. He turned to Dalton. "I take the prisoner to a cell now, Captain."

Hemingway made no answer and in the hallway to the jail section, Dalton spoke hesitantly. "That's fine of you, Lars, but it won't do any good. Nobody will believe you or me either.... I'll swear that gunnie was shooting at you. I didn't know he was an *X*-man and I never hired him."

Larsen said, after him: "You didn't hire him, Jim? But you hired all the *X*-men while you were captain, and told them what to do, didn't you?"

Dalton's eyes narrowed. "Yes, I told them what to do."

LARSEN SAID, VERY carefully, "I am sure I have seen that man before somewhere, this *X-517.*" When Dalton had been locked up, he went back to Hemingway's office and entered without knocking. The captain was lifting a drink to his lips. He set it down hard and liquor slopped on the desk.

"What do you mean, coming in without permission?" he shouted.

Larsen leaned over the desk. "I want to ask you something, Captain," he said. "Why did you put an *X*-man on this? Why did he cover me at Dalton's?"

"What? What do you mean?"

Larsen nodded. "You have charge of the *X*-men. Why did you…?"

"No!" Hemingway cried sharply. "I don't have anything to do with the *X*-men! The commissioner took that over himself. Van Houtten has charge of them, since I came into office."

Larsen straightened, gaze still holding Hemingway's. The captain's eyes seemed sunken a little. Larsen nodded, "I am sorry I came into your office without permission." He saluted, walked out. Downstairs, he shouldered his way through the newspaper men who were waiting for him with questions about the killing of *X-517.* His name, they said, was Riker and the name didn't mean anything to Larsen. He kept his lips shut and went across the street to the saloon. He stood at the bar and stared at his blond, wide-shouldered reflection in the mirror. Very deliberately, he put sentences of thought together.

Helga had said that Van Houtten wanted Dalton and himself out of the way, wanted the Rangers smashed. Van Houtten had an interest in a lot of cabarets and was closing down rivals. Van Houtten, Hemingway said, had charge of the Undercover men. And a new undercover man, hired since Dalton left office, had tried to kill him, Larsen.

That seemed crazy, yet if the undercover man did not intend that, why had he slapped down Helga? And why had Dalton shot him? Larsen began to feel a warmth in him that was not from the *brændevin* he had downed. He cursed deep in his chest. It added up, it made sense. The undercover man *had* tried to kill him, and Dalton had saved his life… and put his own neck into the noose. It was a sweet frame-up, a beautiful frame-up. If the undercover man had killed Larsen, Dalton would have been blamed. Maybe Dalton would have killed the undercover man and then he would have been up for the murder of two policemen, and all Van Houtten had to do was….

Larsen's eyes narrowed abruptly. He was going pretty fast, wasn't he? Quinn had said that Van Houtten had a part of the night clubs around town, but Quinn was supposed to own a big part of them himself. Helga had been repeating what Quinn had told her probably, and…. How did he know that Hemingway had told the truth? Maybe Hemingway was still in charge of the *X*-men, and had lied! If that were true, then Quinn had a hand in the frame-up, too. Damn it, either way, Quinn had a hand in it. He had shouted, as he bent over the dead *X*-man, that Dalton had killed him, and he had had no way of knowing that, no way at all….

Larsen laughed sharply. He crashed a big fist down on the bar and his bottle jumped. And he remembered now where he had seen the *X*-man, Riker. The last time Quinn had been questioned on a racket charge, Riker had been his bodyguard. Now that same man seemed to be an undercover policeman…. Larsen, his lips tight, poured himself another brimming glass. He lifted it to his reflection in the glass.

"Jim!" he said, and tossed it off.

Beside him, Helga's voice said, "Something is rotten in Denmark. I think I know who it is."

Larsen turned to her slowly. He had to make himself do it slowly. "*Lille* Helga"…. He said it softly and stood looking at her. She was talking, but he couldn't hear the words. He smiled. "Do you love Jim Dalton, then?" he asked deeply.

Helga stared at him, mouth open a little. She shook her head vehemently. "He was kind to me, gave me a job when I was down and out. He is a fine man."

Larsen nodded cheerfully. "You are a fool, Helga," he said. "This night, I will…" he laughed. "Tomorrow I shall be a famous one! For I shall put a famous one in prison—or in hell!"

5

—or in Hell!

THERE WERE TIRED lines about her mouth, but Helga was a bright fire in the somber, almost empty bar room. Her blue eyes darkened with anger as she stared up in Larsen's big face. Before she could begin the tirade he could see impended, he stalked off. No woman could stand that, Larsen thought. She would follow. At the phone booth in the row against the back of the room, he paused to glance over his shoulder. Helga had followed all right, was only a dozen feet away. He faced her.

"You cannot follow me," he told her shortly. "I have work to do."

Helga lifted her firm chin.

"Go away," Larsen insisted. He waited until she had gone a reluctant half dozen feet away, then he entered the booth and, with a final glance over his shoulder, drew the door shut. Thereafter, he appeared to become engrossed in dialing a number. The glass sides of the booth furnished an excellent mirror and he saw Helga move out of his line of vision. He waited until he heard her enter the booth next to his, then he deposited a coin and actually dialed a number—the number of Captain Hemingway.

"Larsen, Captain Hemingway," he said excitedly. "Listen, I've got the break in this whole business. Who killed the *X*-man. Everything. I've got enough on Quinn to hang him, and I'm going over now for a showdown. I would like you to be there,

Captain. I think we can even make him tell where he gets protection. Yes...."

That much he poured into Hemingway's ear, then he depressed the hook that disconnected the call and continued to talk.

"That's big news, Captain," he said. "You say that the man who was killed wasn't really an undercover man at all? Just a hood Quinn has hired before to do his dirty work, eh? Man, you're certainly putting him on the spot! We've got enough stuff to put Quinn and Dalton behind the bars for life....

"Sure, I know me and Dalton used to be friends. But this is business. Yeah, I'll go right over to Quinn's apartment fast. See you there, Captain."

Larsen hung up the receiver, grinning widely, then he opened the door of the booth a slit and listened. From the next booth, he could hear Helga's low, excited voice as she talked rapidly over the telephone. Maybe he was crazy, eh? He closed the door tightly and made another call. It got Commissioner Van Houtten out of bed, but that was a small matter....

"Mr. Commissioner, this is Larsen," he said. "Yes, one of the Rangers. You remember you sent me to arrest Dalton and close his place...." He told all that had happened, the shooting of the undercover man. "I got something makes me think that Rocks Quinn had a big hand in it, Mr. Commissioner. I'm on my way over there now to blow this case wide open, but I'll need the private file of officer *X-517,* his prints and photographs, you know. I know Hemingway has the files, but he isn't at his office and I can't locate him. Why don't you get the file and come on over to Quinn's apartment? Yes, sir, I'm going to blow this case wide open, right now. Good night. See you there."

He strode out of the booth without a glance at the one in which the girl hid, his brows drawn in a tight frown. Hemingway had lied then in denying he directed the *X*-men! Or else Van Houtten had lied to him a moment ago when he said Hemingway had charge. Larsen laughed. He would soon know. But if he were wrong in his deductions, he was as good as fired off the Rangers right now. He couldn't be wrong. He couldn't be.... Still, if he were, Dalton would die in the electric chair!

But he was right. Quinn was certainly involved and, with him, either Van Houtten or Hemingway. Quinn couldn't get away with things as he did without police protection. Hemingway, if he were Quinn's ally, would get in touch with Quinn right away. If he thought that Larsen actually could blow the whole thing open, he would want to make sure that Quinn wasn't in a position to confess. That meant killing either Quinn or Larsen. The same applied to Van Houtten.

In a dark doorway, a half dozen doors from the saloon, Larsen drew his revolver and checked it, filled the sixth chamber. *That meant killing either Quinn or Larsen.*

The odds were that they would gun for Larsen. Larsen hoped they would. Violently, he hoped they would. He kept the revolver in his hand, tucked under his coat, as he stretched his long legs out toward Quinn's apartment. Walking was better than a taxi. He didn't want to get there too early, and walking, he could keep closer to cover....

THE BLOCKS REELED past under Larsen's feet. Twice he thought he detected a trailing taxi, but each time the cab disappeared. He didn't worry about it. The men who were after him wanted him murdered, not trailed. He reached Quinn's apartment house without interference. The desk man was almost as burly as Larsen as he stood in front of him, arms crooked a little in belligerence, head pulled down.

"Nobody goes in without he gives his name," the man said surlily.

"That's all right," Larsen nodded. He flicked his gold star with his left hand. "I'm Lars Larsen, here to see Rocks Quinn. I may arrest him. Want to phone that up?"

The man smiled slowly, "Sure. Sure, I'll phone that up."

He turned away, and Larsen's hand flashed to the man's shoulder, whirled him about to meet the up-swing of a knotted fist. The man's head wrenched back on his shoulders and he slumped into Larsen's arms. Larsen carried him with effortless ease and laid him behind his desk.

The elevator was automatic and Larsen grumbled under his breath as it loafed upward. There was a warmth over his whole body that he knew and liked. He blew happily on his knuckles, then got his gun in his fist again.... The guns started blasting up above when he was halfway to the tenth floor, where Quinn had rooms. Was he too late? When the girl relayed to Quinn what she had overheard Larsen say, Quinn would recognize instantly that he had been double-crossed either by Hemingway or Van Houtten, whichever was his ally. Larsen had hoped to precipitate a quarrel among them which he could overhear, find out enough to free Dalton. If the quarrel had begun with shooting....

Larsen strode up to the door of the slowly moving elevator, stepped back again. He threw a quick glance about him and clutched his revolver. The elevator kept drifting upward at the same inexorable pace, Larsen cursed. He got his left hand on the handle of the inner grating of the elevator and waited with his shoulders tense. Upstairs, the guns had stopped. Five sharp explosions, then silence. Was he too late, or had he just stumbled on something, and....

The elevator sighed to a stop and Larsen wrenched back the grating, kicked open the outer door.... and there was nothing. Nothing at all. The hall was empty. Behind him, the elevator door clicked shut and Larsen started, cursed under his breath. He sniffed and slowly a smile spread over his lips. He hadn't been wrong then. The shooting was here or else his nose didn't know the acrid reek of cordite! He pulled his big head down a little and went toward Quinn's door on his toes. Just by the sill, there was a single dark brown smear!... One thing sure, he'd be alone in this. No tenants in Quinn's building would report gun shots. Not if they were smart. Well, that was all right, too. The Rangers had always been able to work alone.

Larsen thoughtfully slid a pin out of his coat lapel and jammed it in the bell button. Inside the apartment, it set up a continuous, maddening clamor. Larsen stood to one side of the door and waited, hand out of sight under his coat, gripping his revolver. It was Quinn who opened the door. He was smiling genially.

"Up to your little tricks, eh, Larsen?" he said pleasantly. "You ought not to ring people's bells like that at night."

Larsen grinned. "That's right." He stepped up close and dug the muzzle of his revolver into Quinn's belly. "Let's go inside, Quinn. Sorry you have to walk backwards."

Quinn's smile did not fade, but it became wolfish. "Sure," he said softly. "Sure, let's go inside and talk this over, whatever it is. Van Houtten called me up and said that you had some silly idea...."

Larsen's lips drew tight and cold against his teeth. So Van

Houtten was Quinn's ally? That made it bad. Anything he did tonight would be wrong. If he killed Quinn.... There was nobody in sight when Larsen walked into Quinn's living room. Two seconds later, there were four men with guns on him. One rose from behind a davenport, one from a closet and one in the kitchen doorway. The fourth man was seated in a deep, wing chair that had hidden him.

"Now," said Quinn, "let's talk this over. What is it you've got against me?"

Larsen looked slowly at the four men and their guns. He was pretty close to the one in the chair. He turned his back on him. Larsen's eyes were wide and there were fires in their blue depths. Color began to creep up into his face and it made Quinn wary. He drew a gun deliberately.

"Don't try any of your berserk stuff on me, Swede," he said heatedly, "or I'll pump you full of lead."

Larsen put a smile on his lips. It showed his teeth almost in a snarl.

"Sure, I'll tell you what I've got against you. The man I killed in Dalton's place isn't an undercover cop in spite of his *X* badge. He's a gunnie you've used before this for dirty jobs like shooting me in the back. He tried to do that in Dalton's office, but he was too slow."

"Go on, Larsen," Quinn insisted softly.

"Your buddy who gave you the badge to pin on the gunnie has gone back on you, Quinn," Larsen went on. "He admitted before witnesses that the gunnie wasn't an *X*-man. He's on his way here now to cross you and help me show you up." He remembered the shooting, but this brag would force Quinn's hand. If he had gunned out his ally....

6

Death Pays Off

THE KITCHEN DOOR batted open and a fifth man thrust Hemingway into the room. Blood sogged Hemingway's left trouser leg and his face contorted with pain at every step.

"That's a lie," he said hoarsely. "That's a lie, Larsen. I wouldn't go back on Quinn...." His face turned white as he saw the flame leap in Larsen's eyes and realized he had confessed their partnership in crime. He laughed. "That's okay. You won't live to leave here, Larsen, and...."

Quinn was looking at Hemingway and only two of the men that Larsen could see had guns on him. Larsen acted without a moment of warning. He hurled himself violently backward on the man who sat in the chair. There was a chance the gun would go off in his back, of course, but he had to take it. His shoulders hit against the man's face and the gun blasted, but Larsen didn't feel any slug. The chair pitched over backward and spilled the two men to the floor. Larsen let his legs come up over his head and landed on his knees, his gun ready in his fist. The man on whom he had thrown himself didn't stir.

For a split-second, the whole room stood in tableau, heads wrenched toward the scene of the commotion. Hemingway's head was tossed high, his neck terribly strained, his hands rising toward his chest, and Larsen saw that the bullet from the gun of the hood he had crushed under his heavy body had bored Hemingway under the breastbone. He saw that and he laughed. The sound was deep and guttural, strangely menacing. There was one of Quinn's killers in a position to shoot behind the chair which was Larsen's shield. That was the gunnie who stood behind the davenport. Larsen bent his wrist and squeezed the trigger. The bullet caught the man just on the point of the jaw and his teeth popped shut, then sagged apart as he stiffened up. Blood spurted from his mouth and he pitched forward over the back of the davenport like a boy propped up for parental reprimand with a razor strop. He was already quite dead.

Larsen laughed again, and lead poured at him. There were three more men, one there in the closet doorway, one behind the toppling Hemingway, and Quinn. The two hoods were pegging bullets around the edge of the overstuffed chair, but Quinn was smarter. He had a powerful Luger and he shot right through the stuffing. One of the slugs glanced off wire and ploughed through Larsen's thigh, whirled him off-balance against the wall. The hood in the closet let out a yelp and sprang toward him, throwing down on him with his automatic.

Pitching backward, Larsen still managed to squeeze off another shot. The man kept coming, but the eager glee on his face became mild surprise. His mouth twisted with pain and his left foot swung wildly to the side, out of stride. He tried to pull it down and couldn't. He hit the floor on his right shoulder, rolled over completely and lay on his back, with his legs twisted. It was nice shooting, Larsen thought detachedly, but Quinn had lifted his Luger deliberately for a sight on him and the other crazy fool was emptying his automatic in a swift drumroll of death.

Larsen jerked his revolver about... and the man under his legs, the man he had crushed unconscious with his body, reared up and grabbed his wrist. Quinn's shot came in that split-second. It missed Larsen's heart, because the hold on his wrist had jerked him aside, but it took him just under the collar bone on the right-hand side, smashed out through his shoulder blade. Larsen couldn't know that at the time, of course, couldn't know anything except blackness and pain swarmed over him and his whole chest went numb. He had felt that way before, the time he had been fighting beside Dalton and had been hit. Dalton had stepped in front of him.... But there wasn't any Dalton now. Only Quinn and his two enemies....

Larsen realized that Quinn was standing over him, leering while he leveled the Luger once more, not at his head for a mercy shot, but at his belly!

"...your guts out," Quinn was saying. It sounded like a whisper. A man flanked Quinn on each side, grinning men with guns in their hands. He was going out and the frame on Dalton would stand! Hemingway was out of the picture....

Larsen still had the gun in his hand, but there wasn't any strength in that arm at all. It was numb from his shoulder down. Sweat popped out on Larsen's forehead. Quinn laughed....

"You and that fool Dalton!" Quinn jeered. "You're both out of my way now. *Take it, copper!*"

HIS FACE TIGHTENED and the Luger pointed at Larsen's belly. Larsen rasped out an oath. He heard an explosion and felt a jar in his right hand. He looked at it slowly and saw that the gun lay beside it, and there was a wisp of greasy smoke oozing from the barrel. Why, he had fired it! Quinn.... Larsen stared at him and saw that his bullet had crossed Quinn's body just below the short-ribs. It had gone in on the left and plowed to the right and upward.... He gasped as Quinn's body smacked down on top of him.

There was some more shooting, but it was as distant as thunder when the storm is over. His eyes were shut. But, by God, he had done it. Hemingway, not Van Houtten, was guilty. He had admitted that before the two punks that were still alive. They'd talk now that their chief was dead. Hemingway and Quinn were both dead. Dalton was in the clear. That was what really mattered.

Why, it was Helga, bending over him! He murmured, *"Lille* Helga, little one...." Tears were rolling down her cheeks. She rocked his head like a baby's. He looked beyond her and saw Van Houtten holding a gun on the two Quinn gunmen. The Commissioner jerked his head at Larsen.

"What the hell you mean?" he demanded. "Papers on *X-517.* Aren't any papers on him. Never were. That guy killed with that badge, Riker. Just a fake, is all. You get me out on a wild-goose chase like this? Hmpf! Who's the young lady? Said she followed you here. Met me at the door crying. Warned me to get my gun out. Some girl!"

Larsen looked up at her blue eyes and smiled. He nodded at her a little. "Kind of figured it like that, Commissioner, I mean about the *X*-man's papers," he said. "Dalton wouldn't kill a cop. Now he's in the clear. Those prisoners. Make them talk. Quinn and Hemingway confessed... framed things to kill us... Dalton and me."

Van Houtten snorted. "Can't kill a dumb Swede like you!"

Helga lifted her head. "Of course, they can't," she said. "But he's not a Swede, Mr. Van Houtten. He's... he's... a Dane." She began unexpectedly to sob. She bent over and kissed Larsen's mouth.

How I Write

Norvell Page is best known for the adventures of pulp hero The Spider, but he also wrote science fiction, sword and sorcery, and even dabbled in the spicies. In the midst of the Great Depression, Page became a millionaire thanks to his high output and penchant for weird menace. In 1935, Page was asked to contribute an article on the nuts and bolts of writing. Here is Norvell Page's response:

PEOPLE WHO TALK of "art for art's sake" annoy me. I did it once myself, but I learned better. I write now for two reasons: because I like to, and because I earn a better living writing fiction for magazine editors than I did working for newspaper editors.

I begin this way to avoid misunderstandings. This is an article about how a writer-for-money produces manuscripts which sell.

I turn out 100,000 to 120,000 words a month for the "pulps"—magazines (so called because they are printed on "wood pulp" paper). These words—the pulp writer always talks of words—because he's paid on a wordage basis—are written as well as I am able to write them. I try constantly to improve the quality, the forcefulness and the keenness of character interpretation in my stories. I spend twice as much time on rewriting as on writing.

To me, these things and pride in my work are art enough...

But let's get on with the article.

When the editor asked me for three or four thousand words on "How I Write," I smiled. "I don't know how I write," I told him, "I've been too busy writing to analyze my methods."

The editor chased me to my files, looked over some of the stories I had written, and picked out one.

"Tell me how you wrote this one," he said.

I looked at the carbon copy of the story—I file a carbon copy of every story until I can cut the printed story out of the magazine, then I compare them to see how the editor edited my work. Well, here was the carbon copy, and I looked from it to the wall of my office, where hung the covers of the magazines which illustrate stories I have written. It was there, the illustration that went with this story.

It shows a man hanging from a rope over a bloody pool in which floats a skeleton. To the left, a man in a black robe and a hood is holding a red-headed girl clothed only in a scant yellow sheathe of silk. The hooded man is trying to make the red-headed girl cut the rope and drop the man into the bloody pool. You have an idea it would prove fatal if she did.

I grinned at the editor. "Okay, if that's what you want, you can have it."

THAT STORY IS titled "Dance of the Skeletons" and it's of the pulp type called "Mystery-Horror"; that is, it's about foul deeds which are to make the reader's blood run cold and to keep him guessing as to who actually committed those deeds.

The history of this particular story began one evening when I climbed three steep flights to a Greenwich Village attic and invited a writer friend to visit a new speakeasy with me.

My friend was depressed. He sat before a table on which sheets of manuscript were scattered.

"The editor wants me to cut my sixty-thousand word novel to thirty-six thousand," he said bitterly, "and get it in by next Monday. I've only written ten thousand and I like the plot as it is."

My friend decided he wouldn't cut his story and that he couldn't plot and write another in seven days.

"Mind if I have a shot at it?" I asked. "I've never written for that editor, but I can give him thirty-five thousand words in a week, if that's what he wants."

My friend said morosely, "Go ahead," and the drinks were on me.

They have a saying: When you want trout for breakfast, you first catch your trout. Or maybe it's a bear. The same thing applies to writing. When I began writing, I didn't believe that. I'd see a market note in a writer's magazine that a magazine was buying western (or mystery or what have you) stories of a certain length and I'd sit down and write a story which I thought filled the bill and send it in. I didn't read his magazine first—why should I when my story had to be original? But in those days I didn't sell.

Now, when I want to sell a new magazine, I pick up a market tip, and then buy that magazine and read it from cover to cover, with especial reference to the lead story and the blurbs—the score or so of words that the editor writes at the top of a yarn to sell it to the reader.

When you see a blurb like this:

"Through the fog-choked grayness these horrors prowled. Their faces were pale as the fog itself and even knives could draw from them no blood. Yet it was blood they sought, blood they sucked from their victims' headless corpses…."

Well, you get the idea that the editor wants it sca-a-arry.

There's more to it than that, of course. You go through your magazine and find that the editor uses some first person stuff; that he has a woman interest in all his yarns, maybe a bit of sex; that the girl should be in danger from the chief menace of your story—this is what is known as "slant" or "formula." Actually it is what the editor likes or thinks his readers like. When a story has it, he buys it. When it doesn't, it goes back to the author.

Having learned this magazine's "formula," I next sought an idea for a story. A story idea is the most nebulous and elusive thing in the world, yet its acquisition can be simple. I believe it is a matter of habit, of training your mind to think in certain grooves.

It is doubtful if any two writers come by their story ideas the same way. A friend of mine saw a corollary between the song "Smoke Gets In Your Eyes" and the fact that a gangster would talk of "smoking down" an adversary. Another writer went walking and noticed the shadows of people, who passed him, sliding along the pavement. He got a story out of that. I looked out of the window once and noticed the unconscionable number of dogs that clutter the parks of New York. I was seeking a horror story with an overwhelming menace. I thought, "Suppose all those dogs had hydrophobia...."

But these are haphazard methods. There are few writers, I believe, who can pull a story out of their brain by staring at a blank wall. Most writers have some system of jotting down ideas. I have a file into which I drop clippings from newspapers, cards on which I have scribbled ideas that occurred to me from time to time, many of which were of no particular use at the time.

This night, when I had finished reading the magazine, I ran through my file. I was looking for some clipping that might suggest horror, that would give me a menace to make the reader's blood run cold. I soon found what I wanted, a typewritten note made after coming home from a motion picture. The movie concerned some lad who had gone up the Amazon for something or another. My note stated that the explorer lowered the carcass of a forty-pound pig into the waters of the river and, forty seconds later, lifted it out a clean white skeleton.

The answer to the stripping of the skeleton was a species of fish known as caribs. The particular type found in the Amazon headwaters are called piranha, and they are cannibals. Only as large as a man's hand, they have remarkably large mouths fitted with a row of razor-like teeth top and bottom.

That much I jotted down after seeing the picture. It was an idea, nothing more. Now, let's see how I maneuvered that into a story. My thoughts ran something like this: I must have a background of terror and mystery. Obviously, these carib fish, operating in the Amazon River, would involve little terror. Furthermore, the solution would be too obvious, hence no mystery either. Then the necessary murders via the caribs must be committed somewhere else, preferably against a city background. So much for locale.

Now then, how shall I use the fish? Obviously, if they are seen at work on the carcasses of the victims, there's no mystery. The point about these fish is the speed with which they work. It becomes apparent then that the maximum of terror would be obtained by converting living men into nice white skeletons within a few minutes, and concealing the method by which this was done. There's the menace decided upon.

Next we turn to motive and the villain. The two are inseparable. The usual resort in terror stories is to devise a "mad scientist" who is making experiments. I've used that. So have thousands of others. It is trite because it is the simplest explanation for unspeakable horrors. Editors don't want it anymore.

I sought frantically for a possible and logical reason for killing people by turning them mysteriously into nice, fresh skeletons (and incidentally, I think motivating stories of this type is the most difficult part of the plotting). My mind flitted to murders for various kinds, torch murders where bodies were soaked in gasoline and burned, murders in which bodies were dismembered and tossed into rivers... ah!

People who commit that kind of murder frequently desire to destroy the identity of the victim. You couldn't do a much more thorough job of hiding identity than by removing all the clothing—and the flesh too. So much for that. Our villain wanted to prevent identification.

But to have the horror of the story to the full, these skeletons must be flaunted in the face of the city, they must appear at the festive board, thud at the feet of the police commissioner entering headquarters. That is obvious intensification.

To motivate such activity, the murderer not only must want to hide the identity of his victims, but he must want publicity for his skeletons. That was rather a tough problem. Also the motive must not be too apparent. That made it tougher. The tip came from the daily newspaper. The stock exchange was fighting Washington over some threatened publicity move. It would ruin the stock market, it was contended, and send shares crashing....

This, then, was what I had: The villain feeds his victims to the carib fish because he wants to hide the identity of his victims; he wants publicity for his skeletons also. From the newspaper I learn that publicity harms the value of stocks. Non-sequitur? Well, here's what I worked out of it, though I'll admit the publicity part of it stumped me for a while:

An unscrupulous capitalist who has fallen on hard times sets out to clean up in the stock market by foul means. He kills off certain captains of industry to make the stock of their companies decline. However, mere murder of these men would not depress the stocks. He must contrive to kill them and make it seem they have merely disappeared because the financial condition of their companies is no longer sound. To accomplish this, he kidnaps them and feeds them to carib fish, piranha, which can within a course of minutes eat all the flesh from the bones. The villain then tosses the skeletons in various conspicuous places. By this means, he not only depresses stocks through the mysterious disappearances of leading men, but he distracts the attention of police from the stock market manipulations, by which alone he could be traced. When the skeletons finally are identified, stocks rise again and the villain cashes in both ways. The hero is a detective from a Midwestern city studying New York methods. The girl would be the daughter of a victim, and for a time, a suspect also.

My agent showed the above to an editor who needed a story and he said he'd be glad to see a detailed outline of the novelette.

He'd like to see a detailed outline! Yeah, so would I. There is nothing on earth I hate more than an outline. Some writers never use them, but I find that an outline holds me to the course of my story, keeps me in the right length, helps in a thousand ways. But it's still a job.

I can't compose outlines leaning back on a soft pillow with my eyes closed. I'd go to sleep. I have to sit down at the typewriter and watch the words beaten out by the flying keys. Then my mind works story-wise. The first thing I do is pick my characters. I had already chosen the type of hero, but that was all. I hammered out a character sketch of him, including the old folks back home in the Midwest and the size of his hat. Most of it never was used, but it planted the character firmly in my mind, brought him to life. I never have been able to write a salable story unless the character "comes to life" and actually at some point in the story takes the action out of my hands and runs it himself. And I've found that the spots where that occurs are the best parts of my stories. Or so the editors tell me, without even knowing that those special bits were "inspiration," if you care for the word.

I also did a sketch of the girl, and of the other leading characters I intended to use. Minor characters might be handled the same way. At current word rates, I never had the time to try it.

The next step was to single out the suspects. After that came the brow-wetting labor of digging up detailed information in the library—this time on caribs—figuring out dramatic incidents, and batting the ball around among the suspects. A tried and true device is to throw all the suspicion on one man, then kill him near the end of the story. But when you do that, be sure you have another suspect all ready and waiting to take the burden of suspicion—and don't let him be the guilty man.

I decided to do that, then I sought a dramatic incident to open the story, a scene also that would introduce the leading characters, and the main theme—the Dance of the Skeletons. And, in this case, I couldn't forget the atmosphere. I knew from analyzing the magazine that the editor likes them eerie.

I started "Dance of the Skeletons" in the police headquarters with our hero and his mentor, a hardboiled New York detective, reading a note that invites them to see the skeletons dance. It's a foggy night, etc. Atmosphere. Hero and mentor go to the spot where the skeleton is to dance. An attack in a dark alley, a glimpse of brown-skinned naked men (I brought in the Amazon Indians, too) and finally, in the dark, our hero touches the bones of the skeleton, dangling from the brick wall beside which the two men stand. He flashes on his light and a cold wind brushes them; the skeleton dances!

Back at headquarters, a detective says he has a clue, but refuses to tell what it is. He goes out to follow it—and an hour later, his skeleton is tossed out in front of the police headquarters! And so on. Another skeleton is dumped on the dance floor of a nightclub. The solution—well, it was easy once the thing got underway. The simplest way to carry the fish northward from the Amazon would be a swimming pool, naturally in a private yacht. The villain tortures our hero by lowering him slowly toward the pool of cannibal fish. (See cover illustration.) One gets his toe, that's all, and in the end, the villain himself dies in his own pool of horrors. Our hero tells who else is guilty and how he figured it out and the hero and the girl clinch. Curtain.

That's the outline of the story, and then the hard work starts, the writing of it. Thirty-five thousand words in a week—with deductions of time for outlining, revision and final typing—a finished product ready to go on the editor's desk.

THERE ARE SOME writers making a living in the pulp market today who turn out no more than three thousand words a day. They may or may not send out the story as it falls from the typewriter. I'm the reverse of that. I once turned out 25,000 words in a fifteen-hour day. In pinches, fifteen and sixteen thousand words a day are not unusual for me. I once wrote a draft of a fifty-five thousand word novel in four days.

But these high production days are spurts. No writer living

can keep that up long. I knew one who was topping 200,000 words a month—one month he beat 250,000—but he cracked after a while. There came a time when 80,000 was a good month for him. He's made his pile, he says, and doesn't care.

An editor told me that the author of the Shadow stories, which run around 50,000 words each, received an outline for a story on Tuesday and turned in the completed manuscript on Friday.

It's a great life if you don't run out of words.

On my Spider stories, fifty-five thousand lead novels for the magazine of that title which I write monthly under a house name, I have written as many as six different opening chapters, and spent a full day getting the first two thousand words on paper. I may have written eight, ten, twelve thousand in getting those two, and even then, I don't always like them.

I STARTED OUT to tell you how a writer-for-money produces his stories. I've tried to tell you how I go about it, but after all, this is my private process. It probably doesn't fit the methods of anyone else. I have a friend—one of the three-thousand-word a day men when he's working at it—who never thinks on paper. He reclines, smokes and builds his stories in his mind. He thinks out his sentences beforehand. When he finishes a scene, he stretches out again and dreams over the next scene, even figures out some of the dialogue. And he, too, revises endlessly. That's the way I used to think "authors" worked.

I have another friend who thinks up his plots pacing the floor with quick, springy strides. Now and then he stops and stares up at a corner of the ceiling and suddenly he flings himself at his typewriter like a hungry man at a steak and pounds out his story. But that "plot" was merely an idea. He'll pour the story on paper with only that idea at the start, and turn out as neat a yarn as any writer I know. He swears he doesn't know from one minute to the next what will happen in his story and he'll often leave the last page of a manuscript in his typewriter overnight while he seeks the right ending, the right "tagline." He's the one who burns them out at 2400 words an hour and sells them as they come from his typewriter without revision.

Personally I stand a little in awe of such men. Turning them out that way is one thing, but selling them is quite another and he does that, too. Be damned if I don't think the man is a genius. (And he'll break my neck if he reads this article and finds I said it.)

They tell of another writer who sits before his typewriter in a dark room and writes his story by touch. He sells them to the "slicks."

But these authors all have several things in common. They study the magazines to which they intend to sell; they are close observers of life; they keep files of notes for stories unless they are possessed of exceptionally retentive memories which can recall not only events but actual conversations which occurred years before; they know what they write about, either from experience or research.

May I speak frankly?

I never turned out a story in my life that wasn't plain, hard work. Not that the writing itself wasn't enjoyable. I don't have to sweat out words, or worry about action when my characters "come to life." But somewhere in that story, the work was hard. Getting the idea, working out the outline, revising the copy, trying to get a fast opening that still would carry all the information it should; straining to tell a scene just as I see it in my mind's eye.

That's "how I write." I hadn't analyzed it before, but that's more or less the course on any story, whether it's a four-thousand word short or an eighty-thousand word novel.

Writing for a living is hard work, but I wouldn't trade with any man I know.

About the Author

NORVELL WORDSWORTH PAGE was born in Richmond, Virginia on July 13, 1906, the son of one of the Old Dominion's first families. He had young aspirations to become the next Edgar Allen Poe. Estranged from his family for eloping from William and Mary College to marry fellow classmate Audrey Rohr circa 1924 at the age of 18, Norvell—contrary to family wishes that he make more of his life—became a Virginia newspaper reporter. Later, he joined the great moonlight migration of newspapermen of that era to Manhattan. While working as a crime reporter for the New York *Herald-Tribune,* he moonlighted as a prolific pulpster.

Page first broke into print—accounts vary—either in *Western Trails* or *Detective-Dragnet,* both Magazine Publishers' titles. It was the early Depression. His father, an executive with the Wurlitzer Music Company, had been wiped out in the Stock Market Crash of 1929.

At first, he wrote as N. Wooten Poge—a nod to his interest in Poe, one imagines—as well as a shield from family concerns. But before long he was himself, Norwell W. Page, a rising star in the pulp firmament, who cracked the prestigious *Black Mask* and penned the popular Ken Carter series in *Ten Detective Aces* in 1933.

Page's big break came that same year, when he was give the opportunity to write a lead novel for the revamped *Dime Mystery Magazine,* making Page a pioneer in the emerging Weird Menace field. This led to him taking over *The Spider* series from the departing R.T.M. Scott.

Over the next ten years, Page was feverishly prolific as Grant Stockbridge, the nominal Spider author, a tenure in which he transformed Richard Wentworth from a 1920s thriller hero into a hardboiled 1930s pulp icon. He also pounded out tales for Popular's *Terror Tales, Horror Stories* and *Ace G-Man.* Occasionally he moonlighted by ghosting a Phantom Detective novel like *Death Glow,* or the odd Spiderized Black Bat tale. He revived N. Wooten Poge for the salacious Bill Carter stories in *Spicy Detective Stories* in 1937. Whenever Popular Publications launched an important new title like *Detective Tales* or *Strange Detective Mysteries,* they tapped Page to help kick off the first issue. For Street & Smith, he wrote the Dick Barrett and Miss Fay detective stories for *Crime Busters,* who gave way to the Death Angel series, starring the lethal but effete pugilist Angus Saint-Cloud.

As the 1930s shaded into the '40s, the fevered Spider novels cooled somewhat. Reader tastes were shifting, and the old "bang-bang" wild action was growing dated. Page retooled as best he could and branched out to writing classic fantasy novels for *Unknown* that are still remembered today, including his masterpiece, *Not Without Horns,* and two Sword and Sorcery epics clearly inspired by Robert E. Howard's Conan the barbarian.

The Spider began winding down in 1943. Twelve years is a long time in the pulp game. Everything had changed. The

Depression was a fading ache. The nation faced another World War. Paper shortages were pounding the pulps. The Spider's days were numbered. Page may or may not have cared. His first wife died of tetanus the previous November. Page fled *The Spider,* and forever abandoned the familiar pulp jungle of Manhattan for a government position in Washington, writing for the Office of War Information. After the war, he wrote speeches for Congressman Lyndon Johnson and reports for the Atomic Energy Commission. He never returned to *Black Mask,* never became the next Edgar Allan Poe—and never looked back. Page passed away on August 14, 1961 at the age of 57.

Remembered today as the soul of the Spider, near the end of his writing career, Norvell Page wrote one fan: "Think of me as Wentworth, if you will. The line between us is not too distinct...."

Perhaps that might as true an epitaph as any.

—Will Murray

www.ingramcontent.com/pod-product-compliance
Lightning Source LLC
LaVergne TN
LVHW091037080826
845145LV00002B/526

* 9 7 8 1 6 1 8 2 7 5 9 5 0 *